SUMMER WINDS

Visit us at www.boldstrokesbooks.com

Praise for Andrews & Austin

"The timely topic of scriptural strictures against same-sex love gets an informed airing in this engaging story about the passion between two women, one leery of love because of her faith, the other wary of that same faith. Andrews & Austin weave religion and romance together in a novel that perfectly balances serious thought and sensual entertainment."—Richard Labonte, *Q-Syndicate*

"Read the prologue to *Uncross My Heart* and you will be hooked, I guarantee it. With one hilarious and devastatingly on-target stroke, Andrews & Austin begin their newest novel, a contemporary romance set on the campus of a fictitious Chicago seminary. The one-liners come fast and furiously, but it's the relationship between two bright, intelligent women that resonates long after the last page has been turned."—Ellen Hart, Lambda Literary Award–winning author

"In a succinct film-style narrative, with scenes that move, a character-driven plot, and crisp dialogue worthy of a screenplay, Andrews & Austin have successfully crafted an engaging Hollywood mystery."—*Midwest Book Review*

"Appealing lead characters that possess wit and intelligence drive this novel. Richfield and Rivers make a wonderful couple who experience the various ups and downs of life with a sense of humor, affection, patience…and an astrology chart."—L-word.com Literature

By the Authors

<u>Romance</u>

Mistress of the Runes

Uncross My Heart

Summer Winds

<u>Richfield & Rivers Mystery Series</u>

Combust The Sun

Stellium in Scorpio

Venus Besieged

SUMMER WINDS

by

Andrews & Austin

2009

ISBN 10: 1-60282-120-8
ISBN 13: 978-1-60282-120-0

This Trade Paperback Original Is Published By
Bold Strokes Books, Inc.
P.O. Box 249
Valley Falls, NY 12185

First Bold Strokes Printing: October 2009

Credits
Editor: Shelley Thrasher
Production Design: Stacia Seaman
Cover Design By Sheri (graphicartist2020@hotmail.com)

Acknowledgments

Dr. Shelley Thrasher has been our editor for so long that working with her is not only comfortable but comforting. She is always there to compliment or correct, delete or delineate, improve or impress. We owe her much. Special thanks to our dear friend and publicist, Connie Ward. Applause for the lovely bookcover design created by Sheri. And to Rad and her entire BSB team, we tip our literary hats in thanks.

Dedication

To Love…life's greatest gift.

CHAPTER ONE

*C*hange is like wind through a screen door tempting you to open up and feel the full force. I let go of that thought and grabbed the metal screen-door handle, stepped onto the front porch, and braced against the wind as it whistled across the prairie and bent the grass to the ground. Late May, and only a few weeks before wet, swollen pastures would dry beneath my feet, ponds would come alive with the hum of cicadas, and chilly evenings would surrender to long, hot nights. Change in the wind made me restless.

"You okay, Maggie Tanner? You look mighty thoughtful." Perry approached from around the corner of the house looking like someone who'd just crawled out of a mine shaft after twenty years missing. His white beard, sweat-stained shirt, suspenders, and baggy jeans belied the romance of unexpected meetings.

I ignored his question because these days I didn't know the answer. Instead I zeroed in on work: what should have been done or needed to be done or had to be re-done. "Did you get that gate repaired so the boom can get through there and Jeremiah can start spraying the south pasture?" I held my hand up to assess the wind's velocity and determine if we'd be wasting weed killer.

"Gate's fixed. Jeremiah's broken. Don't think he's sprayin' or stayin'."

Skipping further discussion, I headed to the bunkhouse two hundred yards to the south where Perry and Jeremiah shared living quarters while Perry gave me a lot of reasons why I shouldn't start "buildin' up a head of steam." Ignoring him, I banged on the door, then pushed it open and blinked into the semi-darkness. Jeremiah, a tall boy in filthy blue jeans and a dirty white T-shirt, lay face down on the bed, his arms spread wide and flopping like a spastic snow angel. The room reeked of drunk-sweat.

"Jeremiah, damn your ass, pack up and get out!" I tried to hoist him by the back of his belt but he was deadweight.

Perry limped in behind me and wedged between us. "Now, Maggie, we're short a hand as it is." Perry half hoisted him to his feet, and Jeremiah staggered once before lurching forward onto the bed again.

"I won't miss him, because I don't know what he looks like, because his drunken face is constantly stuck in the mattress." The blood rushed through my veins and my blood pressure rose.

Perry looked up at the ceiling and gave that little whistling sound he always made when I lost my temper. He used to call me a feisty widow woman, until I threatened to kill him if he ever said it again. Now after nearly two decades of ranching together, no telling what he said about me out of earshot, but he stayed, and that said something.

He caught up with me by the water well where I seesawed the tall pump handle, letting the ice-cold groundwater splatter onto my legs, arms, and face. I could have walked to the house and used the kitchen sink, but I liked the shock of the icy spring-fed water slapping me back to my senses.

"That's three you've fired and the season hasn't even got started." Perry scratched the top of his head as if my decision had irritated his brain.

"Drunks, druggies, womanizers, and lazy asses!"

"Need to hire ourselves some monks," he said evenly, and mopped his brow with the bandana from his rear pocket before he walked away shaking his head.

I wiped my damp hands on my pants, pulled my truck keys out of my pocket, and decided to go into town and blow off some steam. Perry could have the last word, but I didn't have to stand around and listen to it.

My light blue Chevy pickup bounced over the rutted dirt

road for a quarter of a mile before getting traction on the two-lane highway that led into Little Liberty. I sped past miles of flat farmland with white wood-frame houses in the distance and open fields dotted with John Deere equipment. *Can't stand up long enough to work ten acres, much less my twelve hundred. Passed out drunk twice a week, and Perry blames me for firing him. Old coot!*

Thirty minutes later I slowed to twenty-five as I entered the city limits and turned onto Main Street, where I pulled into a graveled spot in front of the Kansas Kafe, or the 2-K, as the locals called it. Advertised as "the best coffee, homemade sweet rolls, and fried hash-brown eatery for miles around," the 2-K had no competition an hour's drive in any direction. I pushed open the glass door bearing the chipped, white-stenciled 2-K, made to look like a cattle brand, and scanned the room for anyone I knew.

Hiram Kendall, my neighbor on the north, his blubbery body lodged into a scarred oak booth in the back, was talking to his employee, Stretch Adams, a tall mid-fifties fellow with thinning hair and muscles as tough and sinewy as beef jerky.

Hiram gave a nonchalant wave as I approached. "Howya doin'?"

I hooked a thumb over the front pocket of my Levi's. "Fair to middlin'." I fell into the colloquial vernacular for "okay, but not great." "Know anybody looking for work?" I asked casually, as if the answer didn't matter. I'd long ago discovered when things mattered too much, people took advantage.

"Everybody I know's tryin' *not* to work." He chuckled and tore into a chicken leg as if the pause for conversation had nearly allowed it to escape.

"I'd be willing to come over there, Maggie, and *do a little work*." Stretch raised an eyebrow, undoubtedly convinced only Hiram would get his meaning, and Hiram chuckled.

"Think the payment might be a bit high, Maggie. I'd look elsewhere." Hiram jiggled from internal mirth and wiped the chicken grease off his chin with the back of his big bear paw.

"How old do men have to get before they stop thinking about sex?" I asked.

"Dead, that's how old." Hiram grunted.

"How old do women have to get before they *start* thinking about it?" Stretch leered.

"If she's in your bed, Stretch, I'd say wake her up and ask her."

"That's a good one." Hiram pounded the table and, in appreciation for my adding humor to his morning, agreed to ask around on my behalf. Unspoken was the fact that men out here would do things for each other when they wouldn't do them for a woman.

Donnetta, a big, dark-haired part-Cherokee wearing a white apron over her tight pink blouse and black stretch pants, hustled between tables and cash register. Catching my eye, she crossed the room to greet me and sang out jovially, "You annoying my diners?"

"Your diners are plenty annoying without my help," I joked.

The breakfast crowd was clearing out, the far-too-fat farm boys hoisting up their overalls and heading out to their trucks. An elderly, bent-over part-timer bussed tables and cleaned up around us as Donnetta indicated a booth that was clean.

"Sit," she ordered in her commanding voice and gestured with one powerful arm that could have been deemed fat, but due to her tight tan skin just seemed strong. "I need a break." Her pie-shaped face beamed as her butt slid across the brown leather seats and her tummy grazed the table edge.

"How's Big Valley, Ms. Stanwyck?" Donnetta had decided years ago that my starched shirts and hard-pressed independence qualified me as the star's double. Ranching had made me tough, but beyond that, I didn't see the resemblance.

"Big Valley needs haying, know anyone?" I asked.

"Sounds like a personal problem to me. My Big Valley needs some attention too." She guffawed, and I wondered if the entire restaurant had a Viagra with their V-8.

"I need ranch hands," I said.

"Well, that works too!" She doubled over with laughter and I waited for her to get serious. "This is where being married again would help you. It would be *his* problem to find ranch hands."

Stretch Adams walked over and bent down to tell me good-bye. "You are looking mighty fine, Maggie." He slipped a stained business card on the table bearing his cell phone number and winked, then slid a toothpick between his lower front teeth and sucked loudly on the wooden shaft before heading out the door.

As if I don't know where to find him in a town of nine hundred people, or that I'd want to. Stretch must have seen a movie where a suave leading man slid his phone number in front of a woman and she jumped his bones, because he glanced back over his shoulder at me as if he thought he was so hot he'd burn a hole in the pavement.

"Imagine 'doing' that one," Donnetta said as he attempted a seductive saunter out the door.

"You imagine it, I gotta go." I downed the rest of my coffee, jumped to my feet, and slapped a dollar bill on the table. As the glass door swung shut behind me, I could still hear her protest my paying for the java.

I turned down Main Street and drove past Benegan's hardware store, which sat diagonal to Olan's gas station, an old movie theater, and a tiny bakery. Down the first side street was the Kendall lumberyard, the corner bar, and directly across from it an old white clapboard house that served as the funeral home where Bea Benegan's husband "Seller" got his nickname after he exited the pub drunk, entered the mortuary, and tried to sell a hand gun to Mrs. McRary, who'd been dead for three days. After that, whenever he walked down the street, people shouted, "Seller, Benegan?"

I approached Main and Fourth, an intersection of churches: Methodist, Baptist, Catholic, and a new one labeled Sinners Church, apparently for those who couldn't settle on a denomination and simply needed a category.

Freedom, religious or otherwise, was hard to come by in this small town, at least the kind of freedom I'd always envisioned finding after graduation. I'd planned to be a reporter or journalist or interpreter for the United Nations but instead ended up married and living on a ranch. After all these years, I still didn't feel like I blended with the locals. But my college education made me the country equivalent of bilingual. I could be comfortable seeing you anon or nigh onto Sunday.

My mental wanderings were simply an excuse to avoid thinking about having fired Jeremiah and leaving myself short a ranch hand. And I was just plain nervous for reasons I couldn't pinpoint other than the wind blowing and stirring everything up off the sidewalks and swirling it around my head. The wind set expectations, but what could you expect in Little Liberty, a town of jobs instead of careers, tasks rather than goals, and duties that displaced dreams.

I drove thirty minutes to the ranch past a landscape sprouting small barns and houses set back off the road. Just enough people to give you comfort that someone might be there when you needed them but not so many that you felt crowded. People were like weeds; a few couldn't hurt, but too many and they choked out anything good that might "come of the ground."

Since we were only weeks from the beginning of summer and blistering heat, I needed someone younger and stronger than Perry, who was probably seventy but guarded his age like a starlet. These days the local kids went away to school and didn't return. Ranch work was hard, and the limping men in the community attested to the dangers of tractors rolling over on you or livestock kicking you. Old-timers knew farming didn't support a family in dollars but paid off in breathtaking sunsets and black starry nights and newborn calves.

I pulled into the long gravel drive and put the truck in park and walked into the house just as the phone rang. The voice on the line took a familiar tone.

"How's the prettiest brunette this side of the Rockies?"

"Tell me who this is or I'll hang up," I demanded, refusing to let strangers trivialize me.

"The eight-second wonder of Texas Tech." Buck Tate tee-heed, then continued to shout as if the telephone wire were nothing more than a Dixie cup tied to a string and volume would ensure transmission. "You miss me, sugar?"

"I'm the *blonde,* Taterhead. Do you even know what woman you're talking to?"

"It's been so long you *are* kind of fadin' from my memory." He laughed at himself.

Just thinking about Buck's Garth Brooks build and little-boy giggle renewed a warm spot in my heart for Tater. "You haven't called me in five years, you crazy fool, and your phone number was disconnected."

"I'm still in Denver but don't advertise it. Second wife's tryin' to kill me. Can you imagine that? Me, of all people. I wouldn't hurt a fly."

Buck was susceptible to volatile women, and during our college days I'd helped him through a dozen broken hearts at the hands of blond cheerleaders and nearly as many broken bones on the backs of rank bulls. He'd gotten a girl pregnant when he was only fifteen, married her quickly, and was in the middle of divorcing her while in college. Despite the disgrace and whispers of that era surrounding unwed pregnancy, his dilemma wasn't as bad as mine as I dealt with the aftermath of losing my parents in a senseless accident.

We sat once and talked about life's irony: I had people leaving the world and didn't want them to go, and he had a baby entering the world and didn't want it to come. "Everybody just got on the wrong train," Buck had said in his simple way. "Now we gotta go on from here."

After that he made it his mission to make me laugh, leading a bull up to my dorm where it relieved itself on the floor. Once when I got called to the dean's office, he wired the dean's door shut and connected it to the fire alarm. Buck Tate was my friend and a shoulder to cry on, the guy who insisted I would take all my troubles, turn them into stories, and become a famous writer for the *New York Times.* Grateful, I encouraged his aspirations to be the world's most famous bull rider. My end of it hadn't exactly panned out, and somehow I didn't think Buck's had either. I asked about his job and his family. On the last topic he drew a deep breath.

"Got a favor to ask. Mary and I don't fight over much but we do fight over the kids, that's for sure. I won't bore you with the domestic details, but basically my teenage boys are spoiled rotten. They've got more computers and software and game toys and bullshit, not to mention a bunch of big-titted, mindless girls chasing after them."

I couldn't contain a chuckle over his distressed tone, as if he'd personally spent his teenage years in an ashram.

"You think it's funny, Mags, but I don't want to wake up one morning and find out that I've raised a bunch of wussy techno-geeks who got up from the computer to go to the john, fell forward, and knocked up big-boob Betty Sue. You oughta see my oldest. He put a stud ring in his nose big as the ones in the bulls I used to ride. I grabbed hold of it and led him around the house and him shoutin' for his mama. Brave enough to staple hardware into his head but yellin' for his mama!"

"Now that's real tragic, Buck."

"Well, this'll wipe the smile off your face. I want you to take one of 'em for the summer. Hell, I'd give you all of them but I don't want to be sued. I could send Hank or Jennings…or hell, even Cash." Buck had named all of his kids after country-western singers and fortunately had stopped reproducing before he got to Slim Pickens.

"I was just in town asking around about a hand for the summer. But the work is hard, you know that, and the heat's fierce out here."

"I guarantee any one of my kids can hold his own."

"You just said they're useless as tits on a boar."

"I was exaggerating to get you to feel sorry for me. Let me go back and pick the right one out of the chute. I promise you'll have the best hand you ever had show up within a week."

By the time I hung up I was elated to have solved my problem, and I nearly skipped out of the house to tell Perry how things had worked out. He was sitting on the bunkhouse cinderblock steps scraping riverbed mud out of his boot treads with a hunting knife. As I finished my announcement he glanced up with one eye.

"He ever work a ranch?"

"Don't know, might have. Buck was a bull rider in college."

"How big's the kid, the one he's sending?" Perry's brow furrowed unhappily.

"Big enough, I guess, or Buck wouldn't send him."

"How long's he stayin'?"

"Don't know that either, but you'd best get the booze-air out of your sleeping quarters."

Perry rose and muttered into his boots, "Nice. Sharing a room with somebody neither me nor you knows nothing about. Could be a killer."

"Or a rocker." I clamped my thumb and middle finger around my nostril as if bolting something to it. "Has a stud stapled through his nose."

Perry snorted. "Guess I'll use a metal detector to find him after dark."

❖

After noon, almost a week later, I stood on the front porch examining my small garden. A few squash, tomatoes, and pepper plants were taking hold now, their dark green shoots becoming stronger by the day. I examined the rich dirt around them to see if it was damp enough, then rose and brushed my hands off on my blue jeans, careful not to get any dirt on my khaki shirt. People often remarked about my crisp shirts, but they just made me feel better so it was a luxury I afforded myself, taking them into town to have them starched and pressed. On cool days I wore a green pullover that had a quilted shooter's patch on the right shoulder with elbow patches to match, old gear from the early days when my husband tried to turn me into a hunter. The soft, worn sweaters always made me feel safe, proof that something could last forever.

A car rolled down the gravel road and I turned my gaze in that direction, shading my eyes with my hand as I rested against the sturdy porch post for support. I didn't recognize the vehicle but thought perhaps Hiram had sent someone from town to inquire about work.

An older black Jeep with the spare tire on the back slowed, then crept onto the dirt-and-rock indention twenty yards from the house. I cocked my head, trying to see the face behind the wheel, then stepped off the porch for a better look and waited.

The motor shut down and the door swung open. The sun's glint obscured the details of the figure climbing out of the vehicle except that he was tall, with dark shiny hair, strong shoulders, and narrow hips. As he turned to face me, I realized even from a distance that he wasn't a teenager, but more like late twenties. The boy wiped his palms on the back of his dark jeans and then sauntered over, squinting up at the sun, seeming to measure its intensity before he extended his hand and looked down into my eyes.

"Cash Tate, Ms. Tanner. Buck said you'd be expecting me." The twinkling eyes were captivatingly pale against the rich, dark hair. "I know you're looking for an experienced hand and I can't say I am one. But I learn real quick." The big, self-assured grin and sturdy handshake unnerved me, but not nearly as much as the fact that this tall, handsome young man was, on close inspection, a woman. And her hand wrapped completely around mine sent a chill through my entire body that felt like the wind blowing back the grass. It caught me by surprise and rendered me momentarily speechless.

She must have realized I was shocked because she grinned wider and said she'd be heading back to the Jeep to get her duffel.

I ran to the phone to call Buck Tate. *What is he doing sending me a girl!*

CHAPTER TWO

First thing is you need to calm down and stop shouting." Buck Tate reasoned with me over the phone as I envisioned he'd done with former wives.

"You told me you were sending me one of your boys," I stage-whispered.

"I said Hank or Jennings or Cash. The boys pitched a fit about leaving home and, well, Cash, she's by my first wife. She's always up for anything."

"This is hard work, Tater, and I don't have time for someone who can't carry her weight, you know that."

"Maggie, you need a strong hand this summer and I'll level with you, Cash does too. She's kind of wild, but nothing a good hot summer can't fix. Bake the hellfire out of her. You work her hard. That's all she needs."

I looked up to see Cash standing in the doorway, her expression asking if something was wrong. "Well, she's safe and sound and right here in the kitchen," I said brightly to Buck for Cash's benefit, then spoke over my shoulder to her. "Want to talk to your, uh…?" My words fell away as I took in her long lean frame. It was nearly impossible to envision this tall, handsome woman being related to Buck. She shrugged, letting me know that talking to him wasn't necessary.

"You two go on and get to know each other. I'll talk to her later,"

Buck said loudly. "You're gonna love her, Maggie, and wonder how you ever got along without her."

I hung up and turned to face the still figure. My worries seemed to leap across the room in telepathic angst because she said quietly, "I know you were expecting one of my brothers."

"No, just someone strong and smart, and you look like you qualify on both fronts, so the only thing I'm worried about is where you'll sleep." It crossed my mind again that Cash Tate looked one moment like a tall slender woman and the next like a handsome boy. I couldn't remember ever seeing a person who was male and female all at once, but Cash Tate was both and right before my eyes. "I can't put you out in the bunkhouse with Perry."

"I don't mind."

"Well, I do. Come on, I'll clean out the guest room and you'll bunk in there."

She didn't move as I crossed in front of her and led the way to a small bedroom I'd used for a dozen different things over the years: Sewing, when I was first married and hadn't realized I'd rather be a nudist than try to master patterns or stitch quilts, then reading as I gazed out the window feeling sorry for myself, followed by easels for oil painting when I'd decided to trade anger for art, and finally workout mats for yoga as I meditated myself into complete boredom. Now the room was a jumble of diversions that hadn't worked. I hoped Cash wouldn't be another one of them.

I apologized for the clutter as I hurriedly scooped up items and jammed them into the closet, then paused. The closet would need to be clear for her clothes.

"There's plenty of room. I don't have that much." She blocked my path and took a blank canvas and jangling wind chimes from my hands, making me nervous for no reason other than her unexpected gender and the fact that she constantly stared at me. "It'll give me something to do. I'll put everything up really neat and I won't break anything."

"I can't imagine what you could break." Other than hearts, I thought. She looked like she could have boys wild for her if any of them ever had the courage to approach someone her height. She had to be at least five foot nine. I gave up trying to put things away, glad to have a reason to leave her alone until I could get used to having her around.

"You hungry?"

"Could or couldn't." She shrugged again.

"If you're going to work here, be decisive." I wanted to shake off the jitters and put myself back in charge. "Are you *hungry*?"

"Yes, ma'am."

I stared at the black wavy hair framing her strong face and high cheekbones. Her mother must be very pretty, perhaps Native American or Irish, having passed on that rare contrast of pale eyes and ebony hair. Buck sure couldn't be expected to have a daughter either this tall or this good-looking.

"Something wrong?" she asked.

"It's Maggie, not ma'am."

"Maggie," she echoed cautiously, as if testing to see that I really meant for her to speak my name. The syllables slowly rolled off her tongue, making my name sound lovely.

Leaving Cash to unpack and straighten her room, I scurried around the kitchen looking for something that might constitute dinner, settling on eggs and sausage since nothing was thawed. As I lifted the old iron skillet I always cooked in, boots on the front porch drew my attention. Wiping my hands off on a tea towel, I went to the door to find Perry standing there, more scrubbed than usual.

"He here?" Perry asked. I stepped outside to keep Cash out of hearing distance. "Saw the Jeep and thought—"

"Buck sent his daughter."

"His daughter! Aw, geez mareeez." Perry yanked his hat off and slapped it on his knee like an old sidekick in a 1950s Western. He then shuffled up and down on the porch's old wooden floor boards like a rabid raccoon. "She ever ranched?"

"I don't know."

"Well, that just beats all, don't it?" He craned his neck to get a look through the screen door. "How big is she?"

His words were no sooner out than Cash appeared in the doorway, and Perry's head snapped up and back as she stepped onto the porch.

"Cash, this is Perry Waits. He runs the ranch."

"Howdyado," Perry said somewhat shyly.

Cash shook his hand energetically. "I can't wait to learn everything you can teach me." She smiled in a way no one could have resisted. "Sorry to interrupt," she added, and went back inside the house.

I thought I saw a glimmer of interest in Perry's eyes, as if he'd taken to her right away.

"*Seems* pretty big," I said wryly, knowing size was always Perry's issue, him being a small man.

"Yeah, tall gal." He shifted his weight uncomfortably side to side, wanting no doubt to find something else bad to say about our situation.

"Looks strong." I pursed my lips as if mulling over whether to throw her out and waiting only for Perry's say-so.

"Yup." He adjusted the beaded hatband on his floppy cowboy hat.

"Green as grass most likely, and not very useful."

It finally dawned on him I was poking fun. "She'll do." He snorted and wandered off toward the bunkhouse. I'd never seen Perry so completely charmed.

I went back inside to find Cash in the middle of the living room looking as if she was waiting for instructions. "So what made you decide to come out here for the summer?" I had no idea how to make conversation with her.

"Buck asked me to. Kind of insisted on it." One hip sagged in a relaxed pose, and as she smiled big again I noted that she referred to her father by his first name.

"What were you doing before?"

"Nothing, really." She sounded politely nonchalant.

The concept of doing nothing and admitting to it was new to me. I paused, taking in her boyish figure: long legs and narrow hips leading to a strong but nearly flat chest and broad shoulders. "Well, then, we'll try to see that your summer is filled with *something*. How about dinner, for starters?"

I pointed to a stool across the wooden counter that served as a rustic breakfast bar, and she sat down and hooked her boot heels on the bottom rung. I ran a paper towel over the eating surface in front of her. "Dust is a way of life out here. You can move it around but you can't get rid of it."

"It's fine." She seemed concerned about me.

I wasn't very talkative, living alone having turned me mute. I cooked sausage and then eggs in the sausage remnants and heated up a few leftover biscuits and slid the whole thing onto a plate in front of her along with butter and jelly and a glass of milk.

"I haven't had milk for dinner in years."

I automatically reached to remove the glass the way women do in a society where male displeasure can be loud and trains them to meet needs quickly. Remove and replace, no harm done. "I think I have some tea."

She reached out and stopped me. "Milk's great." Her hand was soft and much larger than mine. The energy of her touch left my shoulders tingling, and the pleasant sensation drew me to her whether I wanted to be drawn or not. Getting too chummy isn't the goal here, I reminded myself. I would treat her like a ranch hand, not like a visiting relative. No special favors. Buck would never want that. He'd sent her here to learn something this summer, and I was determined to teach her.

"This is the best food I've ever had." She almost swooned. "I mean it. You can really cook."

I was suddenly shy and wondered if I'd caught it from Perry, but I let her praise register. The ardor with which she enjoyed her meal, wolfing it down like a big happy pup, made me smile.

"Well, I'll feed you again in the morning and then you'll be ready to start. The work's pretty simple—driven by the weather. Things have to happen quickly before the rains come. Right now, we're getting ready to spray a couple of the fields for thistles and broadleafs. Have to get those killed out so the good grass can take hold. Our hay's a mixture of prairie grass and Bermuda." I could see some of this information was new to Cash, who looked a little dazed as she pushed back from her empty plate.

"Tell you what. You report to Perry in the morning. If the wind's died down, he can hook up the boom sprayer and you can help him spray. I don't like chemicals, but there's no getting around them a couple of times a year." I explained in detail how we cut, raked, and baled the hay, storing the squares and selling the round bales, putting some up for winter and then rotating our pastures, leasing them out to cattlemen for grazing.

Suddenly realizing her eyelids were at half-mast and she was trying not to drift off, I remembered she'd driven from Denver, which was a good ten hours, so she was probably tired. I slid her plate back and touched her shoulder. She jumped, startled, and reddened with embarrassment, making an excuse about my voice sounding soothing.

"Get to bed. I'll wake you when it's time to hit the floor."

She stumbled off to the guest bedroom, and I cleaned up the kitchen. Afterward I walked out on the front porch and sat in the white slat rocker and looked up at the moon. I hadn't done this in months—taken a moment to merely sit.

Then for no reason, I began to think about my marriage, wondering why I'd never had any surge of excitement when I first met Johnny Blake. And, if he'd stayed alive, would we be on this porch together, a mid-forties married couple swinging and singing and rocking our first grandbaby? Why did that thought horrify me back then and still did today? He hadn't wanted much. Nothing he shouldn't have had. Why did he have to die because of it?

Why am I thinking about that? I shook my head, unable to deal with the memories. Jumping up, I went back in the house and grabbed a notepad and scribbled a few reminders for in the morning. A grocery list, gloves for Cash, tell Perry to clean up his talk around her, show her how the washer/dryer works, get her a set of keys, let her know she's welcome to use the phone. *None of this would be necessary if she was sleeping in the bunkhouse. Her being a woman changes everything.*

Chapter Three

At first light, I went to wake Cash but she wasn't in her room. Her bed was made and her clothes were put away. Good, I thought, she's tidy. I went back into the kitchen and looked out the wide windows over the scarred white iron sink to the back pasture and flecks of sunlight bouncing off the hayfields, but didn't see anyone. I picked up the walkie-talkie from the counter and contacted Perry. He answered, saying he and Cash were starting in the back and spraying five hundred acres before lunch.

"She riding with you?"

"Driving ahead in the Gator picking up limbs and trash and opening gates."

Bouncing over rough ground in the old John Deere Gator wasn't an activity I relished. Somehow the comfort of the venerable old equipment company's tractors hadn't translated to the original Gators. Jumping in and out of a no-frills all-terrain vehicle, lugging tree limbs and logs, would be a good start for her.

"Good, tell her to come on up to the house for lunch after," I shouted over the handheld and signed off due to the static.

I was in a happier frame of mind than I could remember and looked around the big knotty-pine living room, appreciating its simple beauty. The weathered wood was orange in places and gold in others and just plain dirt-worn in spots. Everything about the place was old-fashioned and homey in its ambiance but modern enough to be comfortable. People would give their eye teeth to have this ranch, I thought, and felt so energetic I began to clean up the place, mopping the wide board floors, scrubbing the big battered wood countertop, and airing out the bedrooms, opening the double-hinged casement windows to let the breeze blow through and air out musty corners of the old room.

Then I slung open the fridge and located the fresh cherries Donnetta had given me, pitting them for a pie until the juice ran down my fingers and made me look like a happy axe murderer. I'd sworn I would never go to the trouble to slice every cherry and dig out the pit, but today just begged for a cherry pie and it only took a couple of hours. In fact, the sheer act of making it delighted me. I hadn't occupied my time indoors in months, always spending it with Perry and the workers.

I set the table out on the porch and put an extra plate for Perry, thinking he would enjoy a nice noon meal. It wasn't long before the two of them tromped up the steps chuckling. I hadn't seen Perry grin in so long I'd nearly forgotten he had teeth. On top of that, he'd cut his beard, trimmed it back shorter and neat again, making him look younger.

"Well, you're looking real Sunday slick." I was shocked and amused that he'd obviously shaved for Cash. He cut his eyes at me, daring me to say another word in front of her. I would have, but Cash's looks distracted me—her hair pressed flat and her clothes sticking to her. At first glance I wondered why she was so sweat-covered, the heat certainly not that intense yet.

"You trying to dehydrate her?" I asked, noting the moisture on her body. They eyed each other and giggled.

"She's not overworked, just doesn't move very fast," Perry said as he reached for a glass of iced tea. "This is a mighty nice spread."

A slightly unpleasant odor permeated the air, causing me to inspect her more closely. I pinched the edge of her pant leg and rubbed the cloth between my thumb and forefinger. She was covered in some kind of fluid. When I asked what happened to her clothes they chuckled more.

"Sprayer swung around and caught her before she steered clear," Perry announced.

"This looks delicious!" Cash swooned again, which seemed to be her reaction to anything edible.

"What do you mean, swung around? You mean you sprayed her?" My voice rose.

"Pretty much," Cash said, straight-faced, then looked at Perry and giggled some more.

"Did you get it in your eyes? Go shower! Scrub from head to toe and wash your hair. I mean it. That chemical's nothing to fool around with and you need to get it off your skin right now. Go!"

She jumped up as if hot-wired and darted inside the house, heading for the shower as I addressed Perry. "Why didn't you bring her up here right away?"

"It happened just before we got here, and that last tank was pretty watered down. She was in the lead and I swung around and she hung back instead of going wide."

"Looks like the two of you haven't got the sense God gave a goat." I tried to reason why I was so mad over Cash being sprayed. My mind flashed on Johnny and I shook my head to blow that image away, realizing that must be the cause. I didn't want another terrible accident to happen due to my inattention.

"Not gonna kill her," Perry continued, as if picking up on my thoughts.

"You gonna teach her to ranch or become a kid yourself?"

"Never was one so I might like to try it. You make a great lunch, Maggie Tanner." He spoke my name with his usual supercilious formality and nodded at me appreciatively as he chewed, oblivious to the chewing he was getting.

Minutes later she was out of the shower and back at the table, barefoot in a pair of fresh jeans and a dark tank top, her arms muscled as if she worked out and her hair wet and matted to her head.

"Everything okay?" She looked up with sparkling eyes.

Her presence seemed to drain the angry energy out of me and I settled down, then started to say that few women looked as good as she did with their hair wet but suddenly, self-conscious, changed my phrasing. "You've got good bone structure." I concentrated on my food as I mumbled, "I'm so used to looking for it in livestock that I notice it in people."

"Thank you." She smiled. "I like the way your hair falls down around your face, kind of like you pulled it up but then it decided it had a different plan. And you have really flashy eyes, like you get fired up over things."

"She gets fired up all right." Perry grinned between bites. The casual way she commented on my appearance, unabashedly examining my face, embarrassed me. Frankly, I didn't know if I was attractive or not, since no one around here mentioned how I looked one way or the other, and I wasn't a good judge of myself. "Nobody got anything to say about *my* looks?" Perry paused mid-chew.

"You're rustic," Cash said.

"Rusty?" He seemed indignant.

"Rustic," she repeated, "like this terrific old ranch house."

He thought about that, then started eating again, obviously content to be a ramshackle building.

Dropping the subject of good looks, Cash bubbled over with descriptions of the back pasture as if I'd never seen it. She waved her arms, describing how the scissortails swooped overhead, and she bounced on the bench as she talked about the white-tailed deer that leapt into the woods as she approached. For a moment, I just watched her, thinking how energized she was.

When I brought the cherry pie out, she half rose off the bench waving her arms and nearly caused me to drop the glass pie pan, exclaiming that cherry was her favorite. She apologized as Perry chuckled and said if she kept it up we'd have to eat it off the floor. I cut them both a large slice and eased it onto the plates. She dove in and ate it slowly, rolling her eyes to the heavens.

"You makin' love to that pie or eating it?" Perry asked, and Cash raised an eyebrow but never stopped devouring it.

She looks sexy. Bet Buck had a hell of a time when she was growing up.

She suddenly glanced in my direction. "I hear your mind ticking away. What are you thinking?"

Caught off guard, I stammered. "I've never seen cherry pie so well received."

"I don't think that's what you were thinking," she said.

I felt myself blush and Perry grinned. "She's a pretty smart little gal, Maggie. Better be careful around her." Cash looked right into my eyes and her penetrating gaze gave me chills. Where did someone her age get the confidence to look right through you, and why on God's green earth did she do it? *Too familiar. I'll have to make it a point to teach her some manners. You don't stare at people around here. This is Kansas.*

❖

The following afternoon the big cattle trucks backed into the pasture and dropped their load gates, and dozens of Black Angus cows jogged out of their crowded transport and onto the green grass, pushing and shoving to find their spot in the field. The freckle-faced, dirt-covered driver hopped down out of the cab to greet me, leaving the motor running.

"A hundred head." He nodded toward his wards. "Said he'd send you a check for the lease."

"Tell him he owes me for last season," I said, making eye contact with the young man, who ducked his head.

"He said to tell you he intends to pay you."

"Tell him I intend to *get* paid." I grinned back at him, then signed the paper he held out. He was gone in only minutes and Perry, on his small chestnut mare, Peanuts, signaled that he had them under control. Peanuts knew the drill and almost single-handedly herded the cattle north and into an unsprayed pasture, where I hoped they'd leave my Bermuda alone and eat the rugged Johnson grass.

I stayed away from the cattle herd, not wanting to get attached to them, because they were destined to be bred, calved, and culled—the young males headed for fattening up before slaughter.

Right after I was married, Johnny wanted us to get into the cattle business. He saw them as dumb animals who had no idea where they were headed, but I had deeper feelings for animals than for people. Animals by and large were more honest. If they didn't like you, they kicked you, and their reaction was quick and direct. Plus, they had bigger hearts. Despite the pain inflicted on them, horses, cattle, and dogs all did their jobs when asked and forgave you the treatment they received. Johnny called me a hypocrite for eating beef but being unwilling to support the food chain. In support of my position, I tried being a vegetarian, but failed.

Nowadays, the most I could muster was to lease my pastureland, openly owning the fact that I was a cattle coward and that's why I raised hay and horses.

An hour later I was in the living room as Perry and Cash bounced up the back steps, having secured the cattle in the north pasture. I looked diagonally over their shoulders as they entered and noticed something odd about the herd streaming two abreast north beyond the property line. I grabbed my binoculars to make sure I was seeing right.

"Perry," I shouted, and he jumped, being in closer proximity to me than I realized. "Cattle are going right out the north gate." Perry bounded back out onto the porch and jumped aboard Peanuts, gave her a quick kick, and headed off in the direction of the cows.

I headed out the front door, cranked up the Gator, and sped after him. He swerved left around the outside of the rambling bovine and I swung right, hanging back. The cattle picked up the pace. I pulled wide so I wouldn't scare them, but they were already loping at a steady gait. Perry was skilled at this kind of work and deftly made his way up to the front of the herd, waving his lariat and whistling for Duke, the big gray-and-black Australian shepherd named for his hero, John Wayne. Doing the legendary cowboy proud, Duke quickly moved into position and swung the cattle slowly toward the gate opening.

I jumped out and held the gate wide to accommodate the shoulder-to-shoulder throng streaming through. Duke and Perry dashed back in the opposite direction to head off the last remaining two that had slipped past them. Duke did most the work and soon everybody was safely back inside the fence, and I closed the gate. Perry looked ebullient, obviously missing his cattle-driving youth, and Duke with his tongue hanging out was almost smiling.

Cash approached at a run. "It was me. I left the gate open when we cut through to spray."

Trying not to show my annoyance, I said nothing.

"That was impressive herding, Perry." Her praise clearly warmed him like a bonfire and he tipped his hat to her.

"Mama's 'closing rule': fridge, mouth, gates. Keep 'em all shut." Perry grinned at Cash, who grinned back.

I felt she should be more contrite over the trouble she'd caused, and I couldn't believe Perry was letting her off so easy. He would normally grouse and gritch about the stupidity of even the slightest error anyone made.

"Cash, come ride with me." When I called her away from Perry she jogged over and jumped into the Gator, clanging her boots against the metal interior.

"You're ticked, I know. I'm sorry." She propped one big boot up on the dashboard and held onto the side of the seat as I swerved intentionally to jolt the cockiness out of her.

"You need some working boots. Pointy toes and slick bottoms are for drugstore cowboys," I remarked.

"These are my favorites." She seemed unperturbed by my insult. "I've line danced fifty miles in these boots."

"Well, that's about what they're good for, unless you want your 'Achy Breaky Heart' to extend to your ankles." When she didn't respond I kept probing. "I just assumed, knowing Buck, that you grew up on a ranch."

"But now you know I didn't, because of the gate deal?"

"I know because of your soft hands." I wanted to retract the words. They sounded too personal. I meant that I noticed her hands weren't callused when I handed her the milk and she pulled the glass back. "What I—"

"I know what you meant." I must have appeared flustered because she added, "You thought it sounded funny, the way you said it." She looked at me as if searching my soul for something.

"No harm in wherever you grew up. I simply don't want to tell you things you already know, but I don't want to leave out things you *need* to know." I stopped in front of the house and shut off the engine.

"Tell me anything." Her tone seemed to ask me to confide in her, and while I was trying to summon an offended response, something completely foreign tingled across my shoulders, like electroshock, launching me out of the Gator.

"If you leave another gate open, I'll simply shoot you." *She really doesn't know her place.* I headed into the house, not wanting or needing any more discussion.

Moments later, Cash walked into the living room and I glanced down at her Saturday-night-shuffle boots. "Next time rake the bottoms on the wire boot brush outside the front door." I avoided looking at her and grabbed a broom out of the mud room, trying to sweep the dried dirt chunks off the floor before we walked on them and created a powder that would scatter everywhere.

"I thought I knocked them off, sorry," she said, this time sounding like she meant it. She took the broom from me, looking beautiful: shirt hanging out, pants dirty, her curly short hair half sweat-matted, and still that face and her stature made her look good. *Lucky girl,* I thought.

"Tell you what. Why don't we go down to the southeast pasture and bring the horses up. You might like to ride." *Best thing is to get her mind on horses. That's what summers on a ranch should be about.*

She brightened. "I didn't see horses when we were driving around."

"They stay under the trees in the grove where it's cool. Hard to see them. I'll gas up the XUV while you get the halters and brushes and a few horse cookies out of the tack room, and let's see if we can coax them into being useful."

Twenty minutes later we sped across the pasture in my new

all-terrain vehicle that looked more like a military jeep than ranch transportation, with its heavy-duty grid work, roof-mount searchlights, and shotgun rack.

"Like your ride." She tossed the words into the wind as it whipped our faces.

"For my personal use, but you can use the Gator anytime you need to."

"You realize, if I hit a rut at this speed in the Gator, my stomach will leave my body through my mouth." She was obviously trying to finagle driving permission.

"Then drive slow and keep your mouth shut." I gave her a slight smile, letting her know the pecking order. People, like animals, had to establish who was in charge.

"Good advice." She seemed to mull over my reply.

The horses raised their heads as we approached the grove, but never budged from their spot under the trees, swishing flies away with their tails. Three of them ate grass, and two others scratched their necks against the trunks of the thick oaks. I immediately scanned them for abrasions or cuts or insect bites, quick to end small casualties that could become calamitous.

"Stop right here for a minute. Look at them. I love all the colors—white, black, bay, pinto, and palomino. If you took a picture right now, it would be like some famous painting. It's magical." She held her thumbs and forefingers up, framing an imaginary shot.

I remained still, allowing her to study the animal tableaux as they pretended to ignore us. When the bugs began to swarm I suggested we lead the horses up to the barn where she could brush them. "Get their halters."

A pause ensued. "I forgot them." She made an exaggerated facial expression that seemed to beg me to find her absent-mindedness funny.

"How did you think we were going to catch them?" I frowned.

"Cookies?" She giggled and pulled one from her jeans pocket. "It's okay." She tried to soothe me. "We can just feed them here. I can ride another day."

I refrained from saying it wasn't up to her to decide what was okay. Furthermore, I had planned on getting them up to the barn to give them their ivermectin wormer and check their hooves. *She acts like she's on another planet.* One of the horses blew air through its nostrils, seemingly in loud desultory agreement.

"You like things to work out just like you planned, don't you?" Her constant good humor annoyed me, as if she thought she was smarter or more worldly or the frontier's Dr. Phil.

"If you live on a ranch, you have to plan your work and work your plan—"

"Or there'll be nothing in the frying pan?" She lightly mocked me.

"No," I said, flatly annoyed. "You'll just be majorly screwed, that's all." She blinked. I had clearly one-upped her in the common-vernacular department, and her surprised look gave me pleasure.

For a moment we stared at one another, sizing each other up, and then she giggled. I smirked in response. *You may be young and good-looking, but you're no match for me. Maybe Buck was right, I should work your ass off.*

"Hop out," I said sternly, and she quickly jumped out of the XUV. "Why don't you catch the mare and take her up to the barn. I'll meet you there."

I pulled away in the vehicle as she called plaintively after me. "What will I catch her with?"

The thought of a stranger ever catching Mariah, my haughty white mare, amused me. Even with a halter and lead rope it would be tough, but without one it might become someone's life's work.

"I think you're relying on cookies," I called back over my shoulder and drove away, leaving her standing in the field.

CHAPTER FOUR

Two hours later, I picked up the binoculars resting on the window sill to check on Cash. She'd gone back to the barn, which was about a hundred yards from the house down a dirt path lined with big oaks and the occasional willow that had taken hold in response to the presence of a once-meandering creek.

Cash had gotten a halter and lead rope but the mare was still having none of it, circling her, swishing her tail, staying out of reach. At one point, the magnificent white horse even stole the cookie from Cash's outstretched fingertips and escaped the lead line that flopped over her neck. Cash threw all her gear to the ground and slumped against a tree.

At dusk, Cash was still down in the pasture with the contrary Mariah, trying to talk her into coming up to the barn, I assumed, in order to help Cash save face. She missed dinner and I decided to leave her alone. Apparently, something about Cash's inability to get the mare to come to her fueled her need to stick with the pursuit until she won.

I checked one more time when it was nearly dark, able to make out the white mare who no longer ran but, having assessed all Cash's moves, simply and gracefully sidestepped any capture attempts. I started to head off to bed, then decided to throw on some jeans and tell her to call it a night and give them both a break.

Wandering down the footpath toward the barn was always my favorite journey. Soft dirt covered the ground's barrenness, and the occasional exposed tree root crossed over the rugged dirt lane, sometimes tripping me despite the number of times I'd traversed this trail. Curving slightly around three big shade trees and tilting downhill, it led me toward the small red barn with the lantern lights illuminating it. At the end, I spotted Perry standing about fifteen feet from Cash. Apparently, he too could no longer take the aggravation or feared the mare wouldn't.

"Why don't you try for another horse and give this one a rest?" he groused. "Unless, of course, you just like rejection."

"I'm familiar with it, but can't say that I like it," she said, good-natured despite the circumstance. Somehow I didn't think she was joking, but I couldn't imagine what personal rejection someone as young and attractive as Cash could have experienced.

"You the most stubborn one in your family?" Perry's voice was strained.

"Close." She kicked at the ground with her toe.

"You gotta think like a horse," he said, turning his head to spit chaw onto the ground. "She don't want to get herself into any situation she can't run from. She's got a pretty good idea what you're up to with that rope, and once you got her, she knows she won't be able to run. So you gotta let her know you're a horse like she is. Turn away from her and duck your head and back up a little bit toward her."

Cash did as Perry asked and the mare moved farther away. "Doesn't seem to be working," she said.

"Nothing works right off. But act like a horse and you'll attract a horse."

I backed away, not wanting to disturb the conversation. Perry was a better teacher than I, and it was obvious he liked Cash.

"Don't stare at her. Horses don't like you to stare at 'em. Check out the grass like you're interested in something down there and then kind of sidle up to her like you're just looking for a better spot for both of you to stare at the grass together."

Perry's instructions faded off into the night as I walked slowly back up to the house, checking my watch along the way. Cash had been at it with that horse for a solid six hours. She had tenacity, which was a good thing out here on the prairie. People who gave up were done in. *Now if she just had common sense to go with it, we might* actually *be able to have a conversation.*

❖

The following morning, I found a scribbled note on the counter that said, "I'm down with the horses." The handwriting was less like writing and more like elegant printing—straight short strokes penned with an occasional flourish. I studied the artistic writing for a moment before I picked up a pen and wrote across the bottom of the page that I'd gone to town and would be back in a few hours. I grabbed the keys to the truck and backed out of the driveway, anxious to get away from my new responsibility.

The drive gave me a minute alone to think. Cash had only been here forty-eight hours and already life was crazy, routine upended, my days filled with what she was doing or not doing.

Well, you knew what you were getting when you agreed to let her stay on, the voice in my head admonished. What I didn't know is that she wasn't raised on a ranch, I defended myself to myself. She can be taught like anyone else, the voice in my head insisted. Sure, if I had the time, or the desire, to be a camp counselor or women's dean or God knows what. We have nothing in common so I have no idea what to talk to her about. We could discuss ranching if she knew a damned thing about anything.

I stopped talking to myself when the 2-K appeared on my left, and I realized I'd driven all the way to town without knowing it. *How had I managed to avoid being hit on the highway? I'm as goofy as she is.*

I pushed open the café's heavy glass door and Donnetta greeted me with a whoop. She poured two cups of coffee and joined me in the booth, beaming.

"So how's the new worker doing?" she said, without preliminaries, and I was reminded again of the verbal incestuousness of this small town. Perry must have gone in to get diesel for the tractor and mentioned Cash to Sven Olan, the gas-station attendant, and that's all it took to have the entire town informed in a few hours.

"Not good?" Her tone mirrored my dejected expression. "She'll catch on. Remember when you first came out here."

"She got in the way of the sprayer and was doused in chemicals, she left the gates open and let the cows out, she goes to get the horses and forgets their halters. I'm afraid she'll fall in the damned pond and drown. She doesn't know up from down."

"I seem to remember a story about you trying to can apples and the pressure cooker exploded and applesauce covered the ceiling."

"That was twenty years ago." I smiled, thinking about how many decades I'd been telling Donnetta my troubles.

"Can she work cattle or horses?"

"She doesn't know their ass from their eyeballs. She's been trying to catch my mare for eighteen straight hours."

Donnetta laughed and I joined in. "You're just not used to women workers. You hire good ole boys and throw them out there with Perry and never have to think about 'em. Don't sell women short."

"What are you, the local chapter of NOW?"

"My group's the National Organization of Weirdos." She whirled on the skinny guy bussing tables as if he was the organization's poster boy. "Wash that rag before you use it on the counter." He scurried off into the back room. "Wipes something off the floor and then uses it on the tables."

"So long as he doesn't wipe out the coffee pot with it," I said under my breath.

"Can't guarantee it."

A short, hefty man with close-cropped facial hair and wearing jeans and a striped shirt, the buttons straining from holding in his bulk, broadsided me with his hip, playfully shoving me over in the booth.

"Buddy, don't squash her," Donnetta yelped at her considerably shorter and wider husband.

A big hairy arm encircled my shoulder. "She likes being squashed by a hunk, a hunk a burning love." Buddy gave me a big lip smack on the cheek and squeezed me. "How ya doin', baby?"

"Let go of her, Buddy." Donnetta slapped at his arm from

across the table. "She's got trouble with the new ranch hand and we're talking, so you don't need to be interrupting."

"What's city girl doing?" he asked, letting me know Cash's city status had obviously made it from the gas station to the café.

"What city girls do," Donnetta interjected. "Trying to learn how to get along in the country, only she's got Ms. Stanwyck here doing the teaching, and Miss Barbara's not the most patient woman on the planet."

"Why can't Perry teach her?" Buddy asked Donnetta, the two of them leaving me out of the conversation.

"Perry's got less patience than she does, and who needs to pay a worker to teach another worker. You end up with fifty percent of the former and zero percent of the latter," Donnetta replied. "She hired the gal because she needed more help, not less."

"When you two get this thoroughly discussed, let me know the solution. I've got to get back to the ranch before she sets the place on fire."

I tried to get out of the booth but Buddy wouldn't let me, pestering being his modus operandi with women. I couldn't count the number of times Buddy had trapped me in a damned booth at the 2-K, and if he hadn't been Donnetta's husband, I would have straightened him out on how tired I was of being played with like a Barbie Doll.

I flicked a teaspoon onto the floor when he wasn't looking, and he bent to pick it up. I pushed his behind with my foot, catching him off balance and sending him to his knees and out onto the floor.

"Hey, I'm being a gentleman," he barked, picking himself up.

"Flattened by prairie-boy politeness."

As I escaped the booth and headed for the door, they were still discussing Cash. My dilemma would keep them occupied for a few days and give Jonas Wiley, my neighbor to the south, a break. He'd been the topic of conversation for a week because his kid got himself trapped in a sewer drain at school and the volunteer fire department had to fish him out.

I walked down the sidewalk to the hardware store the Benegan family had owned for forty years and, as far as I could tell, their slogan was accurate: America's last great collection of necessary items under one roof. Sewing machines, raccoon traps, moccasins, roofing nails, hand cream, taxidermy services, and prom dresses. Walmart of the Woods.

I entered and headed for the section of the store with all the hunting and fishing equipment and directly to a rack with soft deerskin gloves in bright yellow. Picking out a women's large, I held it up, then placed it against my own hand for sizing. As the soft animal hide brushed my palm, I recalled how Cash's hand felt that day I first shook it and a tingling sensation crossed my body. I put the gloves back, as if that particular pair had caused it, and quickly picked up a men's medium. Laying my hand against it, I closed my eyes and again felt the sensation, as if I were excited about something. *What, a dead deer?* I mocked myself.

"Maggie, can I help you with anything?" I jumped. Bea Benegan was a friendly, middle-aged woman who wore heavy black shoes built to compensate for one shorter leg, which gave her walk an odd swing. Her flowered polyester dress fit tight across her large bosom, and her braided gray hair sat coiled atop her head as if waiting to break loose and strike.

"No, no. Just, uh…I have a new worker and need to buy them some gloves."

"Well, you can get cheaper ones than this for a worker."

"It's the daughter of a friend who's out for the summer."

"The Tate girl, of course," Bea said assuredly, proving she was still tapped into the Little Liberty party line. "You think those will fit her? Does she have big hands?"

"Larger than mine by probably an inch or so."

Bea wiggled as if titillated by the fact that I knew the size of Cash's hands, information that provided her with a thread of gossip that could be woven into several stories—can't run a ranch, treats workers like guests, spends money like water.

Bea interrupted my thoughts. "Well, these gloves are the nicest ones in the store. And if they don't fit, you know you can bring them back."

"I'll take them." I was anxious to pay and leave and felt self-conscious for no reason. She rang up the purchase and chatted about everything under the sun before I finally escaped, the gloves tucked safely away in their sack. Regaining my composure, I put my thoughts back onto the errands at hand and drove over to the gas station.

Sven Olan, a tall skinny Swede ran the station, its logo so chipped and worn the *S* could no longer be discerned, making people believe their gas came from hell, a higher octane for sure. Sven hurried over as if he'd been sitting at the window waiting for me to arrive. Grabbing the pump handle and inserting the nozzle into my truck's gas tank, he happily controlled the flow of fuel so he could get his fill of conversation.

His sister, Verta, a tall blond gal with huge breasts and tight leather pants, stood twenty feet behind him and waved at me. Not a duo that made me very comfortable, both of them always kind of eyed me as if they wanted to talk about something they couldn't quite get around to—her in particular. "Heard you got some help out there now," he shouted into the wind.

"You heard right," I replied, intentionally keeping information to a minimum.

He rubbed his oily fingers on a gasoline rag and tucked it into the back pocket of his rust-orange bib overalls. "She's tall, I hear." His tone encouraged me to fill in the blanks for him.

"Didn't measure her." I grinned, thinking height was an odd place to start, but both Verta and Sven were tall Nordic types in a community of somewhat squat folk so maybe her height really interested them.

"Perry seems to like her."

"Seems to."

"How long she staying?" He'd finally found a phrase that required I submit new information.

"Long as she likes it, I guess."

"She like it, you guess?" This was the point in a Kansas conversation where I could always feel my hackles rising.

"Have to ask her the next time you see her."

"Ain't never seen her or I'd a known she was tall without asking." The final statement let me know his feelings were hurt.

"I'm sure she'll come into town one of these days and you can see for yourself." I thanked him for the service, cranked up the engine, and headed back to the ranch, wishing I'd learned to be more social and invite people out when they were angling for an invitation, but I couldn't find it in me. And conversations for the sake of hearing yourself talk just annoyed me.

It was dusk when I pulled into the main gates and under the metal arch that welcomed me home. Cash was carrying something toward her Jeep, and for a panicked moment I thought maybe someone had told her I wasn't happy with her and she'd decided to leave. My heartbeat increased as I stopped the truck and got out and walked toward her.

"What are you doing?" I asked, a bit breathless.

"Going to put this in the back of the Gator." I glanced down at what she was carrying: thermos, blanket, wrapped foil package, and a few other indistinguishable items. "Perry and I are about to cook some hotdogs down by the pond and then go fishing."

"How do you intend to cook by the pond?"

"Campfire."

"In this wind, you'll catch the whole place on fire." My mind jumped to the random joke I'd made to Donnetta about Cash's setting the ranch ablaze. Was I somehow prescient? *Perry knows better than that, he's acting like a schoolboy.*

"He's got some kind of contained hibachi thing and that's why we're doing it by the pond bank, to be safe. Want to come?"

"No." I bit off the word to avoid saying how ridiculous I thought their plan was. "And look out for snakes." Now she'd made Perry completely useless. *A cookout, for God's sake.* I didn't pay my ranch foreman to be a cruise director. Why in hell was he spending time entertaining her instead of training her?

"Sure? It'll be fun." Her smile coaxed me.

I shook my head only slightly, indicating my first response

stood and that I didn't need to repeat it. She started to say something more but probably felt she was pressing her luck.

I busied myself in the kitchen and the living room straightening and cleaning. Then I pulled a book on horse care off the shelf and tried to read it. Finally I went out the back door and walked down to the pasture.

Warm and sticky, the air blew around me as I walked briskly, intent on getting rid of the nervous energy that seemed to have taken over my skin, arriving with the impending summer heat and Cash Tate.

The horses were gathered under the same trees, and I longed for a life that simple. Sebastian, the black part-Percheron, ambled over to see me. He was kin to the old horse Johnny had taught to pull a plow after he decided he wanted to know how to do things the way his grandfather had done them. Sebastian didn't pull his own weight, much less a plow, but I filled his days with hay and hugs and scratched his huge forehead. He briefly acknowledged me before deciding I had nothing interesting to add to his life and returned to the clumps of rich green grass I'd left uncut to accommodate late grazing in the grove.

I hung over the fence, my boot on the bottom rail, and just breathed. Knight, the bay gelding, strolled over and nuzzled me across the white vinyl slats of the paddock.

"Hey, you." I greeted the sweet horse whose name bespoke his mannerly behavior and kissed him on the muzzle. "How's the rest of the gang treating you?" I glanced at Mariah, the white mare who glared in our direction, ears flattened, jealous over the attention I was giving Knight. Mariah seemed to be warning him that he'd stepped out of line in the pecking order and hadn't received permission from the higher-ranking horse to visit me.

"Stop it, Mariah." I spoke sharply and her ears pricked up. She went back to grazing as if she'd decided neither of us was worth the effort. "Don't take any crap from her, Knight," I warned the bay. "You come see me any time you want." He blew air out through his nostrils in a large sigh, and I waited when he walked away, wanting to make sure Mariah wouldn't attack him. "You could come see me yourself, you know," I said to the arrogant white mare, who turned her butt to me in disdain. I pivoted and wandered back to the house, noting that she was already making her way to the fence, no doubt sorry she'd let me go.

For a moment I thought about Cash's experience with the mare and how Cash had stayed for hours, trying to win her over, while I gave Mariah only a brief moment to make up her mind and then moved on to other things. Living out here had taught me that holding onto anything too tight in the prairie wind only enabled the forces of nature to shred it.

Near dusk, the setting sun cast an exquisite glow on the western horizon. I looked up at the sky in time to see streaks of orange and purple slowly reveal strange-shaped animals and landscapes that remained for only minutes, then morphed into something else before disappearing altogether.

As I approached the house, I heard laughter in the distance over by the pond and paused to listen. While I couldn't make out the words, it was clear Perry and Cash were having a good time. I stepped up on the porch, sat down in a rocker, and continued to watch the light drift below the horizon line, leaving only shadows to play out their last act before the curtain of darkness fell.

Duke ambled around the side of the house and took up residence beside my chair, and I scratched the mass of gray ticking around his neck. Like most herd dogs, he was smart and obedient and came when I called him. He nudged me with his pointed nose, inquiring about food. I took a Milk-Bone out of my pocket that I carried just for his late-evening snack. He crunched on it slowly, perhaps to make it last.

Out of the darkness, the tall lean figure approached, shirt askew, hair rumpled and blowing slightly in the wind. She stopped at seeing me.

"Hi. Could I join you?"

"You live here too," I said.

"That sounds nice." Her voice was soft. She moved to the porch steps and sat down on the top one, slouching against the newel post.

As she watched the sunset, I feasted on her profile. She looked as if an invisible photographer had asked her to pose for a Ralph Lauren ad. No matter how disheveled, she always looked great. An elegant masculinity.

"Sounded like you were having a good time." I spoke kindly, mellowed by the moment.

"Catch and release. Only every time we'd catch one, it would release itself."

I actually enjoyed her mountains of energy for mundane activities. I made an effort to conserve mine, or at least monitor it, and make sure I had enough to spread across the entire day. Her fingers moved lightly across the wooden step with their dried plank ridges, once smooth and painted, now appearing like inland driftwood, porous and weathered.

"How old is this place?" she asked.

"Older than dirt. Settled in the late 1800s, farmed by three generations of Blakes, the third my husband, John."

She looked up when I said his name. "It's so magical out here. I can see why you didn't leave." Her remark made me wonder how much Buck had told her about my having decided to stay on after John died. Buck knew Johnny because we were all in college together. In fact, he'd encouraged me to date him. I often wondered if he hadn't, where I would be and with whom. And now here I was looking into the eyes of Buck's daughter, the wheel of time having taken a strange turn.

"You have this great ranch, you can cook, you're good-looking…how come you never remarried?"

I was glad to have the darkness cover my embarrassment. "I guess I never fell in love."

"Were you in love the first time?"

"That's kind of a personal question, don't you think, Ms. Tate?" I tried to sound more mature in my response than she had been in her question.

"Yes." The word and her gaze were unabashedly direct.

"Do you have a boyfriend?" I quickly reversed the questioning to put her on the spot.

"We broke up."

"So you're here to heal a broken heart." I was feeling more in control now, on the offensive.

"I don't know. But I'm glad I'm here. Or I wouldn't have met you."

Before I could respond, Perry approached, carrying the hibachi, and stopped at the porch rail to announce, "Didn't catch anything."

"Couldn't land anything, you mean." She stood up and dusted off her pants and dashed inside, waving a playful good night to him.

"Need to teach that girl not to rat me out. Tomorrow we'll get to it. Just needed a break," he said, referring to the ranch work that was always on my mind. He wandered off to the bunkhouse. "You might think about taking a break, yourself." He tossed the words over his shoulder like spilt salt. The only failing for which he ever admonished me, and lately he'd been doing it more often.

"I'm fine." I gave my standard reply. But the truth was, I wasn't. Even I had come to that realization. Most of the time I felt so hollow the wind could blow right through me. I tried to fill the hole inside me with activity, things that didn't matter, but the wind still whistled as if trying desperately to get my attention. I sat for a moment, thinking about what Perry had said and then about Cash, who complimented me whenever she got the chance, and I felt a little guilty for having told Donnetta she was incompetent. *But she is incompetent.* My inner voice refused to let me go soft on her. "But *charmingly* incompetent," I said into the darkness to no one but myself.

Chapter Five

B y the first of June coyotes nesting down by the pond had babies big enough to venture out. This morning a large, skinny, slope-shouldered adult slinked across the pasture and came too near the house long after sunrise. Left unchecked, he might be joined by his mate and gang up on one of the barn cats, so I headed out in my XUV to ward off trouble. Cash spotted me and ran alongside, grabbed the ceiling handle, and swung her long body in.

"Very cushy ride. Tell me again why you get the XUV?"

"Cuz I'm the ranch owner and you're the ranch *hand*." I raised an eyebrow in her direction, only half kidding.

"So where are we going, ranch owner?" she asked as cheerily as if she'd been invited.

"Lean down," I ordered, as I reached behind her for the shotgun hooked on the metal mesh divider. I stopped abruptly, throwing her forward and giving myself room to load two shells, and pumped the first one into the chamber.

"Damn." She laughed as I stepped on the gas, snapping her head back intentionally as I barreled toward the high growth around the pond. Suddenly two coyotes sprang into action and I fired a shot just behind them as they skittered off into the field ahead and down into the trees on Hiram's land.

"You missed." Cash whooped.

"I intended to miss."

"Now that's the worst excuse I've ever heard." Her devilish expression tempted me into sparring with her.

"I don't like to kill things when scaring them will do."

"I've never *seen* such a wild shot!"

"Then you don't get out much." I swerved left suddenly, pitching her right and nearly out of the vehicle as she shrieked. Seconds later, I slammed on the brakes as we arrived at the house.

"I'm kidding, don't kill me," she said, as she tumbled out of the vehicle and then managed to get her feet under her.

I pulled away and headed down to the pasture. By myself again, I could physically relax. *Completely inappropriate. She's my ranch hand, not my friend, for God's sake. Maybe she's just having trouble finding her center. After all, sounds like she kind of got shipped out here as a favor. I was probably a smart-ass myself when I first arrived, using jaded humor to cover up for plenty of times when I wanted to kill people for their cruelty or cry from loneliness or simply run away.* The prairie had grounded me and held me to the earth, and the wind whipped me back into shape, reminding me that if small, helpless creatures could survive on the prairie alone, I should be ashamed to do anything but thrive. Maybe with time Cash would even out. Perhaps that's why Buck sent her—thinking I could possibly help her.

Restless, I made a U-turn, parked the XUV, hopped out, and got into my truck, the destination unimportant, moving rather than thinking, perhaps "driving myself out of my mind."

Exiting the front gates, I drove two miles south of the ranch, then west down a dirt road to a twenty- by thirty-foot white metal building with a hand-drawn sign nailed to a post saying Feed Store. The makeshift store was run by a young couple, Jock and Sara Goodie, who'd just moved to the area. She was a petite blonde who often worked behind the new plywood counter, and her stocky, buffed husband was nowhere in sight, by his own admission on the road every Thursday night to satisfy his rodeo habit.

Like a lot of local boys, he welded pipe and plowed fields during the week to earn entry fees and gas money for weekend bronc riding. Farming and ranching were high-risk businesses that after twenty years could often end in broken equipment, bones, and marriages, but the rodeo circuit seemed to deliver the same pain in record time. And I wondered if Sara and Jock Goodie would be married in five years, much less in business.

I hopped out of the truck and walked past a pickup with a bumper sticker proclaiming BEHIND EVERY SUCCESSFUL RANCHER IS A WIFE WHO WORKS IN TOWN.

Sara brightened on seeing me, greeting me with a smile and a strong handshake, as if I was the only customer she'd had today. She quickly went about locating the fifty-pound sack of sweet feed, another of rolled oats, and an equally large sack of dog food. I dropped the tailgate and she slung them into the truck bed with ease.

"You like this old baby blue bomber?" She patted the faded truck fender as if it were an animal, and I told her I liked it when it ran. "We're looking at a really cute Ford truck for me. If Jock gets into the money on his next ride, I think we'll buy it."

"I'll keep my fingers crossed," I said, as a gust of wind blew loose dirt and hay up from the adjoining field and slapped it into my face. I turned and sputtered, trying to get it out of my mouth.

"Been blowing like this for weeks. Don't know if it'll ever stop."

"You doing okay out here?" I asked somewhat obliquely, looking out over the prairie as if I might be asking about her chosen location and not her sales figures.

"I think business will pick up once people know we're here." Her doubt was evident behind the cheerfulness. I wanted to tell her that folks knew she was here but hadn't decided if they wanted to let her in. A hazing period seemed to follow the warm welcome a person got when they moved to Little Liberty. Just because town folks welcomed you didn't mean they were encouraging you to stay. They waited to see if the grit in your teeth would make its way to your resolve. No need to start liking somebody only to feel sorry for them and be downhearted when they left.

I thanked Sara and wished her well as I climbed into the truck cab. Dust kicked up on the driveway ahead of me, and Stretch

Adams's shiny fifth wheel approached head-on and pulled up alongside me so he could hang out his truck window and greet me eye to eye two feet from my left elbow.

"Stopped over at your place and your gal said you were out. Didn't expect to run into you, my lucky day." Stretch showed his uneven front teeth and leered at me as if waiting for me to make the next move.

"What can I do you for?" I joked.

"You could do me for nothing." He kind of snickered like he had something in mind he couldn't discuss in broad daylight. "I was wondering if you wanted to go out for dinner Saturday night. Maybe drive into Maze City and go to a movie or something after."

"That's very thoughtful of you, Stretch, but I've got company now and more coming." I mentally referenced Cash but threw Buck into the imaginary guest list rather than say straight out that I didn't want to go on a date with him.

He looked a little put out. "Another time, then." He yanked the truck's gear into reverse, wheeled his vehicle around, and sprayed gravel into the air as he fishtailed onto the highway. Pipes, propane tanks, and other paraphernalia slid across the back of his truck bed and banged into each other in metallic displeasure.

Sara wandered over to my truck window. "You know Mr. Adams?" When I nodded, she said, "He ran up a bill when we first came out here and I think he's forgotten to pay it. I was hoping to catch him."

Stretch hadn't forgotten, he'd just gotten by. "Sorry I ran him off. He works for Hiram Kendall at the lumber mill in town. Next time you're in there, you might stop and ask."

She nodded and I headed back to the ranch. Something about Stretch Adams gave me the creeps, especially the way he wasn't embarrassed to look me over like he was sizing up a piece of meat. I chastised myself for being so critical. Stretch Adams had made two trips out to the ranch in an ice storm last winter to help me with an injured cow when Perry was so sick with the flu he couldn't move a muscle.

Face it, down deep you always think men want to take you out to get a piece of your land or a piece of your ass, the little voice in my head said. "I do suspect people's motives," I answered firmly to the dashboard, as if something outside myself had framed the question.

A few minutes later I pulled into the ranch, got out, and started to unload the feed, but then thought better. Cash should do it. Being treated like any other worker was part of her ranch-hand experience.

I walked through the house and didn't see her, so I went straight through the living room and out the back door, catching sight of her in the distance under the barn overhang where hay bales were stacked. As I approached, I saw she was bent over, snipping baling wire to break open square bales for the horses, and her jeans hung off her behind, showing an expanse of muscular lower back and a tight butt. *I swear she's built like a boy.*

"What are you up to?"

She ducked her head and answered into the hay. "Just doing some work for Perry. That Stretch guy was out here asking where you were."

"Yes, I ran into him."

"I think he's got the hots for you." She held her palms together and winced slightly.

"What makes you think that?"

"Maybe it was the drool around the edge of his mouth. Or maybe that's just him." She grinned wickedly, apparently undeterred in her attempts to torment me, and I chuckled in spite of myself. Looking down, I noticed the way she was holding her hand.

"What'd you do?"

"Nothing. Told him where you were, that's all." She sounded defensive.

"To your hand. Let me see it." I held out mine and she turned hers over, revealing a bloody slice across the left palm. "How the hell did you do that?"

"Wire snapped up and cut me like a razor."

I glanced down at the baling wire that had rusted during the winter. "Come on." I entered the barn and she followed me to the tack room, where I opened a small overhead cabinet.

"When you cut baling wire, keep your left hand—"

"I know how to do it. This was just a freak thing and the wire was really tight."

"Wear gloves." I reached for the hydrogen peroxide.

"No, not that, it'll burn like hell!" she yelled as I poured it over her palm.

"Better put a Band-Aid on it if you're going to mess around out here." I reached up on the shelf and located the box. "When was your last tetanus shot?" I could tell from her look and the way she backed up a couple of feet that she was long overdue and didn't want one.

"I'm running you up to Doc's office."

"No, it's nothing."

I ignored her on-going protests as we headed back up the path to the ranch and I dialed Doc Flanders on my cell phone. He was the town doctor and a squirrelly guy by any criteria. Not someone you wanted to sew up your face, but a tetanus shot was safe enough. I checked my watch; he shut his doors at four p.m. sharp on Fridays.

He answered, telling me he was heading out and seeing no more patients today. I swore if he'd wait I'd be there in five minutes. Doc had a time fetish. Some said it was his Olympic medal race where he lost by one one-hundredth of a second. Others said he wasn't even in the Olympics and concocted the whole story to mask a serious obsession with the clock. I'd never bothered to check one way or the other. He was the only doctor for miles so we had to deal with him, warts and all.

We got in the truck and I immediately floored the gas pedal and careened out of the drive, spinning my wheels as I turned the corner onto the highway. The car ahead of me was pulling a tractor and I whipped around it, giving a friendly wave to the gaping driver. Cash pushed her back against the seat as if retreating from the windshield, her foot braced on the floorboard seeking a nonexistent brake.

"Hey, no rush, the wire cut my hand, not my eyeball," Cash said, but I didn't slow down. Doc Flanders was so crazy he wouldn't wait for anyone. He'd walked out while Mrs. Wiley was in labor with her twins—said they were taking too long.

Minutes later I took a tight turn and skidded into the gravel drive of the medical office. Doc Flanders was on the porch locking the door. His six-foot-six frame was bent over, a shock of white rooster-comb hair unattended for what appeared to be weeks, and his baggy pants and sloppy shirt stained beyond color recognition.

"We're here, Doc. Five minutes," I lied.

"Seven," he replied sternly.

"Hey, no problem. We'll come back another time." Cash turned and I caught her arm, holding her in place while the doc made up his mind.

"You want to get tetanus, young lady?" Now that he knew she didn't want treatment, it appeared he was intent on giving it to her. Unlocking the door, he continued his dour lecture. "Not pretty, I can tell you that. Your jaw goes rigid, body convulses, eyes roll back, you foam at the mouth. Some live like that for months, entire jaw goes purple and pieces of your skin fall off."

"I don't recall tetanus having exactly those symptoms," Cash whispered as Doc led us across the waiting area's faded yellow linoleum floor and pushed open a Formica door leading to his examining room. The long wooden table was littered with used cotton balls and blood-stained gauze.

"This place is a mess, where's Stella?" I asked of the old nurse who kept him organized.

"Vacation. She's on vacation every day of her life as far as I can tell." He groused about the only woman in town who would work for him and deal with his insanity. She once confided in me that he got his patients confused and she had to be there to make sure he treated the right person for the right thing. New people in town wondered why we all still went to Doc Flanders. Beyond simple geography was the plain fact that he was ours—a local character, a man who survived out here making little money and fewer friends, yet when someone was in trouble, he showed up. That was one of the measures of a person's worth out on the prairie. When you were down, who showed up.

"What's this?" I pushed several paper towels off the table into a wastebasket.

"Treated Bo Waters's hunting dog awhile ago. Got tore up in some underwater barbed wire."

He picked up a used needle next to the debris and ran water over it as if he were going to use it again.

Cash looked downright green. "You're not using that on me."

She drew back in the face of the contaminated needle as I reassured her under my breath that everything was fine.

"No?" Doc looked playful for the first time. "Bo's old hound doesn't have any communicable diseases. Probably cleaner than some of the boys you've dated." He opened the fridge and took out a tiny see-through jar of liquid and acted like he was going to use the dog's needle to extract serum, then at the last minute tossed the old syringe in the trash and took a clean package out of the drawer. "She's a squeamish one." He eyed me and I shook my head, having seen this ruse before.

I reached for the vial of serum, reading the label on it to make sure he was giving her the right thing, then handed it back to him. "You're not allergic to anything, are you?" I asked the question Doc should have been asking.

Cash shook her head no.

He grabbed her arm and pushed up her sleeve and, before she could say anything else, jabbed the needle in roughly, then swabbed it off with an alcohol rub. "There you go."

"Thanks, Doc, what do we owe you?" I asked.

"You owe me the courtesy of not calling me late on a Friday. If your workers want to do something stupid to themselves, keep it within hours." He didn't look up and I slid a twenty-dollar bill onto the counter just before Cash and I headed out the door. As we climbed into the truck, she rooted around in her jeans pocket for money to pay me back and I refused.

"Think of it as ranchman's comp. Your arm hurt?"

"Yeah. And you took me to a witch doctor! He treats dogs on the table where he treats patients."

"But they're *clean* dogs," I joked. "Want to stop at the Dairy Queen?" I turned the truck around and headed in the opposite direction, outside town. Cash sagged back in her seat, her eyes half closed.

I pulled into a spot in front of the giant swirl of ice cream that formed the top of the building and turned off the ignition. "You stay. I'll get it."

"How do you know what I want?" Her brow furrowed.

"I'll get what I think you should have."

I bounced out of the truck and up to the window. The young boy behind the counter was Donnetta's chubby nephew, Spiff, and he greeted me jovially.

"Coming right up," he said as he made the cones. "That your new gal?" He nodded toward the car.

"My ranch hand."

"Driving her around buying her dip cones. I want to work your ranch."

"Gave everybody in town the chance but no takers," I said to the soft teenager who wouldn't lift a bale of hay if it were lying on top of his grandma.

"She dating anybody?" He goose-necked to get a better look into the vehicle.

"Too old for you, Spiffo."

"I like older women."

"I'll let her know that, and if she's interested I'm sure she'll call you, but I think your cell-phone minutes are safe."

I paid him and headed back to the truck, handing Cash her cone through the window. She was smiling now.

"I heard what he said."

"Small gene pool constantly in search of new material." I sat back in the seat, not starting the truck, and bit into the dark chocolate tip and down into the cold ice cream. "What?" I stopped mid-chew, seeing Cash watching me.

"Very telling about the way people eat." Something about her made me grin all the time and I felt foolish. "You bite right into the cold center."

I shrugged at her comment and spoke between bites. "Which means?"

"Means some guy's missing out." She raised a playful eyebrow and I felt my face flush.

"Then there are those who eat off their shirt." I nodded toward the drops of ice cream hitting her shirt front.

She glanced at her chest and began to devour the dripping cone, trying to mop herself up at the same time, talking in between. "Meaning I eat like a kid?"

"Now why would I think that?" She looked at me for a moment and a giant chunk of chocolate fell into her lap. We both giggled.

Her remark about the way I ate ice cream reminded me that she seemed to have sex on her mind all the time, but didn't all young women. I'd missed that stage of sheer lusting. Instead I'd gone from dreaming of Prince Charming to suddenly being pursued by a guy who seemed to know, way ahead of me, that we were meant for each other. I remembered having to get used to his taste and his smells more than being attracted to them.

"You don't talk a lot," Cash said, crunching the remainder of her cone.

"I do if I have something to say." I finished off my ice cream and started to put the truck in gear.

She grinned, seeming, for some mysterious reason, amused by me. She suddenly wriggled around in her seat looking for a napkin and pulled out the sack I'd brought from the dry-goods store. "Hope I didn't squash something in here or I'll never hear the end of it."

"Actually, it's yours." I tried to sound casual. She looked surprised and opened the sack, extracting the soft, yellow deerskin gloves. "I wasn't sure of the size. Don't try them on now with your hand hurt."

"These are beautiful." Her tone changed to wonder as she laid them against her cheek as I had done, as if caressing the deer who gave them to her. She tried to put the right glove on but her left hand obviously stung. "Would you?" She handed me the glove. I held it open and she slid her hand in easily, but after that, she couldn't tighten the fit, so I slipped my finger between each of hers, slowly pressing the doeskin into the curves of her hand to avoid hurting her. As I fitted the last finger, she grasped my hand in her gloved one. "Isn't that the most amazing feeling ever?"

"Deerskin." My breathing momentarily halted but my heart raced as if I were a dove trapped by kindly hands, nonetheless fearful, having no knowledge the frightening pressure signaled safety.

"How did you know my size?"

I pulled away. "Good guesser."

"Thank you for the gloves and the tetanus shot, which now hurts worse than my palm—"

"Sorry about that."

"—and for letting me stay with you."

"You'll earn your way this summer. No need to thank me."

Talking with her made me want to run away. Yet another part of me wanted to drive her somewhere farther from the city where no one knew me and just sit like this forever. Maybe after so many years without a female friend, I yearned to be able to say what I was feeling to someone who might understand.

"What are you thinking?" she asked softly.

"That we both have work to do." I put the truck in gear and headed back to the ranch, keeping my conversation to a minimum. What little I said related to the things I'd like Cash to get to work on, starting with unloading the feed sacks from the back of the truck, despite her hurt hand. She'd just have to cowgirl up.

CHAPTER SIX

A few days later I drove into town for what I fondly referred to as my dose of Donnetta, traipsing into the 2-K, where I slugged down a cup of her rich ground coffee.

"I don't know how she managed it but she busted open the feed sack while unloading it, which is damned near impossible because the sacks are double lined. She didn't notice she'd torn it until she'd strung half the sweet feed across the driveway. Then she tried to sweep it up and got dirt, gravel, and wind-blown garbage into the mix and would have put it into the feed bin and fed it to the horses, who probably would have colicked on old roofing nails, if I hadn't noticed. Half the time she's off barbecuing down by the pond with Perry, for God's sake!"

"What's wrong with Perry that he's doing that?"

"She's so damned charming—and damned-near useless."

"You look more alive than I've seen you in years." Donnetta ignored my lamentation as her dark eyes drilled into mine. "I haven't seen you get this excited about anything, well, in forever."

"What I'm excited about is that I have this, this kid—"

"She's not really a kid, is she? Didn't you say she was twenty-eight?"

"Acts eighteen."

"Maybe you're treating her like she's eighteen, which could be the problem, as I see it." I was drawn up short by that remark. "Boys around here say she's a grown woman. Spiffo, anyway."

"Spiffo would sleep with a goat and you know it."

"It's genetic. That's how I ended up with Buddy, it was the beard. You ever spend time talking to her?" Donnetta pressed on. "My recommendation here at the café-shrink is that you take a hiatus from work and go have a little fun."

"And leave her to manage things?" My voice rose in shock.

"Go have fun with *her*. A night out. Get to know her. You probably scare the hell out of her."

"She scares the hell out of me." I spoke before I realized what I was saying.

"And why would that be, Ms. Stanwyck?" Donnetta's gaze bore in on me. She was thinking something she wasn't saying, and I was glad she wasn't saying it because I intuitively knew I didn't want to hear it. "Come on, what's going on with you?"

"Too many raging hormones, I suspect."

"Hers or yours?"

"Wish I had that problem. My hormones don't rage any more, they just bitch." I finished off the coffee as she slid out of the booth.

"I've got the perfect thing." She scurried over to the cash-register drawer and pulled it open, scrounged around under the money, and came back with two tickets. "River Festival tomorrow night. I bet she'd like to go." I took the tickets from her and offered to pay for them, but she held her hand up. "Hey, the pleasure's on me."

I drove home thinking about a night out at the River Festival. I'd always avoided it: *a place where good old boys let off steam and do things they'll regret in the morning. Not worth battling mosquito bites and half-drunk guys. I'll give the tickets to Perry and let him go.*

As I pulled into the drive, I glanced over at the south pasture and saw Cash three feet off the ground standing on the top rail of the fence balancing herself like an acrobat.

"Oh, for the love of God," I said out loud. *I wish I had a camera so I could take this to Donnetta. What adult do I know who does this kind of stuff? She's a freaking kid.*

I drove the truck across the open field to within shouting distance of Cash, who waggled her arms wildly to regain her balance as she saw me and flashed a quick smile. When I opened the truck door the tickets went airborne, and I managed to grab them before I got out.

"You'll break your neck," I called to her as the wind whistled around us and I hurried toward her to tell her to get off. The old wooden fence made of weathered logs barely supported the winter snow, much less someone her size, and furthermore I didn't want her to break it down so that it sagged and fell, making it useless as a cattle pen.

"I always wondered how gymnasts kept their balance on the beam. It's…not…that…easy," she said, trying not to topple off. Suddenly steadying herself, she threw her head back, struck a pose, and the late-afternoon light caught the sheen in her dark curls. The wind blew them erratically, revealing her exquisitely high cheekbones, and her shirt flapped in the breeze, like a great mainsail.

"And now, ladies and gentlemen, the dismount!" She jumped high into the air and I gasped as she landed on both feet in front of me, grinning broadly. I clapped despite myself and she bowed.

"I'm applauding your not breaking an ankle or my fence," I said, to recover.

"You were applauding my dismount," she said, looking down at me, breathing heavily. "I promised myself I wouldn't fall." She froze, gazing into my eyes.

The wind suddenly shifted, and I could smell her cologne blended with her body heat and I was sensually aroused. The prairie wind bent blades of spring grass to the ground around us and swirled beneath my cotton shirt like the hot breath of an impatient lover. She reached for my hand and I let her slowly open my fingers, my muscles weakening at the intensity of her gaze and the tenderness of her touch.

"What's this?" She took the slips of paper from me.

"Tickets to the River Festival. I was—"

"Could we?"

Could we what? My mind raced. At this moment, my answer

might be yes to almost anything. "Yes." I let all the air out of my body as if confirming that thought to myself, then hurried back to the truck muttering something about needing to get dinner ready.

An hour later, I'd left her a hamburger on the countertop with a note saying I was going to bed early. I needed time to regroup. I wasn't that naïve. I knew I was in the danger zone. Something about her left me on edge and excited, a condition I'd occasionally wished for, but not now, and not from a younger woman. *Not from a woman of any age.*

Fleeting forbidden thoughts blew through my brain and I replaced them with more appropriate ones. *Maybe I should partition off the bunkhouse and move her out there. Not have her underfoot all the time.*

A light tap on my bedroom door and I froze, pretending to be asleep. The tap grew louder. "Maggie, are you okay?"

"I'm fine." I tried to sound slightly annoyed.

"You sure you're not sick or something?"

"Just trying to get some sleep."

"Sorry. Thanks for the burger." Her voice trailed off and I felt bad about the brusqueness of my tone. But in truth, I *was* trying to get some sleep. I hadn't slept well since she'd been here. The idea that someone was prowling around my house at night, not that she prowled, but *potentially* prowling, opening the refrigerator, flushing toilets, opening screen doors, apparently, at a subconscious level, made me feel unsafe or violated or whatever.

Three hours later I looked at the clock, wondering why I wasn't getting any sleep. *I will take her to the River Festival, demonstrate that I'm her friend as well as her employer so she's not afraid of me, as Donnetta suggested, and then have Perry partition off the bunkhouse and move her out there. If she doesn't want to share his bathroom, she can come in the house in the morning to shower.* Resolving all that, I was finally able to get a few hours' sleep.

I awoke long before sunrise, threw on some jeans, and headed out to bang on Perry's sleeping quarters, hoping he was up early. He opened the battered wooden door looking askew and listened to my plaintive harangue.

"Why does she have to move out *here*?" Perry said, standing on the bunkhouse porch in the predawn light in what could only be described as gray long johns.

"It'll be better for her and give me some room, better for everybody, actually." I tried to sound casual, as if I were suggesting a spontaneous campout.

"Except me...the person who has to cut his personal space in half."

I hadn't really considered that with a male worker the bunkhouse was fairly large, both men sharing the main room, but to accommodate Cash, I would be putting up a wall and removing half of Perry's living area. "You're right, you're right." I turned and went back to the house as Perry asked questions of my back.

"She cause you any trouble?"

"Of course not."

"You feeling okay?"

"Of course."

"I guess I'm the only one who's confused, not that that's unusual," he muttered.

❖

Mid-morning, Cash went into town with a laundry list of items Perry asked her to pick up from the lumberyard, along with filling up two empty diesel drums at the gas station. She was gone for several hours and I was restless. A million chores beckoned, but instead, I took a halter and went down to the grove and pulled Mariah out of the herd and into an alley between pastures. She had long ago decided I was the one person she would tolerate, and it was a rare occasion when she was uncooperative, despite what Cash had experienced with her.

Too lazy to go get a saddle, I found a tree stump and stood on it to climb on her broad white back. Then I rode her slowly down the long grass alley between pastures. She was in a tolerant mood, listening to my commands, seeming happy to have been chosen from the herd.

I edged her up to the end gate, bent over, and lifted the latch before urging her forward. She pushed the gate open with her body and I turned her quickly, after she'd gone through, in order to push it shut again. Certain now she was in a behaving mood, I clicked my heels into her sturdy flanks and moved her out across the prairie. The wind blew her big white mane and she snorted and pranced. It was a beautiful early summer's day. Her damp back, wet from the slight exertion, both of us out of shape from the winter months, and the warmth radiated by her big body felt natural and free beneath me, an emotion only a horse could create.

I'd ridden in college and, in fact, that was the tie that bound Johnny and Buck and me. We all loved horses. Plow horse, bronc, or pleasure horse, they were all kept at the big university barn, and that's where one day Buck Tate encouraged me to give in and marry Johnny Blake. "But I don't think I love him," I remembered saying.

And Buck replied, "Do you know for sure what love is?"

I shook my head sadly, saying I didn't.

Must be Cash's arrival that has caused all these crazy flashbacks, I thought. I turned Mariah in a circle, then signaled her to bend her massive body in figure eights. She bowed her neck and seemed to be performing for an unseen admirer. For a moment, my fantasy put us both in an exhibition ring, flowers entwined in her thick mane and the audience shouting approval.

Out of the corner of my eye, where the ringside seats would be, appeared a vehicle parked in the pasture, a figure resting on the hood, propped up against the windshield. I turned Mariah's head, pointing her in that direction.

"You look awesome," someone shouted, and I recognized Cash lounging on her makeshift metal bleacher. I nodded and tipped an imaginary hat to her.

One leg stretched out in front, the other bent, hands clasped around her knee, she reminded me of a picture I'd once seen of James Dean.

"Taking a day off?" My question was a bit sarcastic, meant to fend off any personal conversation she might be contemplating and to put her image back where it belonged as a ranch hand.

"Took the things Perry needed to him. He said he's through with me for the day. Anything you want me to do for you?"

Was I imagining her tone? Everything she said seemed suggestive of more, as if she was playing with me, coaxing me into something.

Mariah stomped with her right rear leg and I realized she was fighting off a horsefly that was buzzing her shoulder. I swung at it for her and she tensed up, so I patted her reassuringly.

Cash put her hands up to her face, creating an imaginary camera, and with one finger she hit the shutter, at the same time making a clicking sound with her mouth. "Preserving this memory moment and later I'll download it into my virtual photo album of Maggie Tanner, woman rancher." She slid down off the Jeep and walked toward Mariah, who let her reach up and pet her neck. From my vantage point above, I could see how thick her black hair grew, almost like a horse's mane, and how much stronger and broader her shoulders were than I'd realized.

"What are you thinking?" she asked in her invasive way, speaking to me as if we were long-time friends.

"Nice shirt."

"Hard to find one to fit me. I usually have to buy in the men's department. I did a lot of swimming in high school just to get out of the house and have something to do. Speaking of which, what time do you want me ready to go tonight for the festival?"

"Starts at seven. But we don't have to—"

"Let's get there early and stay late." She flashed a big grin. "I've only been here a short time, but now I understand why cowboys wanted to go into town and get drunk and sleep with women. Not that I intend to do either." She reddened, for the first time losing her cool and obviously embarrassed, which made me laugh. She quickly recovered. "But then who knows, I *could*. I hear strange things happen on the prairie."

"No fun being a sheep on a Saturday night." I turned Mariah

toward the house and nudged her forward. "We'll leave at six thirty," I shouted back over my shoulder, pleased I had made her laugh. I was nervous talking to her in an open field and wondered what in the world we'd say to one another tonight.

CHAPTER SEVEN

I'd been jittery all afternoon and stayed near the house, cleaning up, writing out bills, making phone calls, and behaving as if I thought I had to get everything in order because the world was about to change.

When five o'clock rolled around, I was in my closet trying to figure out what to wear. I hadn't been anywhere that required thought about attire in a long time. We'd probably be sitting on a riverbank so I looked through some dark jeans, none of which appeared pressed. The shirts suddenly seemed dowdy and the belts worn. I realized for the first time in years that I didn't like a single piece of clothing in my closet and that I should have come to that conclusion weeks ago when I had time to correct the situation.

After trying on three different outfits, I finally gave up and pulled a clean pair of blue jeans off the shelf with a khaki-colored starched shirt—the same kind of outfit I always wore. Spotting a wide Western belt with ornate leather tooling and a large brass buckle, I slipped that on, sprucing up the jeans. I grabbed a slightly battered pair of brown ostrich boots that matched the belt and checked myself out in the mirror. Acceptable, I thought.

In the bathroom, I put on makeup, which I had to scrounge in drawers to find since I rarely wore it when working on the ranch. *I should wear makeup more often. Makes me look ten years younger.* Even as I thought it, I remembered how right after I married I quit wearing it because Johnny thought women should look "natural."

I heard boots in the living room and checked my watch: 6:15

p.m. *I've been in the damned closet for over an hour? I'm one step away from behaving like a disco diva. But then I haven't been out in ages, so why not spend a little time trying to look good.*

When I pushed the bedroom door open, Cash was standing in the middle of the living room and my heart flew into my throat. Black boots and tight black jeans with a red plaid shirt and a red bandana around her neck.

"Do I look like I should be lying down under a pizza?" she asked, her face scrunched up nervously, and I laughed. "I bought it in town. Now I'm having remorse."

"You look very nice."

"I guess between dorky and sexy, 'very nice' is pretty safe." I took in every piece of her, wanting to remember how she looked, how she stood, how she smiled. "Tell me I look better than 'very nice.'"

"You look better than very nice," I said into the air as I headed for my truck and climbed in. I cranked the engine as Cash hurried to slide onto the seat beside me.

"And what's better than very nice?" she prodded, impishly.

"Winning the lotto," I replied.

"You, by the way, look smashing."

"Thank you." I kept my eyes on the road and avoided her gaze as I merged onto the highway and headed for the riverbank. "Have you talked to your dad lately?" *Now why did I ask her that? This is the night I'm supposed to treat her like a friend, not a kid.*

"No, why?" Not waiting for an answer she added, "He knows if I'm with you, everything's fine. He's a big fan of yours. Did you two ever—"

My neck nearly snapped as I turned to look at her. "No!"

She laughed. "You'd be the type bull riders would like."

"And what type is that?"

"I don't know…full of yourself. Any bull rider ever made the buzzer with you?" she asked playfully.

"I don't want to sleep with anyone whose goal is eight seconds," I replied, and she laughed again. "Did you go to any bull-riding events with Buck?"

"I was born when he was fifteen so, yeah, he's been a friend more than anything, and we pal around sometimes. He married my mom and then they got divorced pretty quick, and then about five years later he married another woman and had a couple of kids, and now he's married again."

"So you spend time with your mom?"

"No idea where she is. Ran off and Buck had to take me in with his new family before I started school and that didn't go over too big, and then he and I left her when I was about ten and…then he dated around, so I had a lot of what we used to call 'mamas du jour,' and then finally he met Mary. Nice enough woman."

I'd always envisioned Buck as a funny, woman-loving guy who went from gal to gal the way a hummingbird heads for nectar. Hearing it from Cash's point of view made Buck's escapades seem sad, and I tried to change the mood by asking what Buck was doing this summer.

"Probably trying to convince Mary not to leave him. Some woman's been calling their house and she thinks he's having an affair."

And suddenly the puzzle pieces began flying in: a kid growing up without a mother, no role model for relationships, and probably always in the way or an afterthought, which explained the way she looked at me so plaintively and wanted to be close to me. *She needs a constant female figure in her life.* Understanding that made me more comfortable and I breathed deeper.

"Let's just go have a good time tonight and forget about everybody else." I smiled at her and Cash's face lit up. *Donnetta was right, get to know her.*

We pulled into a worn spot of ground amid rows of cars and trucks, flagged to a stop by a young boy who wanted to make sure we obeyed his parking instructions. He growled and signaled his unhappiness at my not driving all the way up to the white paint mark on the grass where he pointed his baton.

Cash hung her head out the window. "Hey, parking Nazi. If I give you five bucks will you smile at us instead of shouting?" Cash gave the big-bodied boy a cheesy grin.

"Just pull into the right spot, okay?" he said loudly.

"His name's Bubba," I said, and stretched across Cash's lap and waved so the boy could see me through the passenger window.

"It is not," she murmured, in amused dismay.

He immediately apologized. "Didn't know it was you, Ms. Tanner. No sweat. Enjoy."

"Thanks, Bubba," I said loudly, for Cash's further enjoyment, then said under my breath, "Bubba is derived from the word Bubber, the infantile pronunciation of brother. Bubba also has a very large Mubba." I dead-panned and she laughed. For a second I remained there, across her chest, concealed by battered trucks on either side of us. I finally used her leg to push myself back onto my side of the car. "Sorry," I said, and quickly climbed out of the truck and locked it.

"I used to work out before I became your ranch slave," she said smugly, as if she knew I was thinking about her legs.

"Does that chase the demons away?" I made eye contact.

She paused and dropped the bravado. "No."

"Maybe then it's time for something deeper and more meaningful."

"I'm in favor of deeper," she said.

Must be the air that makes everybody horny, I thought. "Be in favor of more meaningful," I took charge, putting the pressure back on her. Maybe she'd learn some things about life she could take home with her. We trudged toward the colorful tents pitched among the big trees along the distant bank. The music became louder as we got closer, and the smell of hotdogs and brisket filled the air.

"What are you hungry for?" I asked.

"Anything you want."

"How about fish tacos with mayonnaise?" She drew back and wrinkled her face. "Better learn to ask for what you want or you never know what you'll get." I pushed her playfully for no reason.

"I'll remember that," she said. "Make it roast beef."

I stood in line at the Beef Station, a red-and-white tent with overly warm women wearing white aprons and hairnets carving up large sides of beef along a back shelf.

"Our meat is hand-rubbed?" Cash whispered, reading the sign above the Beef Station as she doubled over with laughter.

"With spices." I completed the rest of the sentence as two plates with beef sandwiches covered in barbecue sauce and our drinks slid onto the counter in front of us.

"Like that makes the sign any better?" She continued to giggle as I paid the cashier. Someone on a microphone beckoned revelers to sign up for the river-ropes contest and not to forget the band would be playing in a few minutes.

Cash tried to intervene and offered up a ten-dollar bill, but I ordered her aside and told her to take the food over to a nearby table.

"You're very bossy," she said in between bites as I joined her on the hard benches. "Just an observation. But could be why men are afraid of you." Her eyes twinkled.

I ignored that remark and turned it back on her. "Donnetta said *you're* afraid of me."

"You're a woman who has it figured out. Scares people who don't." She bit into her sandwich. "This is really good."

Bea Benegan passed our table and patted me on the back, shouting hello, then asked Cash how she liked her new deerskin gloves.

"So soft I sleep in them," Cash said, and Bea stiffened. I knew immediately from living out here for decades that Cash had three strikes against her with Bea: she was younger, a hired hand, and new in town. Bea probably believed Cash should be more respectful and less flippant. As if to punctuate that thought, Bea cleared her throat and said archly, "Guess you're learning that it takes more than gloves to make a hand." Then she sailed off in the wind.

Cash shrugged off the remark as Bea disappeared into the crowd. "I'll probably have to kiss her to win her over."

"If you kiss Bea Benegan and live to tell it, I'll pay you fifty bucks," I said nonchalantly.

"She wants to mother me, I can see it. Won't be able to resist my charismatic aura."

"Is that what you call it, charismatic?" I knew she was only partly kidding.

"You don't find me charismatic?"

"Out here, charismatics speak in tongues."

"I have no problem with tongues," she said. At my look she added, "Hey, you brought me to a place where they hand rub their meat."

I laughed. Cash's sense of humor was one of her most delightful attributes.

Suddenly Sven Olan and his sister Verta stood alongside us. I let my eyes travel up her tight pants to her rhinestone belt buckle and Lycra T-shirt under a biker-bar leather vest. Seemed like everyone in town had found their way to the river and they were all drunk, or about to be.

"See you got your gal in town with you," he said, referring to her in the third person as if she weren't present and speaking in that singsong way Scandinavians talk.

"This is Cash Tate, who's working the ranch this summer."

Cash wiped off one barbecue-covered spot on her hand and offered a handshake to Sven. Slightly rising from the bench, she unknowingly answered Sven's query about her height. Verta offered her hand as well.

"I'm Verta, it means truth." She seemed to be purring the words, and for just a second I thought I saw a hint of recognition, as if she and Cash knew each other but were pretending they didn't.

"I'm Cash, it means no credit," Cash said, and I chuckled at her joke.

"How long you in town for?" Verta's lips curled into an appreciative smile and her eyes traveled down the full length of Cash's torso. Then Verta twisted her upper body thirty degrees west, thrust her pelvic bone forward, and tossed her head back as if Madonna had shouted, "Strike a pose."

"Just tonight." Cash seemed a bit flustered now.

"I mean how long are you staying out at the ranch? Maybe you'll come in one night and I'll show you some of the hot spots... well, lukewarm spots, because this is Little Liberty, after all."

"I'll see how things go," Cash said, her voice void of inflection.

I got to my feet and gathered up the dirty plates, tossing them into a nearby trash can. "You two enjoy the evening," I said brightly, as if we had a lot to see and not much time left to see it. Herding Cash away from Verta Olan, I was reminded that the slinky Swede wasn't one of my favorite people, for reasons I couldn't name, and particularly not tonight.

"She acted like she knew you," I said.

"Never saw her before. Why?"

"The expression on your face."

"That was barbecue sauce."

My irritation seemed to please Cash, which only annoyed me more. I forced myself to brighten up as Sara Goodie and husband Jock appeared, Sara gushing over his having made it to the Kansas City bronc-riding finals.

"So you'll be getting that new truck," I said.

"We're going to get some other things we need first—some rodeo gear and a better saddle, I think. Then talk about the truck." She said it as if the purchase priorities were hers. He had his arm around her and looked happy. I introduced Cash and then we all parted, promising to chat more the next time we visited their feed store.

"Yeah, she'll love driving that new pair of chaps." Cash snorted.

"Women first only in lifeboats, darling," I said, and the endearment came out before I could analyze why. Cash turned quickly toward me, obviously savoring the verbal caress. Embarrassed, I ignored her, pointing out more people I knew up ahead and warning they were bearing down on us. All the while I was reminding myself to be more careful about the language I used with her.

"Can we sit over here and listen to the concert?" Cash indicated a grassy spot below an embankment slightly out of sight of the main thoroughfare and up against a wide oak tree. I was delighted to climb down the small knoll, plop down on the ground, and let the rough bark of the ancient tree support my back. Cash sank down beside me, and the wind picked up and fluttered across the silence between us as we let the ground stabilize us and the breeze and the music ripple over us. A cowboy band played a song about a young man's plaintive recollection of love among the wheat fields and how an older woman changed his life forever.

Something about the music created a tension between us, and we remained motionless until the song ended and people around us began to applaud. Cash broke the silence by suddenly repositioning her body and joking that she was sitting on a tree root, which was more intimacy than she could take from an oak.

When she moved over and settled down again, her shoulder was touching mine and I froze, feeling an electrical current, a tingling between us. I sank back into the tree, quiet and breathing. Then involuntarily my breath caught and fell in cadence with hers; our chests lifted and eased in rhythm, each inhalation causing our shoulders to press into one another. When I thought I might not breathe again, she slid her arm through mine, hooking it like two girlfriends might, and pulled me in tight.

"Thanks for everything, Maggie." Her tone was sweet and sincere.

"For nothing," I said softly, almost inaudibly, and closed my eyes as my head swirled. For a moment I couldn't tell if I was standing or sitting or lying down, only tumbling and falling and floating, the music carrying me away. Like cattle in the fields standing shoulder to shoulder, staring off into space as if having left their collective body, floating out into the wind, removing themselves from any pain or discomfort, and ignoring what the future might hold, we stared ahead saying nothing, our shoulders tethered to one another, our breathing synchronized, our bodies in rhythm, and our souls suspended in the wind.

I didn't hear the drink cart rumbling around the side of the tree, but the next thing I knew, Cash had her arms around me and was on top of me, rolling me over as I caught sight of the metal wheels careening past us out of control, two grown men trying to stop it. I sank back onto the ground and let the full weight of her crush me.

My face buried in her shoulder, the smell of her perfume permeated her shirt at the collar and the wind whipped across our skin, cooling my neck, while her essence created an internal heat I could not describe or explain. She didn't offer to pull herself off me until a disembodied voice above us interrupted the air.

"You women all right? Here, let me give you a hand. Close call there."

I tried to get my bearings as Cash nearly lifted me off the ground, and I dusted off my pants, trying not to look at her directly. The voice kept rattling off sentences about our near-accident.

"Probably shouldn't have been sitting here so near the cart path," Stretch Adams, with his sloped shoulders and balding head, bent to tell me personally.

Cash got between him and me and took over the direction of our next move. "We're fine, thanks. Come on, Maggie."

"Hey, wait up!" Stretch called, but Cash was shouting over her shoulder that we were late for something. Moments later we were farther down the river slightly over a hill and she had pushed me up against the trunk of an old tree and was looking me up and down as if inspecting for dings and scratches. "Are you okay, really?"

"Yes, what are we late for?" I was monitoring my breathing.

"I don't know. I just didn't want him around you."

I tried to joke. "One of three unmarried men for fifty miles and you—"

"You don't need to be married." Her tone was serious and her face near mine. She looked deep into my eyes as if searching for something she knew I had but wouldn't give up. I felt as if the prairie winds had taken up residence in my chest and were battering my lungs and fluttering my heart.

"Maggie, have you ever wanted someone. Just to run your hands over their skin and kiss every part of their body?" Cash spoke with an intensity I didn't know she had, and I marveled there could be so much wind swirling around us and yet none in my lungs. I was certain I would pass out. "If you don't feel that with someone, then they're not the one. No matter what. But if you do…if you do feel it, then nothing else matters." She let go of me and I stayed pinned to the tree for support.

"Are you talking about Stretch?"

She suddenly paced up and down in front of me and held her head in her hands as if I gave her a headache. "He's not for you. None of them are."

As if sensing he was the subject of conversation, Stretch approached from the distance and Cash backed away from me. I pulled myself together and walked back toward the festival as Stretch fell into stride alongside me.

"There you are! Thought the near-collision scared you off. Hey, I've got something for you." He fished around in his pocket.

Cash didn't wait to see what he was offering, the mood of our time together broken. Before I could stop her, she disappeared up ahead in the crowd.

Stretch produced a cowboy key ring he said he'd just bought for me. I had to give the man points for persistence, even if he flunked good taste. The yellow plastic cowboy looked demented and his horse satanic. "It's the festival logo," he explained, and I suddenly recognized it. "Thought I might buy you a piece of pie," he added as inducement for spending time with him.

When I refused, he offered up drinks, a drive, or maybe a date later in the week, but all I could think about was where Cash had disappeared and the look on her face when she left. Managing to remain vague and distant, I told Stretch I had a lot on my mind these days and would have to take a rain check. He scowled, but his disposition improved slightly when I thanked him for his gift just before rushing away.

I roamed amid festival performers, mimes with miniature horses, toy twisters who could turn tubular balloons into giraffes, and rows of merchandise tents touting everything from baked-bean wind blockers to corncob door knockers.

Twenty minutes later I finally located Cash, at the far end of chaos, having a beer with Donnetta and talking up a storm. Their conversation died out as I approached.

"Where have you been? I was looking all over for you."

"Giving you some space to talk to Stretch." I could tell she'd had more than a single beer.

"Thanks, but I'll let you know when I need space." My sarcasm surprised even me.

"Well, there you go," Donnetta said, toasting Cash and behaving a little tipsy herself. Cash grinned at her and the two of them seemed to be sharing some barroom secret I wasn't privy to.

"I just don't want you to get lured off into the woods by one of these drunken fools, that's all," I said, to regain my composure.

"Hell, she's so ugly if they took her they'd bring her back come daylight." Donnetta hee-hawed and Cash laughed.

"Glad you two are having such a high time," I said.

"Hey, Missy, have a beer and lighten up." Donnetta handed me a beer and popped the top while it was in my hand. I hated beer, but it was cold and I drank it anyway.

A voice over the loud speaker announced the beginning of the games, drowning out any further conversation. Cash left without comment when the announcer demanded the ropes-course entrants line up by the riverbank.

I glanced over to see several rope configurations spanning the narrowest part of the river. Thick hemp rigged to trees and poles with pulleys and other crazy-man equipment designed to get people killed or at least dunked. My neighbor Jonas Wiley, whose son had to be hauled out of the city sewer, was already clinging to a rope and struggling to catch the flopping end between his knees as the pulley swung him out over the river. He seemed determined to create another water crisis for his family. Midway across, his shorts bagged and his white briefs flapped behind him like a napkin just before he lost his grip and splashed into the water amid whoops and laughter. His fall nearly capsized the raft filled with drunken judges who floated beneath the ropes and gawked at everyone's undies while pretending to rate their rope handling.

"How you doin', Ms. Stanwyck?" Donnetta shouted, sucking on a long-neck bottle and gauging my temperament.

"Fine." I searched for Cash again.

"She's right over there." Donnetta pointed, seeming to know the topic I was most interested in, without my bringing it up. "A strange one, I'll grant you that. And not in a very happy mood tonight. Maybe I was wrong about you getting her out for an evening."

"No, you were right. She's just a little high-strung, that's all."

"Riding high-strung horses is a dangerous deal."

"What the hell does that mean?" I asked, scanning the riverbank.

"Means I'm drunk." She took another long swig of her beer.

A man swung over the water and lost his grip, his hands skidding across the rope, obviously burning them, since he let go, yelping, and fell into the muddy water. The next figure, tall and muscled and wearing black jeans and a checkered red shirt, was obviously Cash clinging to the rope and moving across the river easily. Crossing once without incident, she pushed off from the opposite bank and traveled back, jumping to the ground near us as people applauded. She ambled over, brushing her hands off on her jeans.

"Nicely done, cowgirl!" Donnetta toasted her with her Bud Light. "How'd you learn to do that?"

"I haven't found anything I couldn't hang onto once I wrap my legs around it." She looked right at me before she swaggered off, and a twinge shot through my groin.

"Well now, did you hear that?" Donnetta blew an appreciative whistle across the lip of her beer bottle. "I'd say Ms. Cash might be more like Johnny than June."

I ignored Donnetta's remark as the voice over the microphone summoned Cash Tate to pick up her first prize of a hundred-dollar gift certificate to Benegan's Dry Goods store. Feigning interest in a booth in the distance, I moved away from Donnetta's probing eyes and quickly spotted Cash, hurried over, and put my hand on hers.

"Congratulations!" I beamed as she jammed the gift certificate into her back pocket and stopped to buy another beer. A rope dangled from her neck bearing a cardboard medal with the words 1st Place Winner Knows the Ropes. "Look, Stretch had no idea he was interrupting our conversation." When she didn't say any more, my tone shifted from slightly conciliatory to brusque, and I instinctively whirled, much like I always did with my mare, saying over my shoulder, "Had enough? You ready to go?" She hurried to catch up with me, dancing past me and turning to face me while jogging backward. She stopped, forcing me to stop, and took the rope trophy from around her neck, put it around mine, and gazed at me with her soft eyes.

"I want to go back to that spot by the cart path where the tree is and sit down on the ground and lounge up against that big oak and listen to the music, and I don't want anyone to interfere with that. You said learn to ask for what I want. I want that."

"Okay," I whispered, and she took my hand and my mind chanted a litany of questions: What will people think when they see her holding my hand? Why do I care? Why am I unwilling to pull my hand away? And all the while she was leading me there, to that spot below the embankment where we sat down and sank back against the rough bark, and when our arms touched I closed my eyes and let the wind carry me above the sound of my beating heart. At that moment, I didn't know what I was doing. I didn't want to know. I just wanted to feel something, something I had never felt before, and if it could last only a few minutes on this riverbank, I would take it.

CHAPTER EIGHT

W e drove home silent in the darkness, looking out the truck
window at the stars, and I didn't know what to make of
any of it. How could it be that between six thirty and midnight, Cash
Tate had turned into someone else for me, evoking feelings I didn't
know I was capable of possessing? Maybe I was just waking up
again, and these sensations were all natural. Maybe I'd start dating
again, get married, come out of my shell. I'd heard stories like that,
hadn't I, where people helped others find themselves?

I hated for the night to end. Would there ever be another night
like this one? And I worried about why I was wondering any of
this.

After pulling into the driveway, I put the truck in park. We both
sat for a moment. She flexed her fingers on the legs of her jeans as if
she wanted to say something, grasp something.

"Sooo." She drew out the word and let it linger in the air,
offering me the chance to fill in life's blanks, allowing me to take
this moment in any direction I might choose. Despite the internal
warmth, I was, at the core, a practical woman, and I knew the
consequences of intimacy—too much sharing or too much frivolity
brought about loss of control and lack of respect. So I changed my
tone and became energetic.

"Sooo," I imitated her word and tone, "it was fun. I'm glad I've
gotten to know you better. Donnetta was right. I may have sold you
short. Well, just a little short. You're still pretty green."

"Guess so." Her voice was soft.

"What are you going to buy with your gift certificate? May I suggest boots?"

"Boots it is. No pointy toes or slick bottoms." She mimicked my remark about her line-dancing gear. "We'll go shopping then?" she asked, and I nodded.

Before I could respond, she grabbed the door handle and nearly blasted out of the truck and into the house. By the time I got inside she was in her room.

❖

The next morning Perry was on the front porch with his battered hat in hand, ducking his head and trying to communicate something. "I gave some thought to what you said and it's okay."

"What's okay?" I frowned at his inability to come to the point.

"We can cut my space in half. She can bunk out there with me."

I guided him off the front porch and farther away, out of hearing distance of the house. "That's very nice, Perry, but I've rethought it and I don't believe it's the right thing to do. She needs to stay here."

"Naw, that's crazy. She's a worker and she has every right to the bunkhouse."

"No need. It's all fine. She'll stay here."

"Look, it's your place and if you—"

"Perry, I don't *want* her to leave the house."

"You don't?" His face puzzled up.

"No. I want her here." I bit the corner of my lip.

"Any particular reason, if you don't mind my asking?"

"I like her company."

He paused. "I was kind of thinking that. Well, all right then." He wandered back to the bunkhouse scratching his head.

Cash came into the living room clad only in a man's shirt worn like a nightshirt. I stared at her. She looked raw and stunning, like a big African cat, and she seemed unconcerned that she had on no makeup or pressed clothing or anything else, including pants, beyond her underwear.

"You okay? I heard someone."

"Just Perry. Did you drink too much?" I referenced our evening and desperately wanted the emotions to be tied to excessive alcohol versus anything more serious.

"I might have."

"I would say you did. My daddy always said about drinking, 'Better to deal with your nightmares while it's daylight, than drown your dreams at night.'"

"Your daddy was a smart man. Is he still alive?"

"Both my parents died from carbon monoxide, a freak accident with the heating system when I was a teenager. I was staying overnight with a cousin so I came home to everybody gone."

She looked at me strangely, as if she thought my youth was somehow easier than her own and now realized everyone had baggage. "Any sisters or brothers?"

"None."

"So you married young to have someone?"

"Maybe. Do you think about marriage and children?" My question hung in the air.

"I do. I think it sounds horrible." She laughed. "Families don't work out too well, in my experience." She flopped back down onto an overstuffed chair.

"It doesn't have to be the way Buck did it, Cash, you know that. And you don't want to go through life alone. You'll meet someone."

"You're alone."

"Well, there's your lesson. Don't grow old on the prairie with a crotchety old man and a moody mare," I said.

Her eyes sparkled at me. "Does anyone ever get close enough to really know you, Maggie Tanner?" She asked it suddenly and I knew that if anyone could get close, it might be this tenacious young woman. I cocked an eyebrow and simply locked eyes with her, visually challenging her audacity. "If you'll tell me all your nightmares, I'll tell you mine."

"One of these nights, maybe. When I've had too much to drink," I said.

"I'll make that my goal." She stood there for a moment just taking me in, then seemed to jolt herself out of her thoughts. "If you've got some time today, could we go get the 'appropriate foot gear'?"

"Get yourself together and let's go now." I was more spontaneous than I could ever remember. Cash sprang to her feet and was ready in five minutes.

Like kids ditching school, we rolled down the road in my old Chevy truck, laughing and talking about last night's festival: how pretty Sara Goodie looked and how her husband didn't seem to appreciate what he had, how Jonas Wiley's underwear hung so far off him that you could see the hair on his butt, which made Cash bless poor Mrs. Wiley.

"The judges were all drunk," I exclaimed.

"Yeah, when I was sailing overhead, I looked down and the old gray-haired guy had his pants unzipped and was peeing into the river right while he was judging me."

"And let's face it, you were judging him." I giggled.

"I gave him a four on a drunk's scale of ten: two for having a dick and two for being able to find it. Six-point penalty for size."

We were, as Bea Benegan would have phrased it, "in stitches" by the time we pulled up and parked in front of her dry-goods store and stumbled in to look for boots. Bea took one look at us and seemed to get stiffer still, worried no doubt that our hilarity meant we'd come straight from the festival, having drunk our breakfast. Cash forked over the folded-up gift certificate, and Bea set about helping her locate the right boots.

"Work, field, hunt, or riding?" She rattled off boot categories as she stood beneath a stuffed moose head, its tongue dangling as if exhausted from busting through the store wall.

"How about a pair of crepe-sole Justins?" I suggested.

Bea registered shock, then whispered, "Wonderful boots, Maggie, but those are higher than a cat's back. Run around four hundred dollars."

"Got any on sale?" Cash asked, unperturbed.

Bea led us over to a stack of boxes that looked a bit dusty and battered, and Cash knelt to read the sizes in the dim light. "Got anything in a 10B?"

"Big foot," Bea exclaimed.

"You calling me a Prairie Yeti?" Bea looked embarrassed and busied herself rummaging around for a pair of boots that would fit Cash. Amid the boot rubble, Cash located a pair. "How much are these?"

"They're green," I said to Cash, as if she'd gone inexplicably color blind and had her taste hijacked.

"That's why they're on sale," Bea whispered.

"You're kidding." Cash insisted on trying to prod Bea into good humor as she tried on the boots. "I'd think boots this color would be so rare you'd charge double."

"You couldn't pay someone to be buried in that color boot," I said.

"And they're real comfortable." Cash grinned. "You said the right boots, Maggie. You didn't say they had to be a particular color."

"They're Justins marked down to one hundred and fifty," Bea said, tilting her glasses to read the slashed price.

"You can put the remainder on my charge," I said.

"Treat your workers awful nice," Bea said sweetly. "Most ranchers around here are tighter than Dick's hatband."

"I'm paying for them." Cash wrestled some bills out of her pocket.

"You can work it off," I said quietly.

"I'd have to stay till Christmas and you wouldn't want that, now, would you?" She cut her eyes at me and plunked her money down. When she stood up, her black jeans came way down over the boots, revealing less lime green than I'd envisioned.

"They actually look very cute," I said.

"Cute?" Cash recoiled as if insulted. "Ms. Benegan, do you think I look cute or do you think I look sexy?"

Bea stepped back and eyed Cash top to bottom. Obviously

appreciating Cash's deference, she'd finally warmed to the light-heartedness of the morning and the possibility of a sale. "Miss Cash Tate, I do believe these boots could qualify you as…sexy."

Cash tilted her head and kissed Bea on the cheek, keeping her eyes trained on me. Bea immediately reddened. "From here on out, I'll shop in your store only, ma'am."

"You come right to me, sweetie pie, and I'll take care of you," Bea said as Cash ambled out the door, her old boots under her arm, and I followed, suppressing laughter.

"Think she liked it?" Cash said, sure of herself. And for some reason I found her cockiness endearing.

"I'll pay you when we get home."

"I like a woman who pays her bets, but keep your money. I'll take it out in trade." When I looked at her in surprise, she said innocently, "Barter."

"What are you thinking of bartering, two tickets to the pond with Perry?"

We climbed into the truck and Cash immediately propped one large foot up on the dashboard where the sunlight glinted off her new boots, revealing that the green leather actually sported scales of some kind.

"Man, I feel like a gigantic lizard," she said proudly, and the insanity of that thought made me laugh. "Fast, ferocious, flexible. Able to survive the heat, find refuge under a rock, move rapidly across the sand." She made a slalom swish with her hands.

Glancing over at the boot top, I said, "That could be snake."

"A little reptilian tweak and you've ruined the whole imagery. I can't say, 'Man, I feel like a gigantic green snake.'"

"Sure you can. A snake is fast, ferocious, flexible. Able to survive the heat, find refuge under a rock, move rapidly across the sand."

"Yeah, but if I'm a big green snake I don't have any feet. Lizards have feet."

"Of course you have feet. You have boots, don't you? How can you have boots if you don't have feet?"

"Right," she said, contemplating my words for a moment before she looked over at me and we laughed.

"You bring out total silliness in me," I said, still chuckling.

"I love that side of you. But then I love all sides of you."

Warmed by her tone and the loving look in her eyes, I sighed, momentarily content. Cash Tate and I were becoming friends and I liked that. I liked it a lot.

❖

Over the next couple of weeks, the heat arrived in earnest. Late June often brought with it a persistent hot wind that dried perspiration in seconds and settled dust into the creases of old men's brows.

The hay was growing at a rapid rate and soon we'd have our first harvest. I rang Hiram, on the north, to make sure he still wanted a supply of round bales, most of his own land torn up by his cattle herd.

The first cutting was usually richer in protein but contained more weeds and wind-blown debris left from the winter months. Therefore, first cuttings were often reserved for cattle, with the second cutting being put up for horses. But the weather was so unpredictable that I liked to put aside two hundred square bales from the first harvest as insurance. For some reason I was less anal about the harvest this year, and certainly my mind spent an inordinate amount of time wandering aimlessly. Even Perry noticed it, saying I'd gone from acting like a trail boss to being, "loose as a goose."

I'd nearly forgotten to run an ad in the *County Journal Record* so people in neighboring towns could come and buy the rounds right out of the field. Winter prices were better, but a lot of that profit could be eaten up in getting the hay ready for storage. Besides, in the very best year, haying was a break-even proposition. I was fortunate my parents had left me money and Johnny had a small insurance policy, so I only had to rely on hay to feed my animals and not myself.

Cash pulled up in the Gator, her headband sweat-soaked and her clothes dusty. Having been here a little over a month now, she was starting to blend in with the scenery, looking less and less like a city girl.

"How many did you dig out?" I shouted above the wind.

She glanced over her shoulder at the pile of thorny thistles in the bed of the vehicle. "I lost count around five hundred."

"Chemicals sure didn't do much to kill them out this year. I'm going over there and warn Jonas Wiley that his thistle seeds are blowing into my pastures."

"I'll do it. I'd *enjoy* telling him."

People around here didn't take to neighbors telling them things, much less strangers, so I didn't want Cash talking to anyone on my behalf. "You help Perry do a quick check for that pipe that was out in the open. I don't think Jeremiah put it up before he got fired and it's laying out there in the north field somewhere just waiting to bust up the haying equipment."

"When I find it, where do you want me to put it?"

"It's thirty-foot lengths of three-inch OD," I said, referencing its outside diameter. "I don't imagine you'll be putting it anywhere without someone else hanging onto the other end. Perry tells me he's got another hand coming out tonight, so you two can most likely handle it. Just stack it up back of the hay shed and put a pipe flag on it so we'll know where we've left it."

She grabbed the steering wheel and winced.

"Something wrong?"

"Not a thing. See you later." She floored the gas pedal and I thought about telling her that she wasted gas every time she hot-rodded around, but I decided to forget it. From the looks of her clothes, she was working hard. Couldn't blame her for wanting to get where she was going fast. And I liked it when she was out working and I could deal with her from afar. I was getting a little more relaxed around her and enjoying our friendship.

Just before sundown, Perry came up the front steps with a big-bodied fellow whose stringy hair looked like it hadn't been washed in a decade. But he took his ball cap off and nodded his hello in a polite way.

"This here's Bo Nightengale, Sven Olan's cousin. He's looking for summer work and I've got him put up out at the bunkhouse."

I shook his big beefy hand and welcomed him, silently hoping he could work faster than his body mass implied as he lumbered off after Perry.

❖

Around midnight, I awoke restless, listening to the faraway thunder rumbling across the sky and wondering if the rain was headed in our direction. A good rain would help the hay grow so long as it didn't last more than a day or so, and then had plenty of heat to dry it out.

My mind flickered like the electricity that bolted across the sky. Where was I going with all these crazy thoughts that ran through my head these days? Restless as the wind, my body would not succumb to sleep. I tossed the sheets back off my legs, got out of bed, and opened the shades to check the night sky. Lightning was streaking across the heavens in a wild electric display of power. No cloud to ground lightning yet, the kind that struck cattle and killed them in their tracks.

A crack of thunder made me drop the shades and head for the living room, where I turned on the computer and checked the radar. If it was going to be really severe, I might bring the horses up out of the grove away from the trees. Silly, I knew. Most ranchers let livestock take its chances, but I feared a dawn that revealed a dead horse.

I looked up to see Cash standing in the doorway of her bedroom, sleepy and worried, her brow more furrowed.

"Storm wake you?" I asked gently.

"I couldn't sleep even before the thunder."

"I was just checking to see if the major part of the weather's going to miss us." I looked down at her hands, cupped as if they might hold a baseball, but they were empty. Something in her look made me hold out my palm and demand that she show me hers. She hesitated and I impatiently signaled her to do as I asked. She turned her hand over and rested it, skyward, in my own. Her right hand was a reddened mass of blisters, some blood-stained.

"What in hell happened to you?" I pulled her hand toward the light of the desk lamp so I could see more clearly.

"It's not a big deal. I got over-zealous with the thistles."

"Were you wearing the gloves I bought you?"

"I used some cloth gloves, and most of this is from the shovel." When I jutted my chin forward in a visual request for an explanation, she quickly complied. "I didn't want to ruin the deerskin."

"Ruin them? That's what they're for. To keep your *hands* from being ruined." I went into my bedroom and rummaged through the medicine cabinet, looking for something that might help.

Moments later I came back with ointment. "You seem intent on destroying your hands. When animals do that to themselves, shows they're nervous and bored and wanting food or freedom or something they can't get to. So you might think about that." She reached for the tube of ointment but couldn't bend her hand to unscrew the lid. I took it from her.

"Sit," I ordered. She plopped onto the couch and her chin rested on her chest as she offered up her hand. I squeezed the medicine onto my fingertips, then gently rubbed it onto her palm.

"I prefer bag balm, if you want to know the truth. I've put it on the swollen udders of cattle, on my horses, and on people, but we're not going out to the barn at this hour so let's start with this." She jumped involuntarily every time I touched a new spot and I apologized. "I should wrap the right hand to keep the medicine on there, or you'll rub it off in the night."

"I'm afraid I'll get it on the sheets."

"Don't worry about that." I took her left hand and began to rub the medicine into its less-damaged surface. She stretched her fingers slightly as I applied pressure, and a tingling sensation rippled from the top of my head along my back and across my shoulders. I closed my eyes for a moment. "You have the strong hands of a woman meant for the country, if we could only get your head there," I said softly. When I looked up, she seemed mesmerized like a pup who'd been rescued and now loved its owner. "I can't believe you didn't wear the gloves I bought you."

"They're just too nice to dig thistles in." Something about the way she said it made me think that her upbringing probably didn't include gifts carefully selected for her. The gloves were too precious to her, a treasure instead of a tool.

"Old leather gloves in different sizes and conditions are out in the tack room. Find a pair and wear them. But for now, baby that right hand."

A loud crash of thunder startled us both and we physically reacted.

"Come on, let's go out and look at the sky." Cash jumped up and bounded onto the front porch before I could remind her that standing in the lightning wasn't a good idea.

The cool north wind whipped our nightshirts around us and sprayed rain on our faces despite the porch overhang.

"Does this feel fabulous or what?" Cash pointed her chin skyward.

"It feels wet."

"Then you're in the wrong spot." She reached for me with damaged hands, clasped me around the waist with her wrists, and jerked me back, causing me to lose my balance and fall against her. "Wind is the breath of heaven whispering to us. Want to know what it's saying?"

And there it was again, that riverbank moment, that electrical buzz, that suspension of time creating a window for pleasure to breeze through. And the wind whispered softly, mocking the stuffy constraints of sexual mores, allowing me for one brief moment to breathe the fresh air of sensual freedom. A gust picked up the rain and hurled it at us.

"It's saying, 'Idiots get off the porch, it's raining sideways.'" I whirled out of her grasp and we ran inside, nearly soaked through.

"Your bandage is wet." I became serious about her hand again, unwrapping it.

"I'm wet everywhere." She panted, out of breath, and I wondered if I heard the sexual innuendo because I feared hearing it, or if a total stranger would hear it in the same way.

I quickly ordered her about. "Go dry your hair and change shirts, and I'll fix your hand."

She left the room and I went to mine and towel-dried my hair and put on another sleep shirt. When I returned I put more ointment on her hand and rewrapped it in gauze.

"I like the attention. I may run out in the rain again right now."

"Don't press your luck."

"I'm lucky to be here in this room with you, on this ranch. Have you ever snuggled into bed on a stormy night with someone you love or awakened on a rainy morning?"

"I can't recall, probably," I said, as if distracted, and moved to the computer screen, focusing intently. "Radar shows the serious part of the storm won't overtake us tonight. If you need something, for your hand, let me know." I turned the computer off and headed for my bedroom, feeling her eyes follow me. I sensed her whole being wanted to follow, which is why I hurried and closed and locked the door, then flopped onto my bed and let out a great sigh.

She was in love with the music on the riverbank, now enamored of rain on the roof. She's obviously a romantic and isn't attracted to any individual in particular, but merely the emotion of the moment surrounding that person. She needs an outlet for her romantic nature and it can't be me, I thought. And suddenly I knew what I wanted to do for her. The thought made me smile and relax.

CHAPTER NINE

Despite a nearly sleepless night, I was up at dawn, had my coffee, and was on the road for Maze City. I left a note on the kitchen counter for Cash telling her to sleep in and rest her hands, that I'd be back shortly after lunch.

Perry's note tucked in the screen door said he and Bo had toured the ranch checking to see that the cattle were all intact after the storm, then driven to town to get some more fencing wire. Since buying a roll of wire didn't require two people, I suspected they were really going to the local bar, but even that didn't perturb me since it left me more time to reveal my surprise to Cash.

The day was rain-wrapped and gray, but I felt exhilarated, singing along with the country station and watching the redbirds dart across the road.

In roughly two hours, I pulled into a shop on the main street of Maze and went inside to select just the right item for Cash. It took me over an hour to discuss it and several hundred dollars out of my bank account, but I was happy to pay for the pleasure I was certain it would bring. I couldn't wait to get home and surprise her. I had the entire evening planned.

Stopping at the 2-K on the way back, I asked Donnetta to pack up a couple of baked-chicken dinners because I didn't have time to cook.

She eyed me suspiciously. "What are you up to, Ms. Stanwyck? No secrets shared, no food packed."

I knew Donnetta wasn't kidding. "Cash hurt her hands working out on the ranch."

"Uh-huh." She reminded me of someone's mom, standing on the porch in an apron, clutching a wooden spoon in a hand propped on her hip, listening to a kid spin a story of half-truths.

"And I'm taking us both dinner."

"Well, now, that's nice." I could see her mind ticking away like a Swiss wall clock.

"May I have my food now?"

"Of course you can. By the way, Stretch was in here and said he's determined to take you out one of these days. You know we kid about him, but he makes a good living and he's not that bad-looking."

"Donnetta—"

"Just wondering if you're getting a little bonkers from lack of company."

"I have company."

"Male company."

"I have Perry and now Bo Nightengale."

"*Company* company, as in sleepovers. I know, I know, mind your own business, Donnetta," she admonished herself.

"I was thinking about a dog instead. He'll keep me warm at night and never leave hair in the shower."

Donnetta waved her arms in the air as if sending me off. Taking the large-handled brown bag, I happily fled, tearing down the dirt road and onto the highway that led to the ranch. I pulled into the driveway, scattering gravel, and Cash pulled up in the Gator from the other side of the property.

"Where've you been?" she asked. "I'm lonesome dove out here. No one's around but me."

"Why don't you get washed up and come in for dinner. I picked something up for us at the café."

She bolted from the vehicle and headed for the hand pump out in the front yard, splashing water everywhere like a spaniel.

I went inside and washed up and got the plates out, putting the gift I had for her to one side. Moments later she came into the living room on the way to her bedroom.

"So you like the old well?"

"Yeah, it's like a time-travel machine or something. Real relaxing," she said as she disappeared into her room.

I smiled, thinking about that. It *was* a time-travel machine. The very first ranchers who lived out here used it as their total source of water, filling buckets for cooking and bathing. It wasn't hard to envision rough, callused hands grasping the rust-iron lever and pumping it up and down impatiently, maybe as a son argued with his father over work in the field, or a mother fretted over the health of a child inside the cabin, or maybe lovers used it as an excuse to meet and talk privately out of earshot of the family.

Cash returned with newly washed hair, still wet and shiny, and a pair of thin drawstring pants. Noticing her small, firm breasts clearly outlined underneath her T-shirt, I glanced at her body as I asked about her hands.

"They hurt like hell. Left one is much better but the right one is swollen and sore."

"Let me see it again." This time she stepped in very close and held the back of her hand against my chest with the palm up for me to examine. My breathing became erratic and I nearly lost my bearings, forgetting what we were looking at. "I'll put something on it after dinner."

I pulled away, disoriented, and focused on dishing up the plates. We sat cross-legged on the leather couch chowing down on the chicken. "Donnetta can cook. Not like you though."

I grinned at her political correctness. The two of us sharing a meal together on this old leather couch as the sun went down felt perfect. Why, I couldn't say. It just did.

"What happened to your husband?" She asked it in that direct way she had, without sympathy, taking the evening in a direction I didn't want it to go.

"He died in an automobile accident."

"Why are you so guilty about that?"

I got up and poured myself a glass of wine and then sat back down, giving myself time to collect my thoughts, eyeing this precocious young woman before I finally addressed her. "And why do you think I have guilt about it?"

"Because you keep your body and your mind running like a jet engine, and when I mentioned him just now, you got irritable." She barely moved and said nothing more. I could hear a clock ticking on the shelf above my desk, a sound I'd never really noticed before, listening for the passage of time a new experience for me.

"We hadn't been married all that long and we had a fight and he left angry and the next call I got was from the highway patrol about twenty miles from here. They used the Jaws of Life and flew him to a Kansas City hospital where he was dead on arrival."

She was silent for a long moment, then spoke unemotionally. "What were you fighting about?"

"I had a very nice night planned for us and it's getting pretty sad."

"I'm sorry."

"I have something for you," I said, and she looked surprised as I went to the counter and produced the medium-sized box and handed it to her with less joy than I'd planned now that she'd clouded my mind with the past.

She began to unwrap her present slowly, pausing every now and then to look up at me. "Why am I getting a gift?"

"I don't know." I shrugged, pleased with myself.

She was on the edge of the chair now, down to the final shreds of paper, and could clearly see the image on the box. Yanking it open, she carefully lifted out the Canon SLR.

"You're always holding your hands up, making that little clicking sound like you're taking a picture, so I thought, while your hands are healing, you could take some real ones. It's not too heavy to hold. It's a single-lens reflex, which the guy said you'd like, and it got a very good consumer rating." As I rattled off the camera's attributes, I could see the tears in her eyes. She looked stunned. "Well, do you like it?"

Setting the camera aside, she stood up and wrapped her long

arms around me and lifted me off the floor in a big bear hug, then swung us both in a three-hundred-sixty-degree whirl. I yelped, telling her to put me down. She set my feet back on the floor and then kissed me, missing my cheek and catching my neck.

"This is the absolute neatest thing I've ever gotten. I can't believe you did this."

A thrill ran through me that began at the very spot where her lips touched me and ran through my heart and even farther south to regions I refused to recognize. She loosened her grip but still had her hands on me, and I shivered. "Careful with your blisters."

"You're a wonderful person, Maggie Tanner. Thank you." She seemed as touched by the gesture as the gift. Obviously, Cash Tate hadn't received many expensive presents in her life since she'd always been an appendage to a surrogate family, an afterthought.

She broke away and picked up the camera again and stroked it lovingly, like a kid with a toy at Christmas. "This is a very expensive camera. Why did you do it?"

"Maybe to see you like this." *Maybe to be lifted off my feet and slung into the air and kissed on the neck, although I had no way to predict her response or my pleasure.*

She looked at me for a moment as if she wanted to say more but then buried herself in the camera instructions, swooning over the many things the camera would do. After thirty minutes, I cleared my throat. "Hey, I'm still here." She swung the camera in my direction, pressed the button, and the shutter snapped crisply. "Sorry, I moved."

"Move all you want. This has a high-speed shutter so I can get action shots. But for now…" She towed me over to the chair and demanded I throw my legs over one arm and rest my head on the other.

As I complied, I could smell her cologne either on the leather pillow or perhaps on me where she'd held me, and the fragrance made me catch my breath. "I don't sit like this."

"Maybe you should." She spoke from behind the view finder. "Because you look real…" Click. "…sexy." Click. Click.

I felt my facial expression change—relax, maybe. That's the

thing about a camera. Anonymous, intimate, infinitely close up, it looks deep into your eyes and finds the truth like a lover who can't be fooled.

She moved my arm, tousled my hair, then came in very close, the shutter grinding away. Ending on her knees in front of the chair where I lounged, she rested her elbows on the edge of the cushion.

"Not so close. I don't want all my wrinkles preserved for posterity."

"You have no wrinkles. I love this camera, thank you."

"You're welcome." The words could just as easily have been "hold me" because I had lost track of what we were talking about. Her eyes danced across my face as if waiting for an opening, an invitation. My breath was coming in short, rapid bursts as I envisioned touching her magnificent dark curls and fantastic features. I couldn't stop myself from grasping her forearm, feeling the strength and size of her. At my touch, she knelt and bent her head as if about to be knighted and pressed her brow into my chest, resting quietly.

Could she hear my runaway heart? Did she know what I was thinking or feeling? And why couldn't we stay like this forever? I ran my fingers through her hair, stroking her scalp. Perhaps she just wanted mothering or sisterly contact or some human connection. It didn't sound as if she'd had much of that growing up. But what was *my* purpose...my wanting? Why was I holding this woman against me, thrilled by her touch?

The deep-voiced conversation in the front yard broke the spell. Cash jumped up and met the men as they swaggered up on the porch. "You okay in there?" Bo asked loudly.

"Yeah, fine," Cash answered, and pushed the screen door open to walk out on the porch.

"Her truck was here," Bo said, referring to me, "but the lights were off in the house. Pretty early to be going to bed."

I realized we'd been so caught up in what we were doing that we hadn't turned the house lights on as it grew dark.

"I got a new camera and was trying the flash at different light levels," Cash said, as I flipped on the overhead lights that now seemed bright and garish. I noted that Cash was instantly ready with the plausible lie, as if she'd spent a good deal of her life finding ways to hide the truth.

"Maggie around?" Perry chimed in, sounding like he was investigating a crime and didn't quite believe the story he was getting. I stepped into view behind Cash. "*There* you are. Anything in particular you want us to start on in the morning?"

A silly question. Perry didn't need me to tell him what to do. He had the whole system down and had done it for years. He was just worried about my whereabouts and checking up on me like an old mother hen. And a part of Perry just liked to be in the know.

"The three of you need to move that pipe out of the fields in the morning and stack it out of the way of the haying equipment." I attempted to straighten my rumpled hair.

"Will do. First thing then, Cash?" Bo said.

"First thing." She closed the door and locked it, turning to look at me.

Standing in the middle of the room with the glaring lights overhead, I was aware that I'd almost lost my senses. "Well, I'm going to bed and read for a while. Unwind."

"Maggie…" She tried to block my way.

"I know, you love it, and I'm so happy you do. Just have fun with it." I patted her arm as you would a friend and disappeared into my bedroom before she could say anything else.

So what happens to me when I'm around her? Something! It's the way she's masculine and then feminine, strong and then vulnerable, young and then old. Magnetic.

I'd held her head against my chest, stroked her hair, bought her a gift. None of those acts, in and of themselves, would have meant anything if she had been Donnetta. So why, doing them with Cash, did I feel like I had something to hide?

I need to get that out of my head. I have nothing at all to hide. Nothing has happened. I'm just fond of her, that's all. Let yourself enjoy giving her a gift, for God's sake.

CHAPTER TEN

It had rained for six straight days and nights and was bordering on biblical. The fields were muddy, the hay bent over, and the animals' hooves grew soft and spongy. Only a few pieces of the landscape remained above the mud. Our vehicles tore up the pastures as we slogged over them to check on horses, cattle, or the hay crop. Weather service said today ended the soggiest June in a decade. While all around me Mother Nature had gone soft, I was determined to harden my resolve—enough of contemplating something I never intended to experience and therefore a fulfillment I wouldn't miss.

I was so determined to put a wall between Cash Tate and my strange urges that perhaps I overreacted, always crossing the living room with a purpose rather than lingering to talk, spending lots of time in the barn and making several trips into town so I could keep my physical and emotional distance from her.

Perry had his own relationship issues as he cussed the skies, the hay, and Bo Nightengale, who got on his nerves as a bunkhouse partner.

"He snores and snorts and hawks and spits and carries on. He's louder and more disgusting than a couple of rutting hogs," Perry complained to me.

"Is he a good worker?" I asked, unloading groceries from the car.

"I'm talkin' about evenings with him and now who knows if he'll be useful for haying because there'll be no haying. We may never get dry enough to hay again. Shoulda knowed we wouldn't be cutting. Almanac predicted it." His complaining always harkened back to the *Farmer's Almanac* and how we'd agreed to abide by it and then hadn't.

"If we get a dry week, we can still round-bale and sell it off for cattle hay," I reasoned.

"Not worth *that*. Oughta just lay it down," he said, wanting to let it mulch the ground or get carried off by the wind.

"It'll look like hell, it's a fire hazard, and I intend to get a second cutting this year so I'm not laying down the first." Perry followed me into the house as I sat the sack down on the counter.

"Don't know what condition I'll be in by then," he groused in reference to Bo and exited seconds after arriving, demonstrating his nervous state.

I put the groceries in the cabinet and glanced at Cash, who sat at the computer ignoring both of us. She'd trudged the fields front to back all day, taking photos of birds and wildlife and loading them into her computer. Once Perry left, she beckoned me to her screen, where she flashed images that looked like a *National Geo* exhibit.

"You have a good eye," I said over her shoulder, being careful not to get too close or too intimate. A large male redbird seemed to be looking right at us, and in another shot, a squirrel swung to its next tree, captured mid-leap.

"I recognize beauty when I see it," she said, turning to look at me.

I ignored the obvious compliment. "You should think about doing it professionally. You can't buck hay for the rest of your life." My tone was crisp and I could tell from her expression she didn't like the frosty distance, but I was getting better at it.

Like all plainswomen, I could compartmentalize things when I needed to. That was how Bea Benegan could have a husband lying at home drunk and still tell customers at the dry-goods store that he was a good man. Being able to compartmentalize is how Betsy Kendall could know for a fact her husband Hiram was having an affair with a gal in town and still swear to anyone who would listen that her family was blessed. And that's how I could wall off my heart, ignore the longing, and tell myself that I had absolutely everything in life I needed.

That's what compartmentalizing could do for a woman—allow her to function and go on living.

❖

The sun finally came out and, a few days after that, the land began to dry. When it did, the intensity of the heat created a world of steam. We were heading toward the Fourth of July, muggy and hot and resigned to the fact that summer was upon us. The ground dried up enough that the haying equipment could get across it, and Perry unlocked the huge equipment barn and began tinkering on the John Deere, then drove it out and hooked up the hay cutter. He waited until the dew was off the grass and the mid-morning sun was at its peak before he fired up the tractor and began to cut. We were weeks late in getting our first cutting, which would mean a late September second cutting in a race with the first frost.

I loved the haying cycle. Tall golden stalks falling over as the tractor chugged up and down in rows, like soldiers of the sun laid to rest in the fields, their ending was the beginning of winter nourishment for the horses and cattle.

By the time the last acres of the day had their haircut, a thin orange band of sky was disappearing below a mass of dark purple clouds, creating a glow that concealed all but the tractor lights guiding the big green machine over the remaining acreage.

I looked up to see Perry walking across the field and the tractor still traveling along the backside of the east pasture. "Getting your money's worth with Bo."

"That's Cash." Perry turned his head and spat on the ground.

"Where's Bo?"

"Family emergency."

I said nothing. Family emergencies only tended to happen out here when the work got backbreaking.

"Be back in the morning," Perry reassured me of Bo's absence.

I stayed up waiting for the tractor lights to shut off and finally, around midnight, they did. Cash came up to the house hot and dust-covered from the field-dirt flying up at her. She gave me a wave and a quick hello before disappearing into her room. I heard the shower crank on and the sound of water streaming down. Shortly thereafter, the bedsprings made one loud bounce and then not another sound. I smiled, thinking she must be exhausted, and I was pleased with myself that I'd gotten us both back on track. Good for her and good for me. The nonsense that had been going on in my head would never make it to my heart. I had created an intelligent detour—keeping everyone's mind on the work at hand.

The next morning Cash and Bo, back from his faux-emergency, took turns driving the tractor that dragged the circular tines of the hay rake over the fallen grass, fluffing up neat rows of prairie hay ready for the baler. The moist heat took its toll and the workers looked spent. I drove out at noon with sandwiches and iced tea for everyone, as I often did during hay season, and served it on the truck tailgate. Cash was all grins, having apparently gotten a good night's sleep. Bo looked hung over and Perry was just plain grouchy.

"You ever have anybody come back two summers in a row?" Cash said under her breath.

"I guess we'll see, won't we," I said, and she smiled.

"Maybe I'll become the town photographer. Easier work, I'm thinking," she said.

"Yeah?" Perry moved in and grabbed two sandwiches. "Most things you'd shoot in this town you'd just want to go ahead and bury."

"You are in one pissy mood, Mr. Waits," I said.

"Porky Pig's gotta get out of my bunkhouse," he whispered hoarsely. Bo came around the corner and snorted as if he had a major sinus infection. "Jeez-Louise!" Perry said to no one in particular and went off to eat his sandwich out of earshot.

"How's it going, Bo?" I asked. Cash pulled her camera out and took a shot of Bo's big battered knuckles reaching into the pile of sandwiches. He turned to look at her.

"Mind if I get a shot?" she asked while snapping it.

He shrugged but seemed pleased. In fact, he stood a little straighter. "Those boots green?" he asked, in a tone that seemed to indicate even his country-boy sensibilities were appalled at the hue.

"Nope, brown," she said of her bright green boots.

"Look green." His face was puzzled.

"Must be the light. Lean up against the truck," she ordered, and he posed for her. For a moment, I felt a pang of jealousy.

"You give me a copy of that?" he asked.

"You bet." She sacked the camera, grabbed a sandwich, and headed back to the truck.

"She married?" Bo asked casually.

"I think she's dating some guy back home," I replied. *Why the hell did I say that? I don't know that she's dating anybody. Well, it's important for Bo not to get the wrong idea about her. Cameras do that, create a personal relationship where there is none. I could vouch for that.*

❖

Two days later, the Fourth of July dawned intensely hot. I looked out the back window to observe the hay baling that had been underway since midday, allowing the noon sunshine to evaporate the morning dew and prevent mold setting into the bales. Perry drove the tractor with the baler on it, Bo drove a smaller tractor with a forklift on the end, and Cash, wearing gloves on her nearly healed hands, hoisted the squares up on the loader fork until she had a stack twenty-four wide. We used to stack them on a wagon, but it was twice the work unstacking them in the hay shed. This way we loaded once and the tractor went back to the hay barn and the lift hoisted them to the top of the stack. We used more gas but saved on hired hands.

Grabbing the binoculars off the shelf, I focused on Cash. She looked tan and muscled and beautiful, but tired. I checked my watch. She'd been at it for three hours. I felt a surge of energy and the desire to get out and do something physical.

I jumped in the truck and drove down to where she was standing in the field. Hopping out, I swung a gallon thermos into her hands. "You take a break. I'll handle it for awhile."

"No, no. I'm fine. You can't do this. I mean…well, I'm bigger."

"Only in your mind," I said dryly.

When Bo pulled the tractor in front of me, I grabbed hay bales off the ground. Making an extra effort, I swung eighteen bales onto the forklift before Cash, who refused to rest, could handle twelve, bucking the second row as if I were tossing pillows and not sixty-pound squares. I wanted to collapse onto the tailgate and pass out, but my pride had the best of me. I grabbed the iced tea and slugged down a glass, standing tall and acting like I wasn't even tired.

I caught Cash out of the corner of my eye watching me with a big grin.

"What's the problem?" I asked in a businesslike tone.

"Don't get her riled." Perry shook his woolly head. "Things are tough enough around here on a good day." For the first time he glanced down at Cash's feet. "Where'd you get those green boots? You look like a damned leprechaun."

"They were my grandfather's. I adored him," Cash lied, straight-faced.

"Didn't know that." Perry looked embarrassed and hurried off.

"You're getting your money's worth out of those boots," I said.

"Not easy being green."

After several hours I was panting but trying to hide it. By a quick count, I estimated that we'd hauled and stacked about half the bales on the ground. I used a walkie-talkie in the truck to call Perry and tell him we were trading out so that Bo could stack for awhile and Cash could drive. She protested but I said it was only fair. Down deep, I thought Bo had taken advantage of her good temperament, letting her do an unequal share of the work.

We stood together waiting for the tractors to return. The wind whipped tarps, our hair, and our shirts, slapping us into awareness of our own filth and fatigue. Unable to hear above the roar of machinery and the intense wind, we merely grinned at one another. She was pulling her weight. More than pulling her weight. In fact, she was working harder than Bo and smarter than Perry. Cash Tate was turning into a hand. *Buck would be proud.*

When I looked up again, the shutter snapped and she'd captured me, dirt and all, in her frame. Before I could complain, she shouted, "Smile, Ms. Stanwyck. Big Valley is nearly hayed." I realized she and Donnetta must be sharing information I wasn't privy to, and despite that, she made me smile. Snap. She had me again.

Cash turned her attention to Bo crawling down out of the cab, his huge back end in full view, then Perry loping across the field. She swung her camera lens toward them. Click. Click. Click. She had captured us all.

Chapter Eleven

By late evening I'd left Cash in the fields working alongside the men to finalize the harvest. Everything was nearly wrapped up and I came in and took a long soaking bath, just to relax my muscles, which were admittedly twitching from my showing off this afternoon. I had to smile thinking about the ridiculousness of my behavior and how I would pay for it in body aches tomorrow. Trying to get a jump on pain, I took wine and some glasses out on the porch, thinking that women, wine, and horses all seemed to go together. Perhaps all were a gamble, and ranchers were the biggest gamblers on the planet, most depending on God and good luck for their survival. I sat down in one of the rockers, enjoying the anonymity of night as Cash staggered up, unable to see me observing her.

"You worked hard today," I said quietly out of the darkness.

"I would have fainted but I'm too damned tired to get back up," she said of my startling her.

"Normally we have a Fourth of July feed, but the haying got in the way of that. We can probably see the celebration in town from here."

"I'm not crazy about fake fireworks." She sagged into a rocking chair a few feet from mine and I contemplated what non-fake fireworks might be. Perhaps fireworks of the human kind, and I was certain Cash could generate those. I reached for the carafe on the table between us and poured the pale liquid into a glass, then handed it to her.

"Kool-Aid?" She looked suspicious.

"Wine."

"Thank God. I thought I'd joined an AA work camp." She slugged down the small glass and held it out. I poured her another.

"Some people sip it," I said slyly.

"Those people have never spent ten hours next to Bo's armpit and Perry's spitting chaw into the wind." She pointed to the stains on her shirt. I chuckled. "So was your husband a…regular guy?"

"Why are you so interested in that topic?"

"It's a piece of your history, of this ranch's history, that's all," she said, but I felt she was interested for other reasons, like wanting to know who someone like me would sleep with.

"By 'regular guy' you mean was he like Bo and Perry?" She didn't answer and I knew that's what she was curious about—were my tastes local. "He died when he was so young that it's hard to say what he would have turned into."

"So he was the love of your life?" Her voice came softly from the shadows. Maybe she was able to ask such personal questions because it was dark and she didn't have to look in my eyes.

"We were only together four years." I avoided answering her directly. "He died when I was younger than you are."

"Must have been hard to go on out here alone."

I poured myself another glass of wine and we sat listening to the comforting cadence of the cicadas as they filled the air with a palpable buzz and the runners on the rockers creaked patiently against the porch boards, summoning secrets. "It wasn't so much about loving him, although I cared for him. It was simply that he was here, present, alive. And then in a matter of minutes he wasn't. When I came back from the funeral, a kind of eerie quiet seemed to have spread across the ranch. He was the last of three generations of laughing and fighting and toiling and then nothing. They were gone, existing only in my memories. Every time I took a breath it echoed like wind in a tunnel. I promised myself I would never hurt like that again."

"How do you make good on that promise?"

"It's where I put my focus. I choose to focus on things that don't hurt."

The hum of the tractor motors filled the night air as the big tires rolled across the field out to the equipment shed and the green monsters' lights went dark. We could just make out two dim figures trudging toward the bunkhouse.

"I've lost eight lovers," she said as I filled her glass and mine. I said nothing, and finally she burst forth with a giggle, as if she could no longer refrain. "Aren't you curious?"

"Kansans think it's impolite to pry."

"Well, I'm prying into *your* love life." The wine had obviously emboldened Cash, and her forwardness made me laugh. "But if it's any guy within a twenty-mile radius, stop before we get to the bedroom part."

"Eight." I shifted the conversation back to her. "Does that mean you took a lover at age fifteen or do you merely fall in love annually?"

"I like the chase more than the capture. And the relationship inevitably gets serious and boring. Settle down, job security, social status, the right house, the right car, the right something that tomorrow is the wrong something and now you need something else. Buck thinks I talk crazy. He swears you'll change me."

"I don't have any more answers than you do."

"But you've changed me." When I didn't respond she continued. "It's just the way you are." She drank the last of her wine and we sat in silence for a long while. I was comforted by her presence but nervous over the energy that seemed to hang in the wind. "Do you ever feel like if you could get that 'one thing' you'd feel great, then you get it and you feel great for one day, then you go right back to feeling the way you did before? It's like a constant search for something and it drives you crazy."

"The wind comes closest to filling that void for me. Blows through and rolls over my skin and thrills me into hanging on, whispering change is coming. Of course later I realize it's just spring turning to summer, or summer to fall, but still the wind enticed me into staying alive."

"I should make the wind my lover."

"The land is mine." I thought about those words after they'd left my lips and realized I'd put every ounce of strength, my heart and my soul into this windblown vista. After that, I had nothing left to give.

In the distance popping sounds, then whistles, then patterns of light exploded into the air and we sat very still watching the Fourth of July display from the porch. The celebration, much like the fireworks inside me, witnessed from afar, were muted, muffled, not nearly what I'd expected when I was young.

"There's your fake fireworks," I said, feeling melancholy for no reason.

"First time they've seemed pretty."

"So tell me about the big eight, your lost loves. Or at least start with the last one."

"Tall, handsome, wild, big drinker," she said with a shrug.

"What attracted you to him?"

"Her." Somewhere in the dark I heard a loud whistle and the sound of something breaking apart and blowing up. My brain exploded along with it, and I fought a physical urge to jerk back as the pronoun bounced around inside my head. The stillness palpitated and I fell momentarily off balance.

Of course "her." I knew that, didn't I?

"Buck says an attraction to a woman is a reversible condition."

"Is it?" My voice quiet, I already knew the answer. *Nothing about Cash Tate would be reversible. In fact, she was completely irreversible. One way, no going back.*

"You know it's not." Her piercing eyes upended my thoughts, seeming to convey she knew how I felt. I looked away.

I took a deep breath and then finished off the wine. "Maybe it's not about whether you're attracted to men or women but that you're not able to be monogamous with either." Not knowing for a certainty that monogamy was the issue, I was nonetheless willing to bet a thousand dollars that with those eyes, opportunity was always knocking at her bedroom door. "We'd better go inside before the mosquitoes eat us alive."

I left the wineglasses by the sink and went immediately to my bedroom, telling Cash good night over my shoulder.

Closing the door quietly, I turned and sagged back against the cool wood. Now the truth was spoken and I could no longer pretend the exhilarating breeze between us didn't exist. Maybe that's why I felt drawn to her; she was accustomed to attracting women, comfortable in her own sensuality, and the attraction I felt was either in response to the energy she was emitting or it was, unfortunately, causing it. *Either way, it's my responsibility to put a stop to it.*

Launching myself away from the door, I paced, trying to decide if I should pick up the phone and dial Buck. He knew she was gay and he didn't have the courtesy or good sense to tell me that.

I plopped down on the bed, grabbed the phone, then hung up. I picked up a book by the bedside table and turned on the adjacent lamp, twisting the plastic knob with such strength that I heard it crack as the light came on. "Damn." I bent under the shade to examine the tortured device, then slapped the book down and flipped the switch off again, unable to concentrate on reading.

From the kitchen came sounds of Cash washing something in the sink—the wineglasses perhaps. The floorboards creaked irregularly as if she was walking softly and trying not to make noise. Then I heard her door latch snap shut and was aware of my own quick breath.

I lay back on the bed and stared at the ceiling. *This doesn't have to change our relationship. She felt comfortable enough to share her past with me, and while it doesn't exactly jibe with my experiences, there's nothing wrong with her being gay. In fact, if I believe television, gay is in. Eighty is the new sixty, and sixty is the new forty, and forty is the new twenty. Good to know I'm twenty again because I'm acting like it.*

I hopped up and went into the bathroom to shower, flipped on the light, and faced myself in the mirror. "You need to get serious about finding some nice man around here, like Donnetta said." I spoke to my slightly flushed face and took a moment to examine my figure. I was well proportioned. Nothing had gone terribly south. I still had a waist and fairly firm breasts. I carried myself erect, if not stiff, and held my head a bit too high, but my eyes were soft and I had good skin. Mid-length ash blond hair was pulled back off my face, although most of the time it escaped. I could still be considered in the game, a thought that immediately amused me since I'd never considered how I looked at all, much less conducted a survey of my naked self.

This is all good because it means I'm physically waking up after all these years. I want someone to love me. Thinking those words made me smile, and standing naked in the bathroom, half drunk, grinning at myself in the mirror caused me to shake my head. "You're an idiot," I said, not unkindly, to my image and stepped into the tub.

After a long, cool shower I rubbed dry with a thick towel, then dried my hair in no particular style before crawling into bed.

I had architected my life to avoid losing someone ever again and, to date, I had been successful. My ranch, my animals, my heart, all intact.

Now Cash comes along and confesses that she moves merrily from person to person as if they're dispensable. What was she like with them…coffee, drinks, bed, good-bye? And when she made love to these women, was she on top, acting the dominant partner—what did they do? I closed my eyes and a mildly erotic sensation ran the length of my body.

Perhaps secretly I longed to get lost for a night in a place where no one knew me and I could experience any lover I chose without strings, without recrimination, without the fear of disease. Just pure pleasure from someone I might enjoy and then never see again. Is that what Cash had done? Among the eight, was there one she barely knew? And after, did she lie beside her looking like a freeze-frame from *Gentleman's Quarterly*, an androgynous god of beauty smug that she had taken the woman or tricked her or been better than the woman had ever thought possible?

The house was quiet except for the faraway boom of fireworks exploding and perhaps scaring horses and cattle. My mind drifted to Cash and the long white shirt she apparently slept in, as she occasionally came out into the living room looking like a rumpled angel. Her luscious black curls would lie in stark contrast to the white pillowcase. Her strong hands would embrace her lover and hold her, precluding escape.

I caressed my body, pleased that I was still smooth and soft to the touch despite my muscled arms and more than occasionally rough hands, and I wondered about the curvature of Cash's tall frame and how she might fit up against a body like mine and if she was as soft in all the hidden places. Then I sat up in bed suddenly and gave a muffled growl and punched my pillow with my fist. *I will find the appropriate outlet for this.*

As if in answer to my plan, a loud burst and then white light flared across my window, followed by a sizzling, searing sound that streaked through the sky, then a bright array of color whistled nearer and nearer. I lay back on the bed and let the flickering display flash over my body. This particular Fourth of July would not end in a simple midnight bang but culminate in a sky-shattering release of pyrotechnics.

Chapter Twelve

Cash kept looking up at me over her morning eggs, making expectant eye contact. What she was expecting, I wasn't sure.

"What?" I finally asked impatiently. She'd reduced me to someone of her age acting as if we were in school and had a crush on one another, and I had happily gone along with it, sharing sexual forays like teenage girls at a dance. I was done with it.

"Just checking to see if you're still okay with my staying here after I told you about myself."

"Does being gay—"

"Lesbian."

The word stopped me. I'd never particularly liked the harshness of it and thought anyone would go out of her way not to label herself with it.

"Does being lesbian in any way inhibit your ability to buck hay, drive a tractor, or feed the horses?"

"Some might say it enhances that ability." She grinned.

"Well, then maybe we need to hire more lesbians in order to get Perry's list of chores done by noon." I handed her a torn piece of lined paper with Perry's schoolboy scrawl on it:

> *Use the weed eater around all the pasture fence posts, mow the east paddocks, and pick up all the loose tree branches down by the grove.*

It was three days' worth of work but I acted as if it were nothing. I rinsed my plate, loaded it into the dishwasher, and went in to take a shower, leaving Cash alone. She needed to stay busy and keep her head on straight and not think I intended to be a nightly sounding board for her failed relationships or titillated by her sexual preference.

At noon the heat was oppressive and Perry was in the back pasture checking the cattle, primarily to see that they were all there. Cattle thieving had surfaced again in our county and we were watchful. It wasn't that hard to back a truck up in the dark, cut the barbed wire, and herd a few cows up a loading ramp, so Perry checked the fences daily and made minor repairs where needed.

I drove over to the east paddocks where Cash was working. My arrival went unnoticed as the whirr of the weed eater overpowered the sound of the XUV. I sat silent and watched her work, slicing away foot-tall weeds around the fence posts that stretched ahead for acres. God, there must be five hundred posts, I thought.

She finally caught sight of me out of the corner of her eye and shut off the motor, slinging the device to the ground, the shoulder strap falling off her sweaty T-shirt. Bits of grass stuck to her wet body and festooned her hair like confetti. Her face was smudged with dirt but the smile greeted me.

She went around to the back of the truck and opened the spigot on the large water tank and washed up before taking the drink I handed her. I offered a tinfoil package as well.

"Can you eat? I brought you a sandwich." Taking the workers something during the day to quench their thirst or feed them was a courtesy I tried to maintain for everyone, including Perry.

"I'm too hot. Think it would make me sick. I'll stick to water. If you'll put that in the fridge, I'll eat it later. Maybe on the porch with a glass of wine?"

"I think by the time you finish you'll be anxious for a hot shower and a good night's sleep."

"I've tended bar, worked at a hospital, taught aerobics classes, and I used to party all night, shower, and go straight to work. But

I've never done anything that's busted my ass like weed-whacking 101." She looked surprisingly happy.

I didn't want to hear about her former life that involved partying all night, and I thought her referencing it was bravado. "Well, I'm going to get out of your hair—"

"Lot of things in my hair..." She yanked at bits of weeds. "... but you're not one of them. Can we talk this evening? I mean, you know, on the porch. Rock?" She suddenly giggled. "I've gone from asking women to rock my world to asking a woman if she'll rock on the porch."

I paused, not certain if she was making fun of me or the old ranch porch. She was clearly comparing her former life experience to her current one, and I was certain ranch life came up short. When the summer ended, we would be part of her repertoire of quaint memories that would make great storytelling in a gay bar: the old guy who spat into the wind and the widow woman who clung to her ranch.

She must have sensed my mood because she tried to amend her statement, but I drove away as if I had other work to do, which in fact I did. *She should walk up to the well if she's thirsty. Let her talk to the wind.*

Around six o'clock I left a sandwich wrapped inside a checkered napkin, along with a pitcher of iced tea on the porch and a note pinned to the chair bottom with a rock. I'd composed another list of activities to keep her busy tomorrow and a postscript: *Into town tonight. Rock on.* A little dig, perhaps, if I analyzed it too deeply.

I made sure I was out of the driveway before she came up from the pasture. I needed to begin thinking about my life and what it could become and who I should share it with. That's what this was all about, this being drawn to conversations with Cash. I was lonely, and good for her that she'd dredged that emotion out of me. I *did* long for conversations in the evening on a porch swing. Maybe it was time.

I had nowhere to go, so I drove in to town and went to the Main Street Movies. The local theater marquee read BUTCH CASSIDY

AND THE SUNDANCE KID. The theater didn't have the clout or money to attract first-run films, or even slightly dated ones, so they'd capitalized on their problem, making outdated films their strategy, specializing in classics.

The glass, phone-booth-sized ticket office was manned by Crystal Adams, a wholesome young woman who worked in the small bakery next door.

"So you're working double shifts, Crystal?"

"Their dough by day, my dough by night." She waved a wad of dollars at me before making change. "You'll love the film. Paul Newman has the sexiest eyes on the planet." I realized the film's debut in 1969 occurred before Crystal was even "crystallized," so she most likely thought everyone was seeing it for the first time and that Paul Newman was still a hunky kid.

Cash has those Newman eyes. She'll have girls falling over her for years. My mind had suddenly jumped track. I worked to bring myself back to the moment. "Did you know this film was voted the seventh best film of all time in the Western genre," I said.

"No waaay."

"Way," I said, in teen speak.

"Who told you that?"

"I minored in film in college."

"Next fall, K-state, and I can't wait."

"Congratulations," I said of her college acceptance.

"And hi to your mom."

In the tiny lobby, I bought popcorn and a Dr Pepper and entered the theater through the double doors, walked a few steps down the slightly sloped cement floor, and took a seat in the back row. Only half a dozen people trickled in, and within minutes the room went dark and the old projector cranked up overhead, throwing an intense light onto the screen and ultimately Paul Newman's handsome face as he set about robbing banks. The 35mm film, festooned with dirt specks that showed up on the screen as giant worms, reminded me that this film dub had no doubt been shipped all over the country and seen more of the world than the people watching it.

Every time Newman looked into the camera with those eyes, I thought of Cash and then pushed her back from my consciousness, forcing myself to become absorbed in the story. Many gunshots later, the classic sepia freeze-frame filled the big screen. Heroes dead but immortalized.

A few people exited the theater and dispersed to their trucks, but I strolled Main Street and peeked into the shop fronts as if I'd never seen them before, thinking about Butch and Sundance's relationship. Risk taken for its own reward.

Benegan's dry-goods store had beaded Minnetonka moose moccasins in the window and a big sweatshirt with KC Chiefs on it. In the corner, a vest caught my eye. Dark brown suede, sheep-lined. It would look great next to Cash's hair. Why was I constantly thinking of her? *Like a curse. She's a furrow in my brain that my mind continues to plow.* I turned to find Stretch Adams standing in front of me, all dressed up as if he'd been to a party.

"Little birdie told me you were alone at the movies. Now that should never happen." As he said it, I remembered Crystal Adams was his niece and she must have picked up the phone and told him I'd just gone into the theater right after she took my money and gave me my ticket.

"I enjoyed it, actually." I tried to move to one side but he pinned me into the glass alcove leading to the front door of the store. "What are you doing in town?"

He inclined his head giraffe-like and whispered, "Looking for *you.* Seems like I'm going to have to ambush you to get a date."

"Stretch, I'm really not interest—"

"Now one thing I've learned about ladies, not that I've had many ladies in my life…" He chuckled and used his laughing gestures as an excuse to fling the other hand up over my head, propping himself against the wall behind me and trapping me underneath his armpits. "I've learned that sometimes when a gal says no, she really just means slow, and I know about slooow…" His lips moved toward my face as he said it, and I felt revulsion, anger, the sense I was trapped and the entire thing was going to happen quickly and be unavoidable and I would hate him and myself. "Get the hell away from me, Stretch." I darted under his arm and ran to my truck.

"Hey, darlin', where are you going? This is waaay early in the relationship to be running away. That doesn't usually happen till later." He joked to save face, I was certain, but I was too mad to respond. *How dare he trap me!* I thought I heard him say "frigid bitch," but more than likely I said it to myself. *He's a guy wanting to date me, kiss me, have some contact with me, that's all.*

I got in the truck, slammed the door, and sped down the highway toward home, checking my rearview mirror to see if he was following me. But there were no truck lights behind me and no lights ahead.

Wanting to shake all over like a rain-covered dog, I remembered that feeling Stretch evoked. In my own bedroom where he'd bring me gifts—flowers, candy, a book—and tell me that my problem was I couldn't relax. He'd put his arms around me and hold me, trap me, and cajole me, and not give in to my excuses. His saliva was thick, his body smells strong, his weight demanding and probing, and I would cry and conceal my tears as he entered me.

I didn't recall the thirty-minute trip that took me into the front gates of the ranch, where I pulled into the drive and shut off the lights. The house was dark, although it was only a little after ten p.m.

Climbing up the front steps, I caught sight of her seated in the rocking chair, lounging in her white nightshirt in the moonlight, a book on the table beside her chair.

"Hey, you look great," she said when I stopped suddenly.

"Reading in the dark?"

"My diary. A habit. Thanks for leaving me the sandwich, it was good." I nodded in response and headed for the screen door, but she bounded from her chair. "Did you have a good time?" Her arm swept wide, momentarily blocking the doorway, just as Stretch had done, and her cologne hung in the night air like honeysuckle. Trapped there, my heart racing, I was excited and unnerved, but not repulsed as I'd been with Stretch. I took a second to let that sink in. *It should be the other way around, but it isn't.*

"I *did* have a good time, thanks. *Sundance Kid*. It was fate, I guess, that Steve McQueen demanded top billing and Jack Lemmon refused to ride a horse, because Redford and Newman were the perfect partners." I was babbling.

"Partners come together in strange ways sometimes." She removed her arm and I attempted to enter the house, brushing up against her. For a moment, I was immobile from the electrical sensation, a mild and pleasant stun-gun effect. She stood still, inches from me.

"I didn't like it here without you." Her voice was quiet.

"There's nothing to be frightened of out here." Maybe I was saying that to myself. Maybe I was the one who was frightened.

"I wasn't afraid. I just missed you." I couldn't escape from the pleading look in her eyes begging me to acknowledge what she wanted me to hear, but I wouldn't listen. The night was too complicated and I needed to deal with it right here, right now, on this porch.

"Cash, you're my friend's daughter. You work for me. And... I'm a straight woman."

"Maybe not all of that's true." Her face was very close to mine.

"Every bit of it's true." I looked her squarely in the eye. "And maybe your life would be better if you stopped trying to have a physical relationship with every woman you meet." She acts just like a man and that part of her I don't like, I thought, and found even that idea confusing.

"You were fighting with him the night he died, because he wanted to have sex with you and you didn't want it." She said it as fact, without emotion, and I knew only one person in the world knew what had happened the night Johnny died and that Donnetta had betrayed my confidence.

"He left the house in anger and died in a car crash, consumed by fire because the two of us could not create our own." I glared at her but she never dropped her gaze. "And my not wanting to sleep with him doesn't make me gay," I managed to whisper.

"How do you know?"

Upset over everything that had happened tonight, I couldn't hold back the anger. "Stop trying to analyze me. You have enough demons of your own without conjuring up mine." I turned and entered the house, leaving her on the porch alone.

Chapter Thirteen

A sticky heat dampened my cotton shirt, and the high winds quickly wicked it away, leaving my skin gritty and me as irritable on the outside as in. But I remained focused on the fields and hollows of the land, as if their contours were the most important in my life. Nothing neater than a newly mown hayfield. The square bales had been put up in the hay barns last week, before the round-baling began in earnest, and now the two-thousand-pound rolls lay on the ground every few hundred feet, like giant shredded wheat.

Within days neighbors arrived hauling flatbeds that lumbered in the front gates. Perry drove the loader with its spear attachment up to the round bales, stabbed them in their circular ends, and hoisted them into the air and onto the long trucks.

By midday, the fields were flat and barren like a well-trimmed lawn and the workers had taken the rest of the day for themselves, to rest up and admire what they'd accomplished. I hadn't seen "hide nor hair" of them even through lunchtime.

The late-afternoon wind was hot and the relentless sunshine beat down on me as I swept out the horse barn and hosed off the walls to get rid of the last of the barn-swallow droppings. Swallows used hay to build bird-condos in the eves and fought one another for their territory, often slinging innocent young out of the nests during their battles. Finding it difficult sometimes to tolerate the noise and mess, and struggles to the death, I still encouraged their presence because they kept the fly and mosquito population under control and therefore helped thwart the deadly equine West Nile virus.

The barn radio played old country tunes and I occasionally glanced up to check the front gates for activity or down to see how much filth I'd splashed on my T-shirt and slacks.

Bo's heavy, sweat-covered face appeared overhead, startling me, and I straightened from my chores to ask what he wanted, but he was already blurting out his needs.

"Cash had an accident."

"Was she driving?" My voice rose as I wiped my hands on my pants and envisioned a pileup on the highway.

"No, ma'am. She's out in the pasture." I could smell alcohol on his breath.

I jumped into the XUV and floorboarded the gas pedal, heading for a pasture we rarely used on the backside of the bunkhouse. As we approached, I could see Perry on his knees on the ground next to Cash. I jumped out of the vehicle before it stopped completely, shouting "What happened?" as I ran toward them, flung myself down beside her, and put my fingers to her jugular. "Is she breathing?"

"Yeah, but I was afraid to move her. Don't know if her back's busted or her neck or what," Perry said of the limp form and closed eyes that lay before us.

Relieved to feel a pulse in her neck, I put my face down next to hers and said loudly, "Cash, I want you to wake up. Do you hear me? I want you to wake up, right now. Open your eyes. Can you see me? Who am I?" She moaned. "Wiggle your fingers for me." A long delay and then she finally did as I ordered. "Now let's see you move your feet. Can you move them side to side?" She tried to raise up on one elbow and I caught her under the shoulder blade as she fell backward. "Feel like you broke anything? How much did you have to drink?" I asked her, and glared at the two men. Perry quickly said she'd drunk nothing.

"What was she doing?" I demanded, catching sight of a man I'd never laid eyes on herding an animal along the fence line.

"Got throwed off a bull," Perry said, and I could tell he'd been drinking as well.

"Get that animal out of here!" I shouted, and Bo hurried off to help the man wrangle the bull and get it back into the Wileys' pasture. I suspected by the way it sauntered off that the bull was less trouble when drunks left him alone. She was out cold again and I checked her pulse. "You could have killed her, Perry. Your job is to be the adult, not her damned drunken playmate! Get that folding cot out of the bunkhouse and let's use it like a stretcher." He scuttled off.

Alone with her now, I examined her still form and my heart pounded wildly. She was out too long and hard, and I was starting to think about things I didn't want to have happen. *What if she needs to be life-flighted to KC General? What if we move her and do some kind of damage to her neck or back or spine? And last night when I snapped at her and told her she had her own demons, did I summon one and cause this?*

Her eyes opened and she gaped at the heavens.

"Cash, can you try to get up?"

"My head," she whimpered. "Can't see very well."

"I quickly examined her eye for bleeding or debris, but it looked clean and I assumed she'd hit her head so hard she'd jarred her eyesight.

She closed her eyes again about the time Perry came back with the army cot, Bo hurrying along behind him. Keeping the legs folded under and flat like a stretcher, they rolled Cash slightly to allow us to wiggle it under her until we had her on it. She complained that it hurt as I jogged alongside her, the two men carrying her up the pathway to the house.

I burst into the house through the back door, two steps ahead of them, and scrounged through the freezer for ice packs as the two men huffed and puffed and set the cot up on the living-room floor.

"Seasick," she said weakly, and rolled off the stretcher, trying desperately to get to her knees. I ran to her just as she tried to stand, lost her balance, and fell forward.

"Get hold of her and sit her on the edge of the bed," I ordered. They obeyed, hoisting her up, one man holding her under each arm, and dragged her like a passed-out drunk to the bedroom.

"Less biscuits, girl," Perry said, and I could tell by his tone that he loved Cash and was worried about her. He settled her onto the bed, then reached down and swung her legs up. "Call Doc Flanders and tell him he needs to come out here right now, and tell him I know what time it is, and I don't give a damn," I said, and Perry hurried away, seeming to have sobered up with worry.

I busied myself taking Cash's pulse, checked her breathing, removed her shoes, and covered her with a quilt. Head injury, I thought, and decided not to call Buck until I had something to tell him versus something to worry him. So I just paced and waited and picked up ice packs and then put them back down, not knowing where to place them on her, and she wasn't alert enough to tell me.

A long hour later, Doc Flanders arrived, stood in the bedroom doorway, and shouted, "What did you do to her, Maggie?" Unzipping his medical case, he took out a stethoscope and pin flashlight and shined the light into her pupils. "Told me you flew off a bull, young lady. You have a strange way of entertaining yourself, stabbing yourself with rusty wires and now this."

"She was awake and talking and then just passed out," I said.

"Could be fear, tension, head injury, slight concussion, or she was just bored with you. I'd say get some coffee in her."

"Don't I need to walk her around or keep her awake?"

"You weren't doing that before I got here, don't know why you'd start now. Besides, she's bigger than you." He let go of her eyelid and it snapped shut like a camera lens. "Give her coffee." Doc Flanders seemed less skilled than Perry, but he showed up and reaffirmed what I suspected, and that affirmation was comforting. "If she vomits or convulses, let me know. And don't let her do that while she's lying on her back—gets down in the lung and it'll kill her. Watch her all night, would be the best thing. Can you sleep in here with her?" I nodded that I could. "I'll write my cell phone on your counter out there and if you need me, think twice before calling." As he shambled out the door he kept talking. "Only my wife is allowed to wake me up in the middle of the night, and that hasn't happened in a hell of a long time." He exited past Perry and shuffled out to the front porch.

I ordered Perry to pull a chair up to her bedside and watch her closely while I grabbed a quick shower. It was going to be a long night.

Closing my bedroom door, I yanked my barn clothes off, showered in minutes, threw on sweats and a fresh T-shirt, and headed back into Cash's bedroom. "Okay, I can take over now," I told him, but he was staring down into her face like he thought she was something special. He didn't move for a moment and I thought I saw him tearing up. I put my hand on his shoulder. "She'll be fine, don't worry."

"Fried chicken or a hamburger?" he asked, still fixated on her face as if he was reading a menu there, but he was obviously trying to get his emotions under control. "I'm gonna bring you some dinner."

"Not hungry."

Dejected, he turned to go. "We egged her on." His shoulders sagged like the old man he'd become before Cash got here, and I missed the cowboy swagger she'd given him.

"It'll give her something to tell her grandkids."

"Don't think they'll be grandkids," he said knowingly, and I realized he must suspect that she would never marry.

I waited for him to leave and then locked the front door and made coffee. Ten minutes later, I took a cup mixed with milk and sugar, and knelt by her bedside.

"Cash, wake up." I slipped my hand under her head and cradled her neck. "Come on, honey, wake up."

Her eyes opened and a slight smile played across her lips. She murmured something that sounded like "honey," and I felt myself redden slightly. "Doc said I should get some coffee down you."

"He's a crazy person, not a doctor," she said as I tilted the coffee cup to her lips and she sipped. "No more, please. You don't give people coffee for head injuries."

"Seems to be working. You're talking sense now. Dr. Flanders said I need to sleep in here with you tonight, in case."

"Brilliant physician," she whispered, and I smiled at her attempts at humor. I told her I was going in search of a more comfortable chair to pull into the room, but she stopped me. "Just sleep on the bed. It would take me two days and a forklift to make a move on you. And you can turn on the TV, it won't bother me."

I was ecstatic she was talking and crawled onto the bed beside her, building the pillows up behind me, but when I turned to her she was out again. I let her rest, content to gaze on her strong, beautiful features, all the while hoping nothing permanent surfaced as a result of this fall. After about fifteen minutes, it appeared she might sleep for hours so I jostled her slightly.

She moaned and put her hand up to her left eye. I instinctively covered her right eye. "Can you see anything?"

"Not with my eyes covered," she joked softly, and I took my hand away. "Blurry."

"We'll check you in the morning. You should be okay. Buck did this one time in a bull-riding event."

"If he finds out a pasture bull threw me, I'll never hear the end of it."

"You can't sleep in this outfit. Let's start by pulling your shirt up over your head, can you do that?" Even with help, it was obvious she couldn't. "Change of plans." I scrambled out of bed and stood at the foot, scrutinizing her. "Pants first." I came around to the side and unbuttoned her jeans at the top, then unzipped them, my hand brushing the satin-soft skin of her tummy. The sensation was riveting, an incredibly intimate moment as I slid the zipper down, my hand above the soft white cotton briefs. But I was too worried about her condition to linger on the sensation. Going quickly to the foot of the bed, I grabbed her pant legs and tugged. She yelped.

"It's painfully evident that it's been awhile since you've undressed someone. Pull them down from my waist," she said, her eyes closed and a pained grimace on her face.

I grasped her jeans at the waist, my fingers over the top edge, and she tried to lift her hips, but the pain wouldn't allow it. Bracing her back, I slid my hand down the inside of her jeans and managed to pull them down a few inches, then rolled her to one side to wriggle them off her hips. She wailed that I was killing her.

"Should have thought of that before you put your ass on a

bull," I said, to keep things light, as I finally managed to wrangle her Wranglers down to her knees and sighed with relief when the job was done.

"Not easy being gay," she quipped. "That's why men like women in dresses." As she spoke, my eyes momentarily lingered on her striking body, slender and smooth and tan, before I pulled the sheets out from under her with less effort and covered her up. "Okay, now the shirt."

"How about if I sleep in it but just get the bra off?" She tried to rise and couldn't so I slid my hands under her tee and wrestled with the bra hooks as she lay flat on her back. Losing my balance, I fell forward. For a second I lay there on top of her and she made no smart remarks—my hands trapped under her body, clasping her smooth back. My face to her chest, I could feel her rapid heartbeat.

"Did I hurt you?"

"No. Here, let me do it." She struggled to get her arm through the T-shirt so the bra strap could be next, and when I tried to help, I touched the edge of her breast. I pretended it didn't happen but the blood rushed to my face.

"I don't think we want to put your arms back through this shirt now that we've gotten this far. How about if I get it off over your head and you sleep—"

"You own anything that fastens with Velcro?" she asked, and I immediately bristled at the idea that clothes for the arthritic would be anywhere in my closet.

"It's a joke." She moaned at my sensitivity. "You're in better shape than I am." Something about the way she said it made me feel younger. "I have to go to the bathroom. All that coffee. Get hold of my arms and pull and ignore the screaming. After that, you leave, I can do the rest."

"Are you sure?"

"Who would know better than me that I have to go to the bathroom?"

"You know, if your body could move as fast as your mouth, you'd be well in three seconds." I pulled with all my might, hoisting her to her feet as she screamed, then left the room to give her privacy and collect myself. "Don't fall," I said over my shoulder, and wondered which of us I was warning.

In my room, standing inside my closet, I sagged against the door to collect myself. After a few minutes, I quit trying to analyze the tidal wave of emotions and concentrated on finding a shirt that would fit her, a seemingly impossible task given our size difference. Rummaging around in the bottom drawers of an old dresser, I located a very large T-shirt I'd won at a drawing at an Indian Casino years ago. I cut the neck open, starting at the neckline and heading six inches down to the chest. Then I took the scissors to the short sleeves, cutting them open underneath so they were nothing more than top-flaps. Ten minutes later, I re-entered Cash's room to find her standing and clutching a small bath towel to her.

"I have constructed a plan." I held the shirt up and, with one move, flopped it over her head, and with minimal arm moves she was in.

"Big Bucks." She read the shirt front upside down.

"Appropriate, when you think about it." I helped her get her legs back on the bed.

Crawling in beside her again, I flipped on the TV. She closed her eyes and before long she was asleep. Glancing at her pretty face, creased in pain, I tried to pretend I was merely a paid nurse, then thought about all the stories of nurses falling in love with their patients so I tried to concentrate on the bad cop drama I'd tuned to, then watched the late nightly news. Tired, I finally clicked off the TV and rolled over to go to sleep. I was warm and restless and decided to sleep on top of the covers. Soon I went from hot to cold, nearly chilled and shaking as if I was nervous.

I inched my way under the covers and slid down next to her, keeping an appropriate distance as she slept. Six inches away, that's how far she was. I could smell her cologne when I moved the sheets. Her face looked pained but perfect. I lay back and focused on the ceiling. She sighed and flung her arm out to her side where it rested against me. I didn't move, nor did I move her arm, and I willed myself to sleep.

CHAPTER FOURTEEN

It felt as if I'd only been asleep a short time when the bed sheet quivered, and I turned to check on her.

She was perspiring and shaking. I jostled her arm to awaken her and ask if she was okay, putting my hand to her forehead, which was hot.

"Cold," she said between clenched teeth.

"You've got chills. You're probably in shock from the fall. Best thing is to take the covers off and let the fever burn out of you. I know you feel cold but you're hot."

"No, I'm freezing." She clutched the covers, refusing to let me pull them off her and demanded more warmth. I got up and located a quilt on the top shelf of the closet and put it over her.

"Hurting any worse? Do you want me to call the doctor?"

"God, no." She continued to quiver despite the quilt, then moaned.

"Eye or head?" I said, trying to isolate the pain.

"I don't know," she whimpered. I hesitated for a moment then rolled over, facing her, and put my arms around her, pulling myself in close to her since she was in too much pain to move. She rested her head on my chest and sighed, seeming to relax. Instead of pulling back, I moved in even closer and buried my face in her hair, suspending all internal conversation about what I was doing or thinking or becoming. Of the five senses, only touch seemed to be functioning, sending rays of warmth throughout my body. She was perspiring and the scent of her was mingled with my own perfume and the bed clothes smelled like wildflowers and she stopped shaking and we both fell asleep.

I awoke feeling cramped and realized I still clung to Cash, who appeared to be unconscious. I pulled away gently and slowly, but her long arms wouldn't release me. Finally, I understood she was only feigning sleep.

"If I let you go, I may never get this back," she said softly, her eyes shut.

"I can see that you're feeling much stronger. You're going to be fine."

"I can never be fine again, because I've held you." Her dreamy eyes opened and the pale blue sea reached out and floated me into her. Her large hands moved under the back of my shirt and the heat from them radiated up my spine as she massaged me. Her warm touch felt so good my body gave in and I relaxed and closed my eyes. Her thumbs ventured down to the base of my spine and she kneaded my lower back, which released all tension in my legs and sent pangs of longing through my groin. And then her palms gripped my buttocks and she squeezed me into her and my groan of pleasure was involuntary and unmistakable. I wanted her and she knew it. I had come alive, ready in that instant to be changed forever. My mind seized control of my helpless body, frightened by how quickly the world might turn upside down, and directed my actions. Now, like the wind, I shifted direction and whirled out of her grasp and sat up on the edge of the bed.

Without looking at her, I jumped up and left the room, but it was too late. Change had caught up with me, affecting not only my body, but trying to break free and make its way to my heart.

Five minutes later, Cash came out to the kitchen and I had no idea how she'd managed to get out of bed in her condition, other than being propelled by passion and youth. She came up behind me as I stood at the sink and slipped her arms around me. I pushed the good sensation out of my mind and steadied my voice.

"Cash, I'm not going to do this." Her hands slipped away, indicating she knew exactly what I meant. I refused to be a summer fling, another of her conquests, a homosexual convert for one seductive summer.

"I didn't ask you to do anything," she said. "You held me and I want to believe that you wanted to."

Of course I'd wanted to. Just crossing the room if she was in it made my body vibrate as if I'd gotten too close to an electrical current. And now holding her had escalated even those feelings.

"You should be fine on your own now," I said, refusing to discuss what had happened, and I went to my room, the only place on the entire ranch where I could count on locking her out.

I hadn't been there five minutes, my mind thrashing around as I tried to determine how I could interact with her now that this sexual tension had bound us more tightly than baling wire, when Cash shouted my name and announced that we had company as a horn honked incessantly in the driveway.

As if I needed more physical proof of my current dilemma, a shiny maroon restored '57 Chevy pulled into the driveway, kicking up dust, and a short, stocky fellow leapt out and whooped, "Where's the owner of the finest ranch in Kansas?" I peered out the front door and saw that Buck Tate had arrived literally minutes after his daughter had clutched me to her and made me want her. Buck, no doubt, thought we were just "the girls of summer," but his timing was split-second. After having suffered the physical and emotional pain of wild bulls and wilder women, he'd ironically chosen to check on his protégé at the exact moment she was suffering from the same.

After bear hugs all around, he tromped up the steps, slung his cowboy hat onto the porch rocker, and shouted to Cash, "Sugar, you look great!"

Cash grimaced from Buck's robust squeeze, never mentioning that it was excruciating for her. I didn't offer up her secret as Buck continued his steady stream of conversation, telling me I looked fabulous too. After that, I would have paid money to have him leave, but Buck propped his feet up on the porch rail, asked for a glass of sweet tea, and settled in like an invited guest.

"So what do you think of my girl?" he asked me in a rowdy, loving way, with Cash standing nearby.

"I think she's remarkably...resilient," I managed to say, and eyed Cash, letting her know I knew she was in pain. I was in some sort of agony myself, about to leap out of my own skin and had no idea what I was saying.

"Resilient? Well, now, I'd say that's a good five-dollar word." Buck laughed easily and whacked her playfully on the shoulder and she almost doubled over.

"Did she tell you I sent her to college to study animal husbandry and she quit after two years. Said it was boring."

"Are you here for a refund?" Cash asked slyly, and Buck put his hands up as if surrendering his position on an old argument.

I executed a verbal separation, demanding Buck tell me everything about his life with Mary and what he was doing visiting Kansas and where in Texas he was headed on his business trip. I followed that with questions about what all his boys were doing, where he and Mary wanted to go on vacation, and how his health had been. I kept him talking about himself until the moon came up over the pasture and Cash was slumped back in a rocker half dozing.

"I don't know about you but I'm tea-d out," he finally said, and staggered up from the rocker and headed for his truck, years of bull riding having made him stiff.

"You're hoping he's leaving," Cash said, "but he's headed for the 'car bar.'"

"Buck never got the hang of good-bye...unless he married you." I sighed.

Moments later, he limped back holding a bottle of Jack Daniels by its golden neck and plopped down in the rocker again and poured the liquor over the remaining ice in his tea glass.

"Now we can get down to some serious talking." He grinned at me and I could see where Cash got her big ready smile and her silliness. "You never remarried."

I marveled at the way Buck could never work up to anything

but instead blurted it out. "I let you marry and remarry for both of us," I replied.

"I think I've had more wives than Henry VIII. Didn't kill any of them, though." He paused for a moment. "Wanted to, mind you, but refrained." He let that statement float out into the darkness before speaking suddenly. "Did you know, Cash, that I set Maggie up with Johnny Blake?" The look on Cash's face clearly illustrated that she didn't know, and she sat up in her chair as if paying attention for the first time. "Yep, the three of us were a strange trio. Anyway, Johnny had the serious 'gotta-have-its' for her and she wouldn't give him the time of day, so Johnny asked me to put in a few words for him."

"Must have been some pretty good words," Cash said quietly, eyeing me.

"Enough to convince her to give it a whirl." He filled his glass again while chuckling over something he apparently remembered but didn't want to share.

"What didn't you like about him?" Cash asked me.

"I didn't think he was much fun," I said, and was aware my eyes softened when I looked at her.

"So you're actually *attracted* to the fun-loving type?" Cash said, obviously referencing her antics, for which I constantly admonished her. I cut my eyes at her, amused she was carrying on a covert conversation with me behind Buck's back.

"I got Maggie to agree she didn't know what love was so she had to admit Johnny could be it." Buck addressed Cash.

I laughed softly at the idea that in those days I was naïve enough to buy a rationale like that. Or maybe back then, I was just looking for an excuse to do what I thought I had to do for love and protection.

"She's not that easy nowadays." Cash's eyes danced playfully over my body.

"Now how the hell do you know? She cause you any trouble?" Buck eyed me next.

"She's been too busy learning about livestock," I said, and Cash smirked at my bull reference.

Buck ignored us, as if his mind was on something else again. Then suddenly he said, "Always wished I hadn't done that. Looking back on it now, just wished I'd stayed out of matchmaking." And it was as if the entire visit had come about because Buck Tate needed to divest himself of that admission, the heavy heart lightened by being able to say those words. "You never did learn to love the guy, did you?"

"Everything happens for a reason," I said, avoiding an answer.

"Yeah, it does, and here I am back with you." He reached over and squeezed my arm. "Damn, you feel good!" Cash cleared her throat and Buck looked over in her direction. "I told Mary I'm committed to righting a wrong and I'm going to find you the right mate."

Cash threw her head back and groaned loudly. "You just said you were sorry you tried to be a matchmaker the first time."

"Yeah, but this time I know someone who's perfect, and, in fact, on my way back from Texas I might stop by and introduce the two of you."

"Buck." Cash's tone was comic but warning.

"Enough said. I'm headed to bed," he said, and I realized I'd have to find a place to put him up.

"You two okay double bunking?" he asked Cash, and I quickly said I thrashed around too much to share a bed with Cash and maybe we could fix him up on the couch. He glanced at the long but somewhat narrow sofa and said, "You got any room in the bunkhouse?" I told him we had a worker out there with Perry so we were full up. "Man, I'm feeling like baby Jesus—'no room at the inn.'"

"Take my bed, I'm fine on the couch," Cash offered, giving me a long look that seemed to plead for a softer sleeping arrangement. Buck laughed and thanked her and displaced her without a qualm. She went into her bedroom, grabbed a pillow and her quilt, and made a place for herself on the sofa, which would probably compound her stiffness.

Telling them both good night, I went to my bedroom and closed the door. The lights in the living room stayed on a long time. After several hours, I cracked the door and peeked out to see if Cash had fallen asleep without turning them off. She was sitting up on the edge of the couch in deep conversation with Buck, who sat in the rocker across from her. They looked like two friends chatting away. In fact, Buck didn't look like anyone's father but more like a big cowboy playboy. What a strange situation, I thought. But maybe Buck's arrival had provided a buffer, taken the heat off and let us both relax. Maybe it would put everything back in place. Remind us all where we fit.

❖

I got up the next morning and cooked a huge breakfast. Buck and Cash were lively and energetic and joking with each other.

"Getting pretty muscled up there for a girl." He bumped into her on purpose, jamming his shoulder into hers, and I was sure she was still sore but refused to show it.

"Sad thing is I'm more muscled up than you, cowboy." She bumped him back.

"Oh, yeah? I can still lift you off the ground with one hand." He grabbed her arm.

"Take it outside," I said, meaning the sparring that was endangering everything in the living room that wasn't bolted down. Both of them tumbled out onto the porch punching and tormenting one another like two teenage boys.

Cash said something I couldn't hear and Buck laughed and gave her a quick fighter's punch in the arm. She ducked and dodged him as he continued to pester her, giggling and talking the entire time. It was clear he'd raised her like a boy and saw himself as her buddy rather than her parent.

I shouted breakfast was ready but they were twenty yards away from the house and couldn't hear me in the high wind. I went to the edge of the porch, balanced over the rail, and grabbed the handle of the rusty old dinner bell that dangled from its tall post. They turned their heads on hearing the clang.

Imitating Michael Buffer's famous prize-fight introduction, I shouted, "Ladies and gentlemen, let's get ready for breakfaaast!"

Cash giggled and jogged in my direction. "I am sooo ready to rumble," she said slyly, and looped her hand over my belt, hooking me and pulling me down off the porch in an unexpected and jolting gesture. I ordered her to let me go, which seemed only to encourage her. "Have you gone soft?" she chided, and I gave her a look that said she was pressing her luck.

"Careful, there, Cash," Buck warned as his cell phone rang and he walked back to the car and crawled inside, out of the wind, to answer it.

"I'm sorry, Buck's right, I don't want to hurt you," she taunted, no doubt referencing my size or age or some damned thing, and her tone set me off. I lunged at her, pushing her backward, and her eyes revealed her shock. Caught off guard and perhaps not expecting such an all-out aggressive response, or my physical strength, she tripped and staggered just before I shoved her over hard, not worrying about her injuries, and dove on top of her. She let out a low moan along with most of the air in her body.

"You need to learn some manners since you obviously don't know how to fight," I said, straddling her and pinning her to the ground. She tried to roll me over in the grass, but I had better balance after years of horseback riding and laughed as she struggled to get up.

"I'm a lover, not a fighter." She surrendered verbally and tensed her abdomen intentionally, I was certain, to let me feel the pressure her muscles created between my thighs. I felt light-headed. For a moment, her hands stopped wrestling me and slid down to my waist, holding me in place on top of her. I tilted my head back, soul-searching the clouds, and closed my eyes, in a near-dream state.

Buck honked the car horn as he hung up the phone, waving to us in mock-referee style, as if trying to separate us, and I snapped back to reality.

"Better stick to loving, then, because your ass is pretty easy to whip." I forced myself to act before I was incapable of it, punching her playfully in the stomach for good measure as I jumped off.

Buck came back huffing and puffing and shouted that his client had called and he had to leave early for Texas. Cash happily bounded to her feet, yanking me to mine, and I felt energized and even wild as the wind whipped my hair around my face. Somehow just releasing the physical energy I felt when I was around her relaxed me.

"She's stronger than she looks," Buck warned Cash. "Used to beat me up all the time." I was only slightly embarrassed that I'd been drawn into a wrestling match with Cash, but Buck seemed to think it was perfectly normal and continued his joking. "Cash tells me she's been an enormous help to you from day one and actually taught you a couple of things about ranching." I cocked an eyebrow, and they both laughed.

"Cash has been an interesting challenge," I said.

"Now that's exactly what she said about you!" Buck laughed loudly. "I'd say you two are quite a pair." Cash caught my eye and her look was sensual and serious, and for a second I thought of our wrestling match, my straddling her body and how that had felt, and I grew weak. Turning away from her, I erased those thoughts in favor of breakfast conversation over the clank of silverware and the sounds of eating.

Right after breakfast Buck kissed me on the cheek and said his good-byes, hitting the road for Texas. He climbed into his vehicle and I told him to drive safe and sent greetings to Mary. Cash came up behind me and I felt myself breathe again as his car pulled away. "I feel like the in-laws just left. Thanks for not outing me."

"You said he knows you're gay."

"The bull-riding accident. He'd never let me live it down, being the self-proclaimed eight-second wonder of Texas Tech, although that could have been a bedroom stat." I couldn't contain a laugh. As much as I tried to remain stern, her sense of humor always won me over. We could have been wonderful friends if she'd lived out here and had a family. The strange feelings between us simply got in the way.

"I was going to ask you to go down to the barn and strip the stalls. However, since you've turned into a PBR reject, how about straightening up the tack room? This is a working ranch, not a bed and breakfast."

"Might as well strip the stalls. That's the only 'stripping' going on around here," she muttered, and I didn't let her see me smiling.

"Here," I said, tossing her the key to the XUV. "No need to bounce around in the Gator. I know, despite the bravado, you're still in pain. And take some Advil." I doled out two tablets from a bottle on the counter, handing her a bottle of water, and she grinned. "What?" I asked innocently.

"Nothing," she said, and refused to stop smiling.

❖

All week long, we suffered the intense mid-July heat and the oppressive humidity that went with it. The wind had died down— not just diminished, but stopped entirely. It happened occasionally on the prairie when, exhausted, the breeze apparently decided no longer to pursue the grasslands. The silence was eerie. The heat, propelled by nothing, refused to move along, hovering in the air, leaving everything moist and sticky. Animals were hangdog and irritable and people not much better. It was that moment when we realized we had taken the wind for granted and now she was gone.

I sidestepped Cash. She must have felt I was ignoring her because Thursday night she trapped me alone on the porch at dusk and insisted I face her and talk to her.

"You have feelings for me, Maggie. Why can't we acknowledge that and do something about it?"

"I don't want to talk about this again, Cash."

"Who in the world is going to care?"

I was braced against the doorframe, and she had her hand on the wall again just above my shoulder, shielding me from view and forcing me to stay put. "I'm not your summer playmate."

"Don't demean it, Maggie." She inclined her head and her lips were infinitesimally close to mine, her sweet breath nearly entering me, ready to resuscitate my heart after years of not knowing it could beat for someone else.

The voice came from over her shoulder. "Maggie, you okay?" Perry lumbered toward us and Cash stood up casually.

"I think we got it out. Better go look in the mirror," she said to me before turning to Perry. "Something blew into her eye."

"Hasn't really been that windy today." His tone was skeptical. "How's *your* eye doing?" he asked Cash.

"Better, good, actually," she said.

"Well, just checking on you gals to see if you need something. I'm headed into the city tonight."

"If I haven't got what I need, I've got all I'm gonna get," Cash replied good-naturedly, sounding more Kansas-colloquial than Perry, who grinned at her. He hesitated, as if sensing something unusual, but then said his good-byes and wandered off.

I escaped into the house, running mostly from myself as Cash followed, begging me to come back and talk to her.

"Cash, I want you to quit it." I spoke quietly, but firmly. "I don't want this. I don't." I stared at her, making every attempt to harden my expression. She looked deep into my soul, as if trying to decide if I meant it. Finally, her shoulders sagged, telling me she believed I did, and without further word she walked away and left me alone.

Now I needed to have that same talk with myself to be convinced that I didn't want this...her...and all that she brought with her. A person couldn't just change so dramatically after all these years. I'd been married. I dated men. What would being with another woman out here get me, or anyone, other than stares and jeers and nothing good. *And that's a ridiculous idea to begin with because Cash isn't staying here. She's going home and, frankly, the sooner the better.*

Chapter Fifteen

Friday she stayed away from me and I knew I'd hurt her feelings, but that was good. One short correction with the reins rather than a constant tug of war. I caught sight of her working with the horses down in the pasture. She had Knight, the bay horse, hooked up on a lunge line and was using a crop to encourage him to circle. She looked graceful and yet rugged, as if she belonged in this rural scenery, *although clearly she doesn't.*

After a few minutes of round-pen work, he must have looked compliant because she saddled him up and rode across the pasture. This was the first time I'd seen her on a horse, and she looked relaxed and natural. I went into the house and picked up the binoculars and followed her figure across the prairie, the wind blowing through her hair and her long legs wrapped around the gelding.

My mind traveled to that night on the riverbank when she'd told me that once she wrapped her legs around anything it never got away, and for a moment I felt as if I were physically floating along with her again, beside her, one with her. I put the binoculars down and turned away from the window before deciding that I would take Mariah out for a ride. The day was too pretty to waste.

I jogged down the dirt path as if this was a priority in my life and waved to Mariah, who brought her elegant white body to the edge of the pasture and gracefully bent her head when I offered the bridle. I swiftly brushed her back, tossed a blanket on her and then a lightweight saddle. Checking the girth to make sure it was tight, I pulled myself up, then bent over and opened the gate. Seconds later the metal latch clanged shut behind us. Up ahead, I saw Cash riding Knight at a walk and I hurried to catch up. She spotted me and we met halfway.

"You and Knight look good together," I said. She fit the horse and he seemed to like working with her.

"I picked Knight at first because he was easy to catch, but now I think he picked me." She patted the big bay's neck, and I thought it was wonderful that a creature had finally picked Cash as its own. I smiled at Knight for his kindness.

Mariah stomped, swished her tail, swung her butt sideways, and Knight nickered and jerked unnecessarily. "Mariah, stop that!"

"What's she doing?"

"Getting him in trouble, probably telling him he should ignore you and do what she wants. She's in heat, which makes her a little moody."

"I completely relate to that," she said flatly.

I ignored the remark. "Walk him along beside me and let's do a little training. I never have anyone to ride with, so he can't get used to listening to the rider instead of the mare."

Cash circled him around and pulled up alongside me on the left. Mariah immediately began nosing him and he stomped. "Tell him to stop that," I ordered, and she echoed my words sternly. Knight looked ahead and we walked on. I relaxed into the saddle and let the sunshine wash over my face.

"About last night, I didn't mean to be so harsh."

"Look, it's my fault. I thought you were giving me signals that you...care about me."

"I do care about you."

"You know what I mean. Anyway, I have a rule and I violated it and that's the problem. So as Buck says, 'only place you can take me is back to apologize.' I apologize, Maggie."

I nodded my acceptance. "What's the rule?"

She grinned. "You have to know everything, don't you? Okay, the rule is, don't get involved with straight women." We slowed the horses even more and they snorted, dropping their heads, and moved along slug-like, seeming happy to have a break. I raised a questioning eyebrow in her direction. "A straight woman's head gets in the way, and guilt follows. She might even go back to men after using you to satisfy her sexual curiosity."

"Have you had affairs with a lot of straight women?"

"Enough to formulate a rule," she said, and we both laughed.

"Aren't there enough gay women out there?"

"It's not an inventory problem." She dropped the subject, urging Knight to move out faster. I asked Mariah to keep up and she kicked it into gear, obviously not wanting Knight to maintain the lead.

"Have you ever had a relationship with a man?" I persisted, knowing I was prying but feeling this was my one opportunity to satisfy my own sexual curiosity.

"Most women's idea of a relationship with a man is that he makes a living, carries heavy objects, handles anything dirty or dangerous, and gets her pregnant before her clock runs out. If women would support themselves, hoist their own bags, learn to set rat traps, and find a sperm bank we wouldn't turn guys into a bunch of wussies in office buildings popping Viagra."

"I guess that means you don't want one," I said.

"I'm just wired differently. I wouldn't even want a guy like Buck. I just…anyway, who cares what I want, that's not what I was saying. I was saying I'm sorry."

"I care," I said. "I'm interested in what you think. You have a sharp mind and you see things differently. That's a gift."

"I don't share it much."

"I'd like you to share it with me whenever you feel like it. I like talking to you, Cash." She looked genuinely pleased and surprised. "There are other ways to communicate, you know, besides having sex." I cocked my head, giving her a playful smile, and she blushed.

We rode along in the sunshine and I felt radiantly happy for no reason. Finally Cash picked up the thread of conversation. "I agree there are other ways to communicate, but I take pride in being bilingual." She turned Knight back toward the barn and I followed her, not having realized how much I liked who she was, or perhaps who she had become.

Around five Cash came up to the house and greeted me with a warm smile, then disappeared into her room where the sound of the shower indicated she was getting cleaned up. Moments later she came into the living room in tight black jeans, a black-and-white Western shirt with red roses at the shoulder, a red bandana at the neck, and black boots. She looked darling. Actually she looked very sexy. For a moment I believed she was dressing for me.

"Don't you look nice," I said.

"I try." She stood awkwardly shifting her weight. "I'm going into town this evening for awhile."

"Really." The low feeling hit the bottom of my stomach. "Well, good. Looks like you're going to a party."

"I have a date."

"I didn't know you'd met anyone."

"You know her. Verta Olan. The sister of the guy who runs the gas station."

"Verta? Why?"

"A night out, that's all."

"She's not someone you should—"

"I won't do anything in public that will embarrass you."

"Where are you going?"

"She says there's a bar about ninety minutes' drive. Beer, pool, a mixed crowd."

"Cash, you have to be careful on the highway at night. And you don't know if she drinks and drives."

Cash's big smile broke open and I smiled in return, despite myself, ducking my head. "You think I'm acting like your mother."

"Believe me when I tell you that I never see you as my mother or anyone else's mother. I see you...I'll see you later tonight."

"Okay. Have fun."

She walked briskly out to her Jeep and drove down the driveway. My heart had rarely been so heavy.

Had Cash known Verta before? How had they had time to

contact each other? It's not that hard, I explained to my tortured self. Perry walked up the other night when we were on the porch. He probably told Bo who told his cousin Sven who told his sister Verta, and she sent word back by Perry, Bo, or some other fool that she was available. You don't need high-tech equipment out here. For instant messaging just *eat* the Blackberries and tell a neighbor.

Furious, I decided to busy myself making food for the weekend and pulled things out of the freezer without any sense of what I was trying to create. I finally threw most of it in the trash, deciding from the expiration dates it needed tossing, and I was in the mood to discard something. I opened a package of fresh ground beef from the fridge and began to make meatloaf with a vengeance. Midway through I realized I didn't know what I'd put in it or left out. Had I already seasoned it or was everything on the counter ready for seasoning? I slapped the meatloaf into a baking dish and shoved it into the oven. After washing my hands I put the timer on and made myself a cup of coffee.

Sitting at the kitchen table, I absorbed the loneliness, not having felt this way in years. Perhaps I was particularly sensitive to the hollowness now that Cash had occupied my life for awhile. Suddenly I spotted her diary on the edge of the kitchen table. She must have been writing in it and forgotten to put it back in her room. I picked it up to take it back to her bedroom, thinking I would leave it on her bedside table, and then without warning I was struck with the need to open the pages. I put the book back down and gave myself a lecture on respecting privacy, but the thought of Cash out partying with Verta Olan temporarily erased my moral code and I opened the book to the very first page.

May 28th, Feels like I've been here two weeks. Out of shape. Perry and I sprayed the field and I got covered in some chemical, probably means I'll grow a third arm. I like him. My bed sucks. Slumps in the middle. Maggie's kind of tense, don't think she's used to people in her house. Good-looking, though.
Signed Cash Tate

I couldn't suppress a smile over her compliment and the fact that she signed her diary pages, as if she thought one might be torn out and stolen and she needed to ensure she got credit for every entry.

I closed the book and sat thinking about the day she arrived, looking so attractive, standing in the doorway wondering what she was to do next. I'd thought she was a big kid with that huge smile she spread over everyone. She'd become serious lately and I missed the more-carefree Cash. Maybe I was too hard on her. Maybe I was too hard on everyone, including myself. I glanced at the diary and then opened it again and began to read.

> May 30th, Left the gate open accidentally. Oh, my God, you would have thought I'd murdered someone. The cows all broke out. I can relate! Perry had to hold an impromptu roundup. Maggie's hair was on fire. She was trying to be nice but I think she wanted to kick my ass.
> Signed Cash Tate

I smiled at her characterization of me, then checked the clock and the meatloaf and settled in at the table, no longer skimming through but reading the diary entirely. She was a smart, insightful, funny woman. Despite how awful I knew I was behaving by reading the pages, I was getting a look inside her that no one else had and that I otherwise might never see. And to keep my mind off what she might be doing with Verta Olan at this very minute, I was happy to trade an hour of morality for weeks of voyeurism.

> June 24th, Hurt my hands again and she doctored them, which was worth getting hurt for. She says animals hurt themselves when they're nervous and bored and want something they can't get to. No shit! That would definitely be me.
> Signed Cash Tate

June 30th, Verta sent word by Bo inviting me to come in to town for an evening. I think Bo saw me on the porch with Maggie and suspects something. Think Verta's got the hots for me. A little rougher than I like them.
    Signed Cash Tate

What a male-chauvinist view, I thought. "Then why did you go out with her?" I said out loud, the sound of my voice startling me and Duke, who jerked his head up from his doggie bed, his big herd-dog eyes penetrating mine, no doubt wondering if he was supposed to answer.

July 9th, she held me all night. Oh, my God, it was the most phenomenal feeling ever. Just being in her arms. I never wanted to leave. I haven't felt like that in my entire life. If I hadn't been so busted she would have been in serious trouble. As it was, she took my pants off and I passed out. When we woke up I got my hands on her terrific ass. If I could just have stayed like that forever. She wants me, I know it, but she says she doesn't.
    Signed Cash Tate

It was toward the end that my eyes lingered.

July 17th, Our lips came so close, I could almost feel hers throbbing. I wanted to kiss her so bad my knees about caved in. All I can think about is making love to her. I would have gotten her in bed but Perry showed up! I know she wants me too but she just won't give in. She won't give in to anything or anybody. Then suddenly she whirls on me and says she's straight and she wants to stay straight

and I'd better leave her alone. Break the rule and get a broken heart. When will I get that through my head?
Signed Cash Tate

July 18th, We are fucking platonicsville. I'm going out tonight to get my mind on something else. I can't stop thinking about her and how her skin feels when I touch her and how good she smells and how she would taste and how phenomenal it would be.
Signed Cash Tate

I pushed my chair back and looked up at the ceiling, jealousy clouding my brain. *Why in hell did this woman ever show up out here? Where is she right now and what's she doing? As a more practical matter, why in hell did I read her private thoughts? Inexcusable. Unlike me.* As I closed the book, I caught a penciled-in line at the bottom of the last page.

I wanted you to read this.
Cash

She left the diary on the table knowing I would read it. My jaw tightened at the audacity. *She thinks she can control my emotions, manipulate my life.* I didn't want her to know I'd read it and was mad that she played me like that. I slapped the book shut and pushed it back to the end of the table, positioning it at just the angle I thought it was in when I picked it up.

Jumping up, I paced. She's still maneuvering me as if I'm another of her conquests. *She isn't going to affect my behavior going forward.* The oven timer shrieked, startling me and reminding me that something was done. *I'm the one who's done. The mere fact that I'm spending my evening sitting here thinking about her tells it all, doesn't it?*

I shut the oven off, sat down, and quieted myself. Her going out tonight was made bearable by the words she'd written in her diary and left there for me. She wanted to be with me, but because that wasn't possible, she was doing as I asked. *Why am I so unhappy that she's doing what I asked?*

CHAPTER SIXTEEN

L ong after two a.m., I heard a truck pull into the driveway and a key in the lock. I lay still in bed wondering if she was drunk or simply satisfied. Had she kissed that woman, taken her shirt off as they parked in her truck, or slept with her in some sleazy hotel? *She probably did sleep with her because Verta would undoubtedly let her. After all, Cash is attractive and not from around here...a notch in everybody's Bible belt.*

Moments later her bedroom door opened and then shut. I didn't hear the shower but merely a short delay before the bedsprings bounced. Did she not shower because she wanted to smell like her? Was she lying in bed thinking of her, wishing she hadn't returned to the ranch but could have stayed over? Hell, it's going on three a.m. Why bother to come back? She should have stayed.

Irritated, I rolled over and punched my down pillow into a tight little knot that I jammed under my head and then yanked out from under me, thinking it felt like a bowling ball. *I should make her leave. If she's just going to use this ranch as her base of operations for sexual forays into the gay...excuse me, lesbian...world, that does neither of us any good. No wonder Buck wanted to send her out here to bake the hellfire out of her. Well, it's not working. About the time she's become useful, she's bored. Bored enough to damn-near kill herself on a bull and then make a pass at me and now she's in town carousing with...well, her.*

The image of a half-naked Verta popped into my brain and I scrunched my eyes shut like a lens. *And now that I'm thinking about lenses, what was I doing buying her a camera. I must have been drugged. She probably took it with her to the hotel room and used it to take fast shots of Verta writhing around on the bed.*

Exhausted and fretful, I let out a large sigh and relaxed against the bed sheets. She would be in here with me, if I would let her, pinning me to the sheets as I stretched naked beneath her. That thought slipped out of my brain as fluidly as the dampness that gathered on my skin and between my legs. A luxurious sensation reminiscent of nothing, because I could never summon it when I slept with my husband, no matter how hard I tried. Gels and creams and valiant efforts on his part, trying to overcome the need for an ever-absent spontaneous reaction. In our first year, he saw me as unnatural, prematurely dry, old before my time. Uninterested and uninteresting. I wanted to please him if only to prove I was normal, but pleasure is its own wind and can't be summoned; it merely blows in unexpectedly.

Ironically, tonight, I felt the erotic breeze, but with no one to enjoy it. I got up and showered to cool off and turned on the TV and watched *Indiana Jones* again…able to relate to the *Temple of Doom*. It ended at four thirty in the morning and I finally passed out as the morning light was illuminating the shutters.

Around ten a.m., I awoke feeling hung over and stiff, as if I'd been out all night instead of Cash. I staggered to the bathroom and took another shower. Circles under my eyes made me look like a raccoon and I tried to cover them with makeup.

A quick tour of the house told me Cash had left, and I glimpsed her returning from the pasture and Perry walking toward the north gate where the cattle were grazing. I checked on her through the binoculars. She was in tight jeans, her hands gesticulating, apparently happy and animated. Glad life is working out for her, I thought sardonically, and then felt bad. *What the hell, Maggie, stop acting like some gal who doesn't want the guy but doesn't want anyone else to have him. Let her be Verta's summer screw!*

Deciding to drive down to the back pasture and check the cattle to get my mind off things, I grabbed a floppy hat from the wall hook and put it on, the brim concealing my face from no one other than myself. As I stepped outside a sudden gust caught my hat and blew it back off my head. The leather strap snapped against my neck as if the wind demanded I face it or it would strangle me. And then I saw her, standing by the pond, her hair tousled by the same breeze, her cotton pants whipped against her legs as she faced the north gale.

Caught off guard, I stopped and could only stare. Something about her was so profoundly strong and beautiful. An assuredness that should only come with age but for unknown reasons had found itself in her stance and the movement of her arm as she skipped a rock across the pond. My heartbeat picked up and I fought the desire to call out to her. After all, right now she was most likely thinking of her tryst last night and what she should do next: pursue the woman, refuse her calls, download the photographs onto her laptop when I wasn't looking, print one out and jam it into the wooden edge of her dresser mirror.

I got into the XUV and headed in her direction, noting Duke was by her side, his nose burrowing into the weeds around the pond bank. She squatted down on the ground slowly, as if not to disturb something, then put her hand into the tall grass. Despite my anger over her midnight antics, I called out to her, not wanting to see her injured by a water moccasin or rattlesnake baking in the summer heat.

She grinned widely when she saw me and waved me toward her as she reached back into the bushes. I winced at those long slender fingers disappearing into the marsh grass. This time she extracted something black-and-white.

"Puppy!" she shouted as I approached and took the wriggling creature from her. "How do you think it got here?"

"People dump puppies all the time but usually something kills them before they get this far in." The puppy made little grunting sounds and I smiled in spite of myself at the tiny flat face, with its bright pink nose. I held the wriggling furball up to check its underside. "Girl."

"I'm going to keep her," Cash insisted, as Duke ran up and gave the small creature a literal top-to-bottom sniff, apparently deciding she was acceptable and could stay.

"Hard to keep small animals safe when there's no fenced yard."

"I can train her. She's smart or she wouldn't have gotten this far and stayed alive. Kind of like us." She looked at me, seeming to want a deeper conversation, but I ignored her.

I handed the squirming ball of fur back to Cash, who nestled the pup under her chin and rubbed her face against it lovingly, then turned the vehicle and headed slowly back to the house, not offering Cash a ride but letting her trail behind. "So what are you going to name her?"

"Moses."

"Because you found her in the bullrushes? Maybe not the best girl name." I spoke over my shoulder and out of the corner of my eye caught sight of something.

"Neither is Cash but it's mine."

"Hold still for a minute, don't move." The snake, about as big around as my wrist, was coiled up in the reeds just ahead of Cash. I lifted the shotgun off its rack in the XUV and fired quickly. The snake exploded, squirming and bleeding, and Cash jumped back and swore. "It's a wonder it didn't get the puppy," I said, and got out to examine it. "Triangular head so it's poisonous. I always hate killing good snakes but this one needed to go." She drew back, startled by the shot, but obviously impressed. "Pretty hard to miss with a shotgun. Although you did think I missed the coyote." I couldn't help but goad her. "It'll be gone tomorrow. Other animals will eat it. Tastes like chicken," I said jauntily as I signaled her to climb in and drove us back to the house, Duke running alongside our vehicle.

"I want to keep Moses indoors unless we're with her, until she's older. I won't let her ruin anything, don't worry."

"I'm not worried about that." I reached over and scratched the pup's warm body as we drove.

"I didn't sleep with her," Cash said, and glanced sideways at me.

Her remark cascaded over me, stunning me that she knew I had given her sexual escapades any thought at all. I paused, avoiding her eyes, and said evenly, "You can sleep with her if you want to."

"You're talking about the puppy and don't pretend you're not."

I looked straight ahead, pretending I couldn't hear above the wind, but my soul let out a great sigh and I felt triumphant, happy… *she didn't sleep with her.*

CHAPTER SEVENTEEN

I crawled up in the attic and located a small wire cage I'd used to hold stray animals and handed it down to Cash. Before letting her put the puppy in it, I washed it out with Lysol and dried it off. She got one of her old black T-shirts and bunched it up in the corner, making a makeshift mattress. We put drinking water inside and Cash ran up to the corner store for some puppy food. Moses squeaked and wiggled and paced as if she'd already decided Cash belonged to her and couldn't bear her absence.

"You're just another woman captivated by her charm, aren't you?" I said as I finally picked her up and cuddled her. She squalled rhythmically for a minute, then let out a big sigh and went to sleep.

I sat in the rocker and held the little pup, wondering why creatures of all shapes and sizes end up on the prairie and how each has to decide if it will fight and then fate decides who will survive. The pup's small warm body against mine soothed me, and I sighed too and closed my eyes, taking a brief break.

No telling how long we slept but when I awoke, it was to the smell of ham and eggs and Cash at the stove. I smiled at her quizzically.

"You two make a cute couple," she said.

I stroked the still-sleeping puppy and didn't move, not wanting to disturb its rest. "What are you cooking?"

"Omelets. One of the few things I've mastered. I also do soup, hamburgers, and tacos, but the ground beef wasn't thawed so I went with eggs. Thank God for chickens. Oh, and I also made fresh biscuits...bet you didn't think I knew how."

"I think you can do anything you set your mind to. An omelet sounds nice." I felt dreamy and relaxed and watched her as she worked in the kitchen as if she belonged there. She slung bowls and plates and frying pans around with speed, not worrying what she splattered or sprayed, then minutes later deftly mopped up the mess with paper towels and scrubbed dishes out at the sink.

"You cook like a man."

"Well, thank you, since it's never been my goal to cook *for* one."

"When did you know you were gay?" The words came out before I could stop them.

She paused in mid-motion. "I can't remember ever not knowing. I always liked women."

"Tell me about the first woman you were ever with."

"My rowing coach and I pursued her."

"Your teacher?" My voice revealed shock and Cash merely shrugged. "So she was quite a bit older."

"That wasn't the issue. The problem was her husband. He threatened to kill me and called Buck, which is how Buck figured everything out."

"What did *coach* have to say about all that?" My emphasis on her title was condescending.

"She was on pain medication and not herself, she loved him dearly, and basically...good-bye." I giggled and she lightened up. "Thus, 'the rule.'"

I got up and put Moses back in her cage before sitting at a barstool across the counter from her. She slid the omelet onto a plate with hot biscuits and honey. "There you are, ma'am. Garnished with chopped salsa made with fresh tomatoes from your garden."

I beamed at her and her face lit up with delight. "So your relationships have been conquests...you convinced women to surrender. Has anyone ever pursued you?"

"Hasn't seemed to work out that way." The puppy squeaked once and I took her out of the cage and gave her a bit of biscuit and honey. She licked the honey with her tiny pink tongue, then gummed the biscuit bit, gobbling it up, and we both laughed.

"She's spoiled," I said, contributing to her condition.

"I've never had a puppy. My apartment doesn't allow pets." Cash came around the counter to stroke the furry little creature's head as I held her. I didn't ask Cash what she planned to do about the apartment rule, or how the puppy would go home with her, or if she intended to leave the tiny creature here. I swallowed at the emotional tide of sadness that suddenly washed over me. She would obviously be leaving in the not-too-distant future, and the puppy represented that moment.

"Do you like where you live?" I asked, looking up at her, driven no doubt by the idea of losing her.

"Not any more." She wrapped her hands around the puppy and in so doing around my own—our fingers entwined, her hands enveloping mine. She leaned over, as I whispered no, and gently put her mouth to mine. An innocent touching of lips that held beneath their pulsing softness a promise of passion if only unleashed. For a moment, we breathed each other's breath, unable to separate, and finally she spoke, barely parting from me. "I want you, Maggie Tanner, like I have never wanted anyone or anything in my life."

"You don't know what you want, Cash," I whispered, at the same time thinking, neither do I.

Her lips close to mine silenced me. "Don't, please. Just think about us. That's all I'm asking. Just think about us together." The puppy squirmed, probably from all the fingers enclosing her. "I think she's too hot." Cash pried the puppy out of my hands and put her in the sleep cage.

"We're all too hot," I said under my breath and headed out to the front porch, where the wind rippled over my body and created a chill. Moments later, the screen door clicked and Cash was on the porch behind me. She put her arms around me just under my breasts, resting her chin on my shoulder and holding me.

"You have to stop this. I'm so confused. I can't function in this state. I can't get anything done." All the while I nestled against her, a warmth running through me that could heat an entire city, and she put her lips to my neck. I bent my head to one side to allow her better access, all the while protesting…as if my mind and my body were no longer communicating with one another.

"It's your ranch, your life. Who are you hurting by making love?"

"I don't know about women together and I don't want to get used to it." Her kisses on my neck were melting me into an incoherent pool of desire. "You're not solid like the land, you're like the seasons that come and go."

He was on us before we heard a sound, booming out, "Anything you need from town, Ms. Tanner? I'm headed in." Bo stood off the south end of the porch and talked loudly to be heard as Cash's arms casually slid away from me. It was hard to tell what he saw or what he might think he saw, and I tried to remain unflustered.

"Thanks for checking, but I think we've got everything we need."

He ambled off, looking back over his shoulder once as if trying to decide what he'd witnessed. I hurried into the house and Cash followed.

"Maggie…" she called out to me, but I was already in my room feeling like a teenager caught necking by her parents. She lightly tapped on my door. "Maggie, let me in, please. Let me just talk to you."

Taking the coward's way out, I said nothing but merely flipped the dead-bolt lock, the only thing I could rely on to keep us apart.

❖

I couldn't sleep and got up before sunrise. The diary Cash had left on the kitchen table was now gone without my ever having confided that I'd read it. In its place was a note saying Moses had been fed early so she should sleep all morning. By ten o'clock the pup seemed as restless and unfocused as I was. Cash wasn't in her room and I realized she must have written the note on her way out. Taking the puppy out on the lawn, I let her relieve her little bladder and walk around. She stumbled on chubby legs as she sniffed the grass, and I inspected all her body parts, trying to figure out her lineage. She looked like the love child of a Boston terrier and a bluetick hound. "If that's true," I said to the pup, "then your parents had their own romantic challenges."

Looking left at the sound of birds chirping, I noticed Cash's Jeep was gone. The morning dew was still on the grass, and lack of tire tracks headed toward the front gate indicated Cash hadn't left the ranch. In fact the damp grass showed distinct tire tracks down toward the pasture. I put Moses up and went back outside, deciding a morning walk would do me good, then followed the fresh trail to see where it led and what Cash and Perry were up to. And if I were honest, just to see Cash.

The Jeep was parked under a grove of trees on the north side of the property down where the cattle stood in the shade. Shadows prevented my seeing inside the front seat, and it appeared she had parked it there and taken a walk. I picked up my pace and fifty feet from the vehicle heard moaning, then movement as if someone was making love. I paused, then decided to see what in hell she was doing. Maybe meeting Verta and, if so, once and for all, I wanted to see it with my own eyes. Get her out of my system. Convince myself she was exactly who I wanted to believe she was, a woman who would screw anything.

The body on top was too large to be Verta and the person beneath was struggling. Without further thought, I yanked open the passenger-side door and was greeted by Bo's half-naked butt. He had Cash down on the driver's seat, her cries muffled amid the struggle. A fury took over my body, an anger I hadn't felt in years. If I'd had a gun, I would have been the headline in one of those news stories about a woman who shot someone fifty times when twice would do. I grabbed the waistband of Bo's pants and jerked back so hard he reared up enough for Cash to get her arm between them and slam his head up against the Jeep's ceiling. Off balance after another violent yank from me, he fell backward out onto the ground, moaning as he hit the hard tree roots of the grove. I glanced at Cash, whose shirt was torn, clothing askew, and her lip bleeding.

"What in hell's going on?" I shouted at her.

"What the hell do you think? He jumped me," she shouted back, her face hurt and angry.

All my sexual frustration and anger blew out of me and into my right foot, which could not stop kicking Bo. I planted my boot in his head, then his shoulder, then his back as he tried to protect himself from the blows. "You sorry, fucking jackass, get off my land. If I had a shotgun I'd blow your brains out and feed you to the snakes. What makes you think you can come in here and take my money and attack my guests."

He managed to scramble up on his hands and knees. "Quit it now. Stop it. She asked for it!" He was on his feet. "You both asked for it. Dykes is what we call it."

Cash swooped up a broken tree limb about the diameter of her arm and swung it like a bat, catching Bo across the chest and throwing him over backward. She pointed the end of the stick to his chest, pinning him to the ground. "Apologize." He looked at her and she glared back. His mouth opened as if to say something but she cut him off. "To *her*."

He turned his eyes to me. "I apologize."

"Get off my ranch."

"I need to get my stuff."

"Perry will bring it. Just get off," I said, weary now with disappointment in human nature. He started walking back across a hundred acres to the front gate. I signaled Cash to get in the Jeep and drive behind him until he was gone, then pulled out my cell phone and rang the bunkhouse. Perry answered and I told him to pack Bo's clothes and catch up with him down the road and drive him the hell away from here.

"Aw, no, what happened?" Perry whimpered.

"Just get him off the ranch." My voice rose and I hung up. Shaking involuntarily, I strode back to the ranch house, unnerved by what had just happened and terrified over the timing. *What if I hadn't been there?*

Twenty minutes later, from the window I could see Bo staggering out through the front gates, Perry headed his way in the truck. Cash pulled up by the house, parked, and bounded up the steps.

"You okay?" I asked, upset. She nodded that she was. "How'd it happen that you two were in the Jeep together?" Nothing like this ever occurred here until Cash arrived: friendly charismatic, sexual. Unlike the rest of us, she was high-voltage wire plugged into a town with low wattage, causing everyone to blow their circuit, starting with me and ending with Bo Nightengale.

"I couldn't sleep and took a drive this morning to think things over. He was out early and flagged me down, asking if he could catch a ride down to the cattle guard. When we got there, he said he could tell from watching me on the porch last night that I needed his services. I'm strong but he caught me off guard. If you hadn't shown up, it wouldn't have been good."

"You see now, don't you, how men out here think about two women together? They can't stop until they get things back the way they think nature intended."

"It's natural to nearly be raped because some guy thinks I should be lusting after him instead of after you?"

Something caught in my chest at the thought of her lusting after me, but I held steady in my gaze and revealed nothing of what my pounding heart signaled. "It's not how it *should* be, it's how it is." I went to the fridge and pulled out an icepack, wrapped it in a kitchen towel, and handed it to her. "Put this on your lip."

"Maybe you've lived in the country too long. Where I come from, it's *not* how it is. You don't escort guys off the ranch. You call the cops and escort them to jail."

"Well, the 'cops' out here are two more guys pretty much like the one we escorted off the ranch and they never heard of a 'significant other' and 'partner' is always preceded by 'howdy.'"

"Good reason, I guess, to just marry one of the bastards. They can promise to protect you along with their land and cattle and other possessions so long as they can fuck you when they want." She whirled and left, muttering over her shoulder. "Not much difference between that and what Bo tried to do, seems to me."

I was snapped back into my marriage and the argument in the bedroom, where it always began. I wouldn't make love when he wanted. That's where the trouble lay. I never desired sex with him.

Like a gay woman in hiding, I had lived an inauthentic life, hadn't I? If my husband were here, he would no doubt agree with Bo that I was just another dyke.

CHAPTER EIGHTEEN

A daily weather check was routine for any rancher, but I'd lost track of time and, along with it, the wind and rain. And so like a siren in the night, the storm swooped down on me, shredding decency and shattering silence, battering the windows of my bedroom, the roaring winds drowning the howling of my soul.

Lightning crashed around the house and I jumped up and put on sweatpants, grabbed a slicker, and drove down to the far pasture where the horses were huddled. I knew ranchers considered it stupid to worry about horses in a storm, but the tall, moisture-rich trees were natural conductors of electricity and the exact spot horses always chose for shelter. I shouted for them and they came running, wondering no doubt where in hell I'd been. I hopped out and opened the gates, and they knew the routine, rushing from the south pasture into the fenced field next to the barn gates and then into the small area around the barn, thundering like trained circus animals through the openings and careening up to the barn before I could get back to greet them.

When I caught up with them, all I had to do was open their stalls and they could stay dry inside or go outside in the attached run, and I could rest without seeing images of stiff, swollen horse bodies lying flat on their sides, electrocuted.

When I parked and slogged back into the house, lamplights were on and coffee was brewing. Cash was standing in her nightshirt holding a towel out for me in exchange for my dripping slicker. "Was this a necessary trip, Ms. Stanwyck?"

"Lightning."

"And that's why you shouldn't be driving a metal vehicle around in it and opening and shutting metal gates."

"Listen to you," I said, amused at her acting like the ranch woman. "Well, normally I'd know the storm was coming. This time I missed it."

"Me too." She reached over and gently helped me dry my hair before giving me a penetrating look that seemed to reference storms raging within that had caught us both unawares. No denying that there was something between us. Something so mysterious to me that it was frightening. How had it happened that this woman attached herself to my every thought and in certain moments made my heart actually ache with longing?

Without another word, I broke away and took the coffee she offered to my room, where I showered and dressed. The warm water took the chill off me and the coffee did the rest.

When I returned to the living room, Cash was there in sweatpants and a T-shirt, she too showered and smelling of some cologne I'd come to associate with sex, as the mere whiff of it made my mind go immediately to that topic.

"Where's Moses?" I asked, trying to be congenial and diversionary.

"Sleeping in her crib. Are we going to pretend that we never kissed?" She interjected the subject I dreaded.

"We *didn't* really kiss. Have you fed her something?" I felt my cheeks flush, and my hands trembled as I tried to get the conversation back on sensible ground.

"I fed her some Puppy Chow and I walked her." She came up behind me. "It felt like kissing to me. What would you call it then?"

"Being caught off guard. Vulnerable. That's all." I moved away quickly. She groaned in desperation at my constantly fending her off. Then why don't you send her away, the voice in my head inquired. Unless of course you want to re-enact some tired scene from *The Graduate*.

"I'm not playing Mrs. Robinson to your Benjamin." The words

popped out without my having time to analyze them. "1967, Anne Bancroft." I responded to the quizzical look with a miserable sigh. "You weren't even born yet."

"Well, I'm here now, in the flesh, and I want to know what you're doing."

"What do you mean?"

"You're completely push-pull. Half the time you're letting me know you want me to take you in my arms and hold you, and the other half you're telling me to leave you alone." Cash searched my eyes for an answer and, receiving none, said quietly, "You're driving me crazy, Maggie. I don't know how much longer I can take it." She whirled and left the room.

❖

For nearly a week the storm clouds threatened and the winds blew as if trying to rid us of the last days of July, sometimes bringing rain and other times stray pieces of hay, debris, and anything else that wasn't bolted down. The fire danger was high despite the water. Small sparks ignited into brushfires south of us, and the local fire department warned of impending threats to adjacent counties. I didn't think the flames would reach us in any significant way, as the rainwater seemed to have pooled in most areas around the ranch.

But only a few days later, the winds increased to gale force, forty-mile-an-hour gusts, and the fires were visible on the horizon. Huge plumes of gray and by nightfall the smell of smoke in the air. No matter where we walked, the smell never left our nostrils. We got in the truck and drove south to see how far away the fires were, but the rolling hills concealed the exact location. Calls to the fire department assured us they'd had men positioned five miles south for the last twenty-four hours. Nonetheless, the high winds were creating jump flames that were igniting new fields, and they admitted they had their hands full.

The animals seemed oblivious to the impending danger as they moved about aimlessly, noses to the ground, chewing on grass. I didn't sleep well. It always worried me when something as big as a tornado or a wildfire approached. Too many animals to save and at what point did we save ourselves.

I drove up to the north pasture, where the cattle grazed on the near-barren grass, and located Perry. He and Cash were down on the ground stringing hot wire to hold the animals in. Cash rolled the big spool of silver wire along the ground, and Perry pulled and clamped it at eight-foot intervals, then ratcheted it up to the next post, taking the sag out. It was backbreaking work if you strung more than a thousand feet, and from the looks of the pasture they were about there.

"Have you checked the horse trailers?" I asked, ignoring Cash, leaving her to her work.

"Aired up the tires on the new one. Old one's floorboards are in decent shape so it's usable. We can jam the horses into 'em if we have to."

"Tight quarters," I told him, "but better than leaving them behind."

"Won't come to that," he said casually. "They'll knock it down. They've got trucks from three counties. Bo told me."

"Why are you still talking to Bo?" My voice rose in anger, and Perry gave Cash a furtive glance.

"He's in the volunteer fire department," he said simply. "I've known him a long time and he must have been drunk or something when that thing happened."

"That thing? *I'm* that thing. Well, that's just great!" Cash threw the spool of wire to the ground. "He hawks and snorts and spits and you can't stand to even bunk with him, but he seriously tries to jump my bones and you don't give a shit. I ought to get him drunk and let him put his big sweaty belly up against your rosy ass and see how you like it!" Cash stomped off and I concealed a grin. Apparently the idea that male bonding superseded female injustice didn't sit well with her.

Perry jerked upright. "What the hell?"

"I was going to ask her to help you get the trailers ready, but I think I'll just stay out of her way." I turned around and headed back to the house, chuckling at Perry's shocked expression. It also crossed my mind that Cash was very sexy when she was fired up.

❖

Overnight the hot winds blew in, bringing the fire on us like a biblical plague, so close the smoke choked us. Oppressive summer heat coupled with intense flames, the wind drying out our eyes. We could only move about restlessly in cotton clothes and work boots, trying to prepare for what might come. Hoses were hooked up to every spigot and horse trailers were backed up to the smallest pasture, where I'd temporarily corralled all the horses in case we had to round them up.

"What do you think?" I asked Perry, as we gathered on the south end of the ranch gazing off into the darkness at the red glow that seemed to be widening and brightening. Not a good sign. Cash was standing next to him and they'd most likely discussed the situation in detail. They seemed to have reached a truce, focusing on the fire, her anger merely scorched earth from which friendship could now be recultivated.

"Well, wind could shift and send it southeast of us." He seemed to be making up unlikely scenarios just to calm me down.

"If it jumps the Wileys' ranch, then I want to open all the cattle gates and herd them out. Give 'em a shot at not being barbecued before their time."

"We'll need an hour to get ready." Cash looked around her with amazing calm. "I can drive one horse trailer and you can drive the other. That'll give Perry the cattle detail. I've already got Moses and you can take Duke. You have insurance?"

"Yes," I whispered, thinking insurance didn't replace memories.

"Any documents or valuables you want out?" she continued.

"Box of photos in the coat closet."

"I'll put them in the truck." Cash went inside, leaving me and Perry on the front steps.

"Let's get some sleep. If it hits Wiley's have them call us," I said, and went back inside to try to get some rest.

❖

It was two a.m. and I'd been asleep only a couple of hours when the phone rang. Jonas Wiley was shouting that the flames were at his south pasture and he was calling everyone he could to ask for help. I told him we'd be there. I ran across the living room floor barefooted and banged on Cash's door. She stepped inside off the porch, fully dressed in jeans and boots. "I've got burlap, shovels, water tanks in the back of the truck ready to go." I realized while I'd slept, she'd been awake and planning. I ran back to my room and threw on jeans and boots and a sweatshirt over a tee. We were in the truck in minutes, headed down the road toward Wiley's. Cash said Perry was already over there, and I wondered how I could have just checked out and slept. So unlike me. *I must be more stressed than I know.*

All the neighboring ranchers were gathered at the property line, beating back the flames with everything they had. People had been trenching for days, trying to create a fire line the flames couldn't jump. The row of ranchers strung out as far as you could see, their shovels tossing dirt on flames.

Cash fell in beside them and I was impressed that she knew where to stand and how to help without being told. A section of flames died down, then a gust and the fire flared somewhere else. A shout went up and men clustered to beat it back. A fire truck finally pulled onto the scene—more like a tank on the back of a pickup. County fire departments were makeshift and volunteer, some of them better than others at the occasional work.

Two men jumped out and dragged a big hose, which shot down the fire line and into the most serious burn. The flames quieted. The tanker, now empty, left to refill. Soon another section of the fire had them in retreat again. The heat and sweat and human noises were insignificant in relation to the sound of the air itself. The wind flung the flames around our feet where they danced between us. I picked up a shovel and joined a group of people trying to toss dirt onto the newly ignited patches of prairie grass.

Hours went by and we seemed no better off than before, just dirtier and sweatier and more tired. Then the wind died down, an omniscient force silenced and the calm unnerving. As the blast furnace simmered, the ranchers knew they had a lull in which to conquer the blaze. Despite fatigue, we double-timed our moves, beating small, recalcitrant flames, dousing them with water and throwing more dirt on the hot spots. After another hour, we began to rise from our bent positions, exhausted, to assess the landscape.

Jonas Wiley shook hands with Jock Goodie, and Sara beamed at her husband. If there was something good about this fire, it gave folks a chance to see that Sara and Jock were here to stay and would pitch in like everyone else, and maybe it would be Jonas Wiley who would help neighbors find their way to the Goodies' store. Wiley's wife hugged him, dirt-stained tears smudging her face. "I think we've saved it." Her husband put his tired arms around her shoulders and held her against him, while men paced up and down the line making sure every little ember was out.

"Couple of us will stay down here," Perry said. "Case of a flare-up." A few other men nodded, indicating they'd hang around in case we'd missed anything.

Moments like this made me proud to be a rancher. People who probably didn't see each other but once a year showed up to save another family's property. Some of us out of self-preservation, but a lot of these folks, as I looked around, were well out of the path of the flames and didn't have to spend their night in the soot.

I caught sight of Cash, as dirty as the fellow next to her, who on closer inspection appeared to be Stretch Adams. Their conversation went on for a moment, and he chuckled and squeezed her arm at the bicep as if measuring her muscle strength.

I waved and she caught sight of me. She didn't look the least bit tired and gave me a sweet smile, as if she too understood what had just happened here when it came to things that counted.

I left drinking water with Perry and offered to go get him anything he needed, but he acted irritated at the idea that he needed more than a rock to sit on and a can of beer, the latter having been handed to him by another rancher smart enough to throw a case in the back of his truck. Cash insisted she would hang out with Perry for a bit and then walk back across the pasture. Nothing left for me to do but pack up and drive home, grateful for a moment to have struck a bargain with nature.

❖

Water, I decided was the world's great luxury, as the shower cascaded down my dirt-streaked arms, washing away grit and grime and fear. We were safe now, the flames doused. Life could resume. I got out, toweled off, and threw on cotton drawstring pants, not bothering to entirely dry my hair, but preferring to step out onto the back porch and let the wind caress it.

In the distance, debris seemed to be piled up around the barn and a light had been left on. The straight winds had undoubtedly upended everything that wasn't bolted down. I poured myself a small glass of wine and donned moccasins to amble down the path to the barn. Relief flooded me, and I said a small prayer of thanks to God for sparing my ranch.

As I approached the barn, I spotted Cash standing in the aisle toweling off. I stopped to observe her half-naked body, the curve of her back. She picked up a clean black T-shirt off the sink's ledge and slipped it over her head, her small breasts not requiring a bra. I waited until she was decently clothed, then approached.

"Cash, is that you?" I acted as if I hadn't seen her but had only suspected it might be she.

She waved and then spoke when I came closer. "I was just washing the soot off."

"You were a big help," I said as I bent to pick up the scattered muck buckets blown down the aisle. Reaching inside the tack room, I set my wineglass on a counter to leave both hands free to collect the debris the wind had wrought: a stack of black plastic garbage bags loose and flapping about, harnesses blown off hooks, along with anything else that had formerly hung from a wall. Cash fell in at the opposite end of the barn, doing her part. "Don't knock yourself out. I'm just collecting the big things that could end up out in the pasture."

Giving the place a quick look, I stepped into the tack room and collected my wineglass, then flopped down on a comfy leather couch. I'd forgotten how cozy this old cowboy settee was, having banished it from the house for ostensible soil and tears. Tired, I swung my legs up and reclined into its smooth softness, then put my head back and let my neck muscles relax for the first time in what seemed days. The quiet was a luxury and I wondered where Cash had gone. Perhaps up to the house to have a real shower.

I glanced at the doorway and she was standing there...her shoulder angled up against the doorjamb as if Annie Leibovitz had posed her, strong and young and beautiful and looking as if she wanted to own me. Like a prey animal, I tried to get up and escape, but she was on the couch in one swift move. Her body above me, her weight aloft as she lowered herself onto me.

She pressed her lips to mine and without prelude devoured me with the heat of her tongue. Inside me, taking me, as surely as if she'd entered through an even more intimate passage. I moaned and twisted beneath her, not to escape but to savor every second of this erotic moment—one I had never experienced and now knew only through this androgynous woman. She slowly pulled her lips away and, eyes glistening, riveted mine. "So there's no mistake, we have now kissed."

"Let me up," I whispered. She hesitated, then got off. I managed to get to my feet and find my balance. "There's no denying what you do to me." I paused, trying to quiet my pounding heart. "But the difference between being my age and yours is that I look down the road, past the passion, and I know the heartache that waits there... and I don't want it."

"You can reject passion for the rest of your life, Maggie, but that won't stop heartache. It's a risk you take to be able to love someone. And if ever there was a risk worth taking, I'm it. I swear to you, I'm it." Her tone was pleading and I couldn't look at her.

We stood there for a long time, in the silence of the night, orchestrated only by the crickets and the plaintive sounds of an old barn owl.

When she spoke again, her voice was sorrowful and held a quiet finality. "All right. I swear to you, on my grave, I won't try to make love to you again."

CHAPTER NINETEEN

The following morning was the first day of August. The fire danger on the ranch seemed a distant memory, but inside me the flames could not be knocked down.

Perry phoned around ten a.m. to say he planned to sack in for the rest of the day. Life would get back to normal, he assured me, but I knew that wasn't true.

I took a cold shower to relieve the throbbing in my body. I had decided to wash Cash and any longing for her out of my life.

But standing in front of the bathroom mirror again, I studied my nakedness, trying to see myself as Cash might see me if we were in bed together. Her taut, firm skin pressed against my slightly sagging breasts, her muscular thighs against my less-than-firm ones. I examined the crow's feet at the corners of my eyes and saw traces of lines that were beginning to form on my forehead and around my mouth. *She's young and you're not. And when her gorgeous skin finally experiences a hint of aging and slight creases line her brow, I will have more lines than the Sunday paper. Ridiculous to have ever kissed her.* Why didn't I simply slug her and demand that she get off me? Because, a small voice residing in my heart whispered, you want her. The air came out of my body and I slumped before the mirror, trying to come to terms with that thought.

If wanting is what it's all about, then I will want someone else. I burst out of the bathroom to escape the dreaded mirror, dashed into the closet, and got dressed, letting action fill my brain so I could avoid dealing with my heart. *She's a horny twenty-eight-year-old looking to have sex with yet another older woman so she'll have something to boast about when the summer is over and she's chasing every barfly in town. The pain now is nothing compared to what it would be, if suddenly you fell for her and then she left. Not that I would fall for her. But I'm not letting this entire summer turn into a setup for sadness. It's sex, really. It's all about sex. Before she arrived here, I hadn't thought about it much, and I certainly haven't had it enough in my life, so that's the issue.*

I flung my bedroom door open with unintentional force and it bounced back against the wall, startling me and making Cash look up in alarm from the counter where she was having lunch.

"You okay?" She looked surprised and I quickly assured her I was fine. "I was thinking, after what you said last night, that I should get on back home. Take the pressure off both of us," she said, looking down at the floor.

My heart pounded and my stomach lurched. "What about the second haying? It's taken a while for you to learn what you're doing, and now about the time you've got it down you want to run—"

"We both know that's not why I'm leaving." Her words sounded final and fear flew into my chest and I panicked at the mere thought of her driving away.

"Well, you don't need to worry about that. Besides, we'll both be very busy. For instance, I won't be here tonight, I'm going out. Stretch Adams asked me. City council fundraiser and he's invited me to attend." The frantic lie rolled off my lips.

"You want to date Stretch Adams about like I want to kiss a pig!"

Dating Stretch was an insane utterance, and Cash was right, but if nothing else, it signaled my desire to find the straight and narrow and to make sure she didn't leave. Those two thoughts might be diametrically opposed, but I was too upset to analyze that possibility.

"You're just running away, Maggie. We're at an impasse here, and for me it's physically and emotionally painful." Her eyes bore into me like a truth meter.

"I simply want you to stay and help me with the second haying," I said evenly.

Snatching her diary from the table, she headed out onto the porch and sat on the swing. After a few minutes she jumped up and walked toward the back pasture and I let out a long sigh, upset with damned near everything, myself at the top of the list.

The phone rang and I grabbed it. Buck's jovial voice came across loud and abrasive, as if he thought the wires had failed and only volume would suffice. He apologized for not stopping back by on his way home from Texas, but wanted me to know that I'd more than fulfilled my obligation with Cash.

"I was intending to call her tomorrow and thought I'd check with you first. Easy for me to suggest she get her tail on back home. What do you think?" And for some reason his tone and the timing of his call made me believe he'd spoken to Cash and she'd said something about being unhappy. His words buzzed through my head like insects and I felt faint.

"There's no rush." I tried to sound casual.

"Well, second haying is probably on you pretty soon. Unless you need her—"

"I do need her." My response was too quick and my heart jammed in my throat at the confession. "Certainly through the next haying anyway. We can talk after that."

The pause on the phone line lasted so long that for a moment I wondered if we'd been disconnected, then he spoke. "She's told you she's into gals, I guess." His tone contained a tension. Not defensiveness or embarrassment, but more like he was worried.

"She told me." I was still breathless and tried to control my breathing during the silence.

"You okay? Does that upset you, because if it does, I could—"

"Stop apologizing for her, Buck. She's a terrific woman and she's worked very hard the whole time she's been here."

"Didn't mean it that way. You just sound nervous, that's all. You know her liking women used to bother me some, but the way I see it now, Maggie, is that we oughta do what makes us feel good in life, what makes us happy. After that, well, hell, there is no after that. You know what I mean?"

"I have a date tonight." I could have punched myself after I said it. One lie always leads to another, and I wasn't a good liar. "Just a fellow in town. No one, really."

"Well, now..." He seemed taken aback by that information. "Cash didn't tell me you were dating anyone."

"Well, I wasn't, or I mean I haven't been."

"Guess I'll need a full report. Anyway, I appreciate your keeping Cash for the summer. She sure admires you and enjoys your company and uh...I think you've taught her a lot."

"That's very nice," I said, and looked for a way to wrap up the conversation. Hanging up, I slumped back against the counter thinking about Cash leaving. *God, God, God. Imagine lusting after Buck's daughter and then lying about dating someone to cover up. I'm fully fucked!*

I got dressed up a little, in case Cash saw me leave, and drove into town around six p.m. as if I were meeting Stretch Adams. Parking my truck out of sight behind the 2-K, I walked around to the front and entered, spotting Donnetta. She was about to close the place down, and one look at me apparently told her I needed private counseling.

"You sit, Missy, have a cup of coffee. I'll get everybody out of here and you and I will talk. I haven't seen you in weeks." I nodded and waited, my mind paddling around in my head looking for a place to stay above water, drowning in my own illicit desires. *What in the world am I to do? How long will this feeling last? How can I get rid of it?*

Twenty minutes later, the last ticket rung up at the cash register, Donnetta threw the lock on the door, turned the Closed sign over, and slid into the booth across from me.

"Heard you narrowly missed the fire," she said, using mundane topics to find out how to get into what was bothering me.

"Yes." I nodded.

"Heard you fired Bo for coming on to Cash."

I nodded again, not able to speak.

"Are you going to talk or just keep acting like a bobble-headed doll?"

I teared up.

"Did somebody die? Get hurt? Do you need money?" She paused. "Are you in love?" The last question came out as if she'd just discovered it and the wonder in her voice amused even her. "Who is it? This isn't good, I can tell from the look on your face. Is he married?"

"We kissed."

"Who? Not Cash!" My expression must have confirmed her fears. "Well, honey, we can take care of that..." Her tone sounded as if she was willing to come out to the ranch and black her eyes.

"Maggie Tanner, look at me."

I raised my head and shook it slightly, as if even I couldn't figure myself out.

"Omigod, don't tell me."

"She just does something to me."

"Does what? Omigod, you slept with her." I shook my head no. "Good. Good. I mean, you know, time out. Maybe you've just been alone too long, you think? Happens to animals if they're penned up away from the opposite sex."

"There's something about her." My tone must have communicated that I was captivated by her because Donnetta shifted from wanting to punch her out to justifying my feelings.

"Okay, well, look, it's no big deal. Bighorn sheep are gay and male giraffes have orgies." Her words tumbled out and my eyes widened. "Although when I looked it up in *National Geo*, I think they said it was a temporary condition. But that's good too, the idea that it's temporary, I mean."

"Why were you looking it up?"

"Well, because I saw the way you were kind of undressing her with your eyes when you went to the River Festival. Even back then, Cash looked like she wanted to rip your clothes off so I started trying to figure it out. According to a lot of studies, most people know they're gay from the time they're very young, but a lot of women find out late in life."

"Could you be less of a sexual encyclopedia and more of a friend?"

"It's not uncommon. Some women even leave their husbands."

"Speaking of husbands, you betrayed me, you know, and told her about my marriage after you swore—"

"I'm sorry! After I did it, I could have killed myself. She just looked so forlorn swinging on ropes to get your attention." She giggled and I managed a smile.

"What am I going to do about her? I don't want to be gay and she's fifteen years younger than I am…and she's from the city and used to nightlife, and she's a carouser with lots of girlfriends, or so she says, and you know how people talk in this town. They'll gossip more than they do about Verta."

"Already are. Don't look so aghast. You yanked Bo right off the top of her and kicked his head in. He's telling everybody who'll stand still for thirty seconds that you beat him up for coming on to your girlfriend."

"He attacked her…" I sank into despair.

"What are you going to do about this?"

"Nothing! Of course, nothing. She'll be leaving for home soon." I began tearing up again and Donnetta tried to comfort me, pulling napkins out of the box on the table for me to use as Kleenex and reaching across to pat my arm.

"Well, look…" Her conversation briefly stalled as if she was about to say something she wasn't sure she should and then finally decided to go ahead with it. "If you're not going to get a disease, or get pregnant, or get killed, then love is supposed to make you feel good."

"I didn't say I was in love."

"Okay, but you haven't felt this good in a long time, admit it." Donnetta jiggled her eyebrows up and down in a comic fashion and I laughed.

"Okay, I feel…really good, except for the crying and the fear."

"If you like it, phone me. I might throw Buddy out and go after Verta."

My cell phone rang at that instant, punctuating the joke, and we both jumped, and I answered. It was Cash saying there'd been an explosion at the ranch. I headed for the door, still talking on the phone while trying to tell Donnetta what was happening.

Cash's voice was panicked. "The house, Maggie. Something exploded and set it on fire."

I ran for the truck as Donnetta shouted for me to call her and tell her what was happening. I sped down the highway toward the ranch, dialing the local fire department to make sure they were on the way.

Chapter Twenty

I careened down the driveway in time to see the fire truck and two volunteer firemen reel hoses back in. Cash was thanking the driver.

"Where was it?" I scanned the side of the building in the evening light for damage.

"Backside on the north. Propane tank blew up," the fireman shouted over the light wind. "If it'd been any closer to the house it would have done more damage. Mostly wallboards to replace. If you're barbecuing, I'd keep the tanks farther out."

"I don't keep propane tanks by the back of the house," I said out loud to no one, as the firefighters were already on their way out, nothing of interest left for them. I walked through the house and out the back door where metal shards, singed grass, and scarred brick signaled the damage.

At that moment, Perry hustled around the side of the building and we made eye contact. "Who do you think?" I asked. "Your good friend Bo?"

"I doubt it. Even he's not that dumb," Perry said, looking a tiny bit remorseful about his associations.

"You think somebody did this on purpose?" Cash asked.

"Country people have their way of expressing displeasure. I'd say somebody's not happy with us, or with me, most likely." I strode across the pasture toward Hiram's house. Cash hurried to catch up, but I waved her off and she fell back with Perry.

Moments later, I banged on the back screen door of their kitchen and Hiram came out wearing dirty, faded blue overalls that formed a ski jump over the top of his enormous belly. He wiped his hand on a stained rag that could have been used as easily to wipe up motor oil as dry dishes, or perhaps both, knowing Hiram.

"Saw you had the fire truck over there. Didn't stay long, though," he said casually, squinting under the glow of the sodium light dangling from a nearby telephone pole.

"Got it out pretty quick, I guess. I wasn't home. I think somebody helped it along."

"What makes you think that?" He turned his head and spat tobacco juice into the bushes by the side of the house and I wondered how much tobacco fertilizer they'd had over the years.

"Propane tank exploded."

"They'll do that," he said, referring to the propane tank as if it had an independent will.

"Not if you don't own one." I strolled over to a weeded area, broke off a long stalk of grass, and sucked on the end of it as I plopped down on a large tree stump Hiram used as an outdoor settee.

"You haven't gone and hacked off any of your suitors lately." He looked down at me kind of funny, like he wanted me to really think about that. Stretch Adams's face popped into my head. "This whole town's ear is wired to its ass, case you forgot." He turned and spat again as his wife, Betsy, stepped out on the porch, a big square woman with worried hands she twisted and wrung when not engaged in a particular task. She greeted me with a hug, telling me she hadn't seen me in a while and was sorry about the fire.

"Did you tell her?" she asked her husband somewhat sternly.

"You tell everything so I thought I'd leave that to you." Hiram walked off to the shed as if he suddenly had important business that had been interrupted, then crossed the pasture and fired up his old truck and drove away.

"He's been talking to Stretch, who said Bo had been talking to Buddy, who told him Donnetta had said she thought maybe you liked living with that young gal…" The way she stopped at the end of the sentence, as if going another syllable farther would crash her into the unneighborly zone, let me know exactly what the rest of that sentence might be: "…more than a man."

"I never trusted Stretch, myself." Her comments wandered on to reassure me that she wouldn't blame me if I liked anyone better than Stretch. I got up suddenly and thanked her. "Now don't go saying I said anything."

I stalked back across the pasture, the blood all zooming to my head until it was hot and buzzing.

Cash and Perry were waiting for me on the front porch. "What'd the neighbors say?" Cash asked.

"Stretch Adams," I replied. "Didn't come out and say it but they might as well have."

"You went out with him." Her voice rose and I didn't bother to correct her misconception. "Any idea why he wants to date you at seven and burn you down at ten?"

"Years back, I'd have told you a lot of her dates kind of ended in flames." Perry grinned and spat, and I glared at him. He turned and walked back to his bunkhouse, knowing apparently all he needed to know. I said nothing, choosing to pace, thinking through what to do that would put a stop to this before it got any further out of hand. But Cash couldn't let go of it, like a dog with a bone. "Did your date go bad? I've heard city-council meetings can be treacherous."

"I didn't go out with him."

"Really?" She looked pleased. "Which could be why he's mad."

"Country boys in heat don't like anything between them and what they think ought to be theirs."

"This is about you and me?" She came to a quick halt and her eyes widened. I didn't answer but grabbed my truck keys, and Cash followed and hopped into the Chevy beside me. I asked her to get out, but she was defiant. "If it's about me, then I'm sure as hell not staying home. In fact, in my current state of mind I would enjoy kicking someone's ass."

"That just stirs up men like Stretch and makes them want to

top whatever you do. They'll shoot your mailbox, put nails in your truck tires, and that's just the warm-up. It's taken me a long time to earn the right to retaliate, and you haven't earned it because you're not from here."

"Where I come from, if someone fucks you over, that earns you the right. Your theory is bullshit," she said, obviously not caring about my reaction at this point. I decided I didn't need a second fight so I said nothing and stayed focused on the road to town, pretty certain that Stretch was on the late shift.

Thirty minutes later, I whipped into the gravel drive of the lumberyard at such speed and so close to the entrance that when I cranked the wheel to the right, gravel sprayed halfway up the side of the metal building and my headlights flooded the workshop where the night shift did their cutting. I spotted Stretch's truck parked alongside the fence, and then I remembered seeing the propane tank in the back of his truck the day he fishtailed out of Sara Goodie's store lot. My blood started boiling.

"Got to be him," I muttered. "Thinks he's creating a perfect alibi for where he was during the fire." I continued talking to myself as I jumped out, and Cash jogged to keep up with me.

Inside the cavernous, drafty building, several nightshift crew were stacking lumber, talking on phones, or working at buzz saws.

Stretch was bent over a huge circular saw, his face goggled as he sliced through large slabs of wood. I marched over and flipped the adjacent wall switch I'd seen Hiram use to shut down the power to equipment and watched the giant industrial blades spin down on Stretch's workbench. Etta Dormer, the lumberyard's dumpy little night manager, stopped to see what was happening.

Stretch pulled his goggles off and propped them on top of his head and lazily arched his back, hands on his spine, stretching like a tall preening waterbird.

"Stretch, I've always treated you like a gentleman." My voice rose, prompting Cash to move in closer in a protective way.

"Too much so, because I'm no gentleman." Stretch tried to make his voice sexy but it was "a stretch," given how he looked.

"You were out of work and I convinced Hiram to hire you." He glanced around, no doubt wondering how many of his co-workers knew I'd gotten him the job. "And the time your mama was sick and you left her and went fishing, I cooked a meatloaf and took it to her so she could have something to eat." My mention of his elderly mother, who went to church services every day and twice on Sunday, took the sexual wind out of his sails. "And to show your appreciation, you blow up a propane tank that sets my house on fire because I won't go out with your sorry ass!"

One of his male co-workers snorted, choking back a laugh, then pretended he was looking at something on the floor to cover up his embarrassment.

"Look, Maggie." Stretch shuffled from side to side and made an effort to regain his bravado. "All I've ever tried to do is come courting but I'm competing with a...different kind of hand." The same fellow snickered again, and Stretch snorted in appreciation just as Cash charged forward and got Stretch by the shirt front.

"Get the hell out of here, you she-he!" His lip curled with the gender slur and she reared back to slug him, but I yelled for her to stop and in the same breath threatened him if he touched her. Stretch put his hands above his head in mock surrender.

"If your mama heard about this she would die. Keel over and die! You've disgraced her and she raised you better than that."

I gave him one big shove backward toward the saw blade, dashed to the wall, and flipped the wall switch while he was stumbling around trying to regain his balance. The revving blades spun wildly a few feet from his back and he flattened to the floor, fearful of being sliced like baloney. Scrambling on hands and knees, he made it to the door in the back. His co-workers remained frozen.

"I'd like you to come over to my house. I need to get my husband in line," Etta said as she turned her back on me and walked away.

Fired up and remembering something else, I shouted at the top of my voice, "And get your ass over and settle up with Sara Goodie. She's running a feed store, not a bank!"

I stormed out of the metal building and Cash followed me back to the truck and crawled inside looking a little shaken. "Will he stop or retaliate?"

"Probably stop. Prairie males are afraid of two things: Jesus and Mama."

"You're hell on wheels when you're mad," Cash said solemnly. I glanced at her stoic expression, then broke into a big grin. "My God, the gravel's spraying, and you storm in, pull the power on his bench saw, start shouting about meatloaf and Mama, and then you nearly slice him up like bad-boy brisket, and to save himself he hits the floor quaking like he's found Jesus. You scared the pee out of him...and me! You won't let me finish punching his lights out, but you try to cut the guy in half with his own power tools."

Her eyes softened and my heart did the same. It felt sexy and wonderful being the object of Cash Tate's admiration. We drove in silence, smiling into the windshield as the radio played a country song about a woman who relished destroying a guy's headlights with a baseball bat and autographing his leather seats with a pen knife.

"Men are trouble," Cash mused.

"And so are some women." I glanced at her.

"They can be..." Cash reached over and took my hand in hers. It enveloped mine in a loving way, and for a second I welcomed the feeling it sent through me.

It's not sex, it's just hand-holding, I said to quiet my mind. Hand-holding that feels like sex. I made an excuse to pull my hand back and dust off my shirt.

"Sorry. Nothing personal," she said. "Kind of like when two football players pat each other on the butt after a big play, then go off and screw a cheerleader."

I cut my eyes at her and hers twinkled in response. With those looks and that sense of humor and the way she could kiss, she could be addictive. Even I could see that.

"You saved that rope I won at the River Festival. I found it in your photo box when I packed for the fire."

"What were you doing looking in my photo box?" I demanded, shocked.

"What were you doing reading my diary?" She grinned at me and I ignored her. "I'll tell you why you kept my River Festival necklace. Because you're sentimental, and you don't want anyone to know that, and you care about me. Just a little, nothing big, just… you care." She smiled at me as if she'd won a significant victory and kept smiling all the way home.

CHAPTER TWENTY-ONE

The following morning, I was having coffee on the front porch and making a list of things we'd need to repair the back of the house when the wrecker turned into my driveway.

"Oh, for God's sake," I said out loud to no one as the vehicle came toward the house, and I recognized it as the one always parked at Olan's Gas Station. As it approached, I could read the lettering painted on the side. *Towing To Keep You Going.*

The driver pulled up, swerved wide, and put the vehicle in idle. The door swung open and Verta Olan, her breasts like two chubby divers poised to make the leap from her tank top, swung her black leather-wrapped derriere to one side, hopped out, and gave me a playful wave.

"Never get out this way but had to tow somebody and thought while I was in the area I'd stop by and see how you're doing, and say hi to Cash." She added the last part as if it was the inconsequential piece, but I knew it was the sole reason for her visit.

"So the two of you had a night out," I said, getting to the point.

"We did." She sighed happily, apparently believing that my brevity indicated approval. "She's a mean dancer." She dragged the words out as if the dancing might have been horizontal. "You like to dance?" When I nodded, she added, "We should all go sometime," and I smiled, thinking I would sooner go to a religious revival involving snake handling than a dance with Verta Olan. "So what's been going on out here?" Her necked stretched, terrapin-like, as she scanned the landscape for signs of Cash. I shrugged and smiled, refusing to give her any information. "So is uh…Cash around?"

I told her I didn't know but I would certainly check. Leaving Verta on the front lawn, I dashed up the steps and knocked sharply on Cash's bedroom door. When she opened up, looking surprised, I said, "Your date from the other night is here." I turned and walked back into the living room, busying myself at the computer while Cash stood at the front door.

"What did she say to you?" Cash didn't take her eyes off Verta.

"That you're a meeean dancer," I said flatly, without looking up.

Cash pushed the door open and went out onto the front porch and began talking to Verta. The wind sent some of the conversation my way, but not all of it. Verta's tone was toying and playful. Twenty minutes later, Cash came back up the steps and the wrecker pulled out of the driveway and headed for town. Without so much as a word, Cash returned to her bedroom.

What in the hell was that about? Obviously Verta thinks they're dating or wants to continue dating or something. And what did Cash tell her? See you later, e-mail me, pick me up at seven?

After a few minutes, Cash came back into the living room, crossed to the kitchen, opened the cabinet and took a jar of peanut butter down, located the bread, and began to make herself a sandwich. The casualness of that act annoyed the hell out of me. I was determined not to let her think I cared what she and Verta had said to one another, and after five minutes it appeared Cash was determined not to tell me. I sighed loudly enough to shock myself, then pretended to be occupied with an animated ad on the Internet. Cash picked up a paper plate with her sandwich on it and headed for her bedroom.

"So did Buck teach you to dance?" I asked just before she disappeared again.

"Dance lessons," she replied, and took a bite from her sandwich.

"You lead or follow?" My tone was a bit haughty as I

contemplated the overly endowed Verta gliding across the floor with Cash.

"Why?" She walked back into the living room, her expression blank as she slumped onto the couch. Another long silence.

Irritable, I began again. "I was just wondering, that's all. Two women dancing, I assume you have to decide who's leading."

"Lead." She picked up a magazine and began nonchalantly reading. *Of course she would lead. She's tall and athletic...and a complete smart-ass.*

"So they have dance classes for gay women who dance the boy's part?" I said, and she looked confused. "I mean, it's...how do you learn it, that's all?"

"I asked my brothers to teach me when we were kids," she said simply, and I realized my questions sounded ridiculous, but I couldn't stop myself. Another long silence while she read and I breathed and focused on my computer, having no idea what I was looking at. "You lead or follow?" she asked, so casually that her tone was almost mocking, and she never looked up.

I swiveled in my chair to face her. "What do you think?"

"How would *I* know? A lot of men can't dance and their wives kind of guide them around the dance floor and make them look like they're leading when they're really following. So I was just curious."

"Follow."

"You lead on the ranch but you follow on the dance floor. I follow on the ranch but I lead on the dance floor. Guess it's all about... geography." She went back to reading, then looked up suddenly as if she'd forgotten to ask something. "Are you good at it?" Her tone sounded as if she were conducting a survey. "Following?" she said, for clarity's sake.

"Anyone who could answer that is dead," I said, coldly.

She got up, tossed the magazine down and stood in front of me, took the computer mouse from my hand, gliding it across an Internet site, then clicked on a button, and then another and another, and finally the video of a 78 rpm recording popped up and spun around on the turntable.

"I'm an oldies freak. You like Gogi Grant?" Suddenly a scratchy rendition of "Wayward Wind" began to play. Cash stepped back and offered her hand, pulling me up. "Let's see," she said, daring me to prove I could follow her.

Slipping her right arm around my waist, she held my right hand in hers, keeping about six inches distance from my body, saying this was her formal-distance stance and exactly how she'd danced with Verta. Before I could say something rude, she twirled me around the living room to the plaintive descriptions of the restless wind and the lover who was born to wander. At one point I tripped and she laughed. I was a good dancer and knew it, so her amusement rankled me.

Perhaps to elevate my dancing above Verta Olan's or merely in defense of my gracefulness, I said, "Dancing is like riding a horse. To follow effectively your bodies have to be in close contact so you feel every move the other person makes." I stepped in and pressed myself to her. She held me so tight I could barely breathe and could feel every muscle as she stepped or turned. I could have simply stopped dancing altogether and she would continue to move me as if I were glued to her body. The sensation was overpoweringly sensual and my head was spinning far faster than my feet. Both of us were warm and ebullient.

The record looped and replayed the same song. This time we danced more slowly, as if the act itself meant something, as if the music was speaking only to us. Every inch of me in contact with her body as we slowed to a mere swaying, so as not to cause the slightest separation of our flesh, which seemed to be pulsing through our clothing. When the music ended, we both stood very still, wrapped around one another, breathing for perhaps thirty seconds, not knowing what was next.

"She's right. You're a mean dancer." I stared up at her, feeling that riverbank moment, that sensation that had returned on the porch in the rain and was now haunting me again. Gazing deeply into her eyes, for a second I thought I saw the depth of what she was feeling for me, but she regained control and the expression quickly faded.

"You're a wonderful dancer. Thank you for that." She broke

the mood and gave a little mock-formal bow. "And here I thought the only thing I was going to get from the living room was a peanut-butter sandwich." She picked up her sandwich, toasted me with it, and headed off to her room.

Whether to honor my demand that she leave me alone, or to protect herself emotionally, Cash Tate had obviously determined to move on with her life, leaving me to mine, and I felt suddenly foolish. I *was* push-pull, as she'd accused me. Only this time as she pulled away from me, I pushed forward…and now, all alone, I was falling.

CHAPTER TWENTY-TWO

August was upon us. Summer would be ending soon, and a sadness had begun to shroud my thoughts because Cash would be leaving. Maybe nature was simply trying to cheer me up and remind me that every season has its rebirths, when two nights later my cell phone rang.

I checked my watch and it was already ten, so I couldn't imagine who was calling. Hiram's wife, Betsy, was on the line, and I thought she might have heard about my foray into the lumberyard and wanted to tell me something about Stretch's reaction to my threatening him, but her need was more immediate. She was alone and her favorite mare, Annie, was in labor. She'd been unable to reach Hiram, and she needed someone to come right away. I couldn't help but wonder if Hiram was in town seeing his girlfriend again, something no one spoke of but everyone knew.

As Cash and I ran across the field in the dark to the small barn east of her house, I told her what was happening. We jogged into the aisle between the four small irregular stalls that housed equipment rather than horses, and at the far end where metal farm implements used to lie rested a distressed white mare on a bed of straw.

"We may lose her" was the first thing Betsy said as she looked up at us, her round face perspiring. She squatted next to the mare, herself bloodied, and patted the poor horse's bottom gently. "I can't get that foal out for the life of me. Been at it awhile."

"Did you call the vet?" I asked.

"I've left word," she replied.

Most people would have wanted assistance right away, but sometimes country pride kept neighbors from calling for help until it was too late. The mare's sides were heaving up and down. At the business end of all of this lay a pool of liquid; the mare's water had broken.

"Getting weak from the contractions. She's in a lot of pain." Betsy was fretting, and it crossed my mind that everyone was in pain: Cash longing for a relationship, me repressing lust, Betsy losing her husband's affection, and the mare losing her foal. Every female in this damned barn was hurting.

"Let's get her up," I said, and yanked off my shirt, ran to the barn hose, and washed up to my armpits, shivering more at the task ahead than the cold water. "Okay, Annie girl, we're getting up, let's go!" I pulled on her halter and her head rose off the straw, her eyes rolling wildly. "Let's try to rock her from the far side."

Betsy and Cash got on the opposite side of her and pushed, and I pulled, and the poor animal made piteous cries and tried to get up. She wasn't getting it done, and I knew if we had to use a crop then we had to, in order to assure that she stood up; otherwise she and the baby would die. And they might anyway.

"Again, let's go!" I ordered, and the mare got to her knees as the three of us shouted at her. We all gave a huge hoist and she staggered to her feet, rocking against us all and knocking us around. I feared at any moment that she would just sag to the ground and die, taking one of us with her.

"If she walks, there's a chance the foal will fall back into the womb and get turned around," I told Cash, then spoke to Betsy. "You got any lard or mineral oil?"

She ran back to the house to see what she could find while Cash and I kept dragging the exhausted mare around in circles. She was screaming and wrinkling her upper lip in a pinched fashion. Occasionally she gave a tortured kick with one hind leg.

"It's coming out!" Cash shouted. "One leg. No nose."

Bad news. The little foal's face—rather than coming out between its legs, pointing toward the ground, in a swan-dive position—was pointed in the wrong direction, most likely facing back up toward the mare's chest, causing its hind leg to come out first: a dreaded breech birth, where almost certainly the mother or baby or both would die.

"Lead her." I handed Cash the halter rope and ran around to the back of Annie. "She's breech. We've got to try to get the baby turned around. Keep her moving." While Cash walked her, I gently inched the little leg back inside the mare, then reached into the birth canal and tried to right the baby, pushing back at the little creature resting inside its mother, but no luck. Hoping the rhythmic walking would turn the baby around, I reached inside again as far as I could, but my arm wasn't strong enough and, with her water broken, the mare was dry now, all fluids out of her. I was fearful of the hideous decision looming—destroy the mare to save the foal. Betsy reappeared carrying a can of lard.

"If we have to put her down, have you got anything?" I asked, and both Betsy and I knew I was asking for something intravenous versus just a bullet. Our only hope then would be to rescue the foal.

"Don't talk about that yet, give it a chance." Cash's voice was reprimanding.

"I found Hiram, he's on his way. And the vet returned my call, if he can just get here. I can't bear to lose Annie. She's been a real good mother and takes such care of her babies."

Something about Betsy's plaintive cry that Annie had been a good mother seemed to ignite Cash, who had never had one.

She handed me the lead rope, stripped down to her bra, scrubbed her arms at the sink, and slathered herself up to the elbow in lard.

"Do you know what you're doing? Have you ever done this?" I asked nervously.

"Actually, no, but I know I can do it. I'm strong enough if someone will walk me through it."

"You've got to be careful with the tissues inside her and don't puncture anything, because you could kill Annie," I said, which wasn't exactly walking her through it but more like warning her against disaster, and I made a mental note to settle down and try to be more instructive.

Betsy led the mare while Cash went to the animal's backside and put her face up against the mare's left hip and her hand inside the weary animal as she continued to drag Annie around. "Okay," Cash said. "I've got my palm up against the baby, I can feel it."

"That's good. As she contracts, you have to go with it. Slide your hand in and around the foal very gently and slowly, as deep as you can. You've got to be patient or you could hurt her," I said.

"And don't pull the baby out," Betsy instructed. "That happened once with a cow man down the road and it destroyed my other mare." Her minute-by-minute coverage was making me nervous and the mare must have felt the same, because her eyes rolled and she looked like she wanted to give up and die.

"Okay, I'm working my way kind of underneath." Cash panted, her arm inside the mare now as the mare kicked one more time and screamed and Cash hung on to her.

"Don't jerk around, Cash, you could injure her," I said.

"Just trying not to get my ass kicked off back here," she replied. "Wait, wow, I just felt something move." Cash momentarily extracted her arm and stepped away from the animal. Betsy held onto the lead rope.

"Keep walking her, maybe something shifted," I said. Another minute of walking and sweating and praying, and suddenly I heard Cash's voice an octave higher than usual. "I see its head. It's coming out!"

"Okay, reach in gently and help guide it." The first little hoof became visible under the head. She reached inside and carefully located the second, protecting the membrane around it so as not to puncture anything vital. Moments later, exaggerated moans came from the mare as she contracted and the baby launched itself at our feet.

"You did it, Annie!" I ran around and hugged the mare's neck as Betsy dropped to the ground and began to pull the placenta back and clear debris from the little foal's nostrils. "And *you* did it," I said with admiration to Cash as we stood there, gazing at the little guy who looked skinny and wobbly and spaced out, as if he'd landed on the moon.

I looked up at Cash and tears had gathered in her eyes. She tried to wipe them away with her forearm.

"I guess Annie got Buck's money's worth on your animal-husbandry stint," I said.

"Yeah, you can go years never knowing why you experienced something, and then suddenly it all becomes clear," she whispered. As we stood side by side, watching the mare lick her foal and the tiny little fellow twitch all over from his sudden arrival into the world, it seemed like a new beginning, certainly for Annie and her foal, but also for Cash and me. A physical birth had taken place tonight, but somewhere inside me was a yearning still unborn.

"It's amazing, isn't it, to see him stand up and walk around after only minutes," I managed to say.

"It's unbelievable how the whole thing went from critical to a miracle. That's how I want my life to be," Cash said softly, almost to herself, and I didn't have anything to add. I wanted my life to be that way too.

Betsy took over now like a midwife, coaxing the colt into standing steadier, talking to the mare about what a fine job she'd done, cleaning up around the stall, and checking every now and then for Hiram. I was exhausted from my ER duties and believed Cash must be in the same condition.

"Guess we ought to name him after one of you," Betsy said, smiling at us.

"You should call him Maggie, after her, but put a C on the end for Cash. That makes him Maggic."

"With your help, he popped out like magic, that's for sure." Betsy grinned.

Hiram and the vet pulled into the drive, their headlights flashing up on the wall of the barn, and Cash and I headed outside to a hose bib to wash up and stay out of the way of the vet, who would be examining the mare to make sure she was okay.

The water splashing on us was cold and we stood shoulder to shoulder getting cleaned up, which was no small task.

"Hey, Maggie, thanks for what you did." I heard Hiram's voice before he rounded the corner of the barn and quickly told him Cash did most of it. "Betsy said she's turned into quite a hand. Better go see if I can help the vet any. Hurry him out of here so I'm not paying for more than one hour of his time." He chortled at his own stinginess.

As Hiram disappeared, having given the most effusive thank-you a country fellow could muster, I turned to Cash. "You were great. You should be very proud. You didn't panic." Both of us dried off on our shirts before putting them back on, and in that moment I contemplated that Cash Tate had, in addition to all her visible attributes, an underlying confidence and courage that was perhaps even more sexy than her high cheekbones and gorgeous curls. She'd stuck with it, out there in the barn, when I'd tried and failed and was nearly certain we would lose the foal or have to put the mare down. She'd stepped up and said she could save them, not knowing if she could, but willing herself to the task. She was, in a strange way, more adapted to this environment than I, because she was unafraid.

"I don't think horses should be named after people. Being that intimate with someone named Annie makes me feel like I've been on a really bad date," Cash said wryly, breaking my thoughts and making me laugh.

"Where else can you have a wildfire, a propane explosion, and a breech birth all in the same week to liven up your summer?" I was ebullient over our success and loved being with Cash and talking about it.

"You've provided a lot of excitement, believe me." That sweltering look that would melt metal had started to coalesce in her eyes, when she suddenly turned away.

I glanced down at her lime-green boots covered in God knows what after tonight's emergency. "Kind of got ruined."

"No, just broken in. I look like a real rancher now."

"You do indeed." I admired her tall, strong frame and the confidence she exuded, and I was not only proud of her but drawn to her.

"Think I'll go take a real shower. Not that afterbirth isn't a fabulous cologne." She smiled at me, then jogged back across the pasture, and my heart raced as I watched her go.

She looked agile and athletic as she bounded across the moonlit prairie, and I wanted to be running alongside her. Free like animals, nothing separating us but the wind. In the distance, she paused in the front yard and seesawed the old pump handle up and down, bending over and putting her mouth to the thick stream of cold water, her body a natural outcropping of the land, a fitting evolution of its harsh strength.

Betsy stepped outside the barn, interrupting my reverie, to say the vet had pronounced her favorite mare tired but healthy and able to reproduce again. She was resting now in another stall with fresh straw beneath her and her new baby struggling to nurse. I peeked in long enough to see the spindly legs of the little colt shake as he tried to steady himself and his little muzzle search blindly for his mother's teats. Betsy talked to him in her rough, kindly way, guiding his little lips to his momma's udder. The mare stood patiently and tolerated his fumbling until finally he could get a drink. I smiled, thinking every one of us human creatures had done that, drunk from a teat to stay alive.

As I ambled back to the house in the dark, my mind fixated on that idea. Why did some of us get weaned and others didn't? Why did Cash want to be at the breast of a woman and I did not? Really? A voice inside me questioned that thought. So you would be repulsed by running your hands over Cash's breasts or putting your lips to them? The warm sensation that washed across my body answered that question decisively.

I entered through the back door, past the lightly snoring Moses curled up in her sleep cage, and went straight to my room. Summer had consisted of Cash in the flesh, mental images of Cash, changes in my tone when speaking to her, lectures to myself about her, followed by gay fantasies and cold showers, and none of this seemed to change my nervous condition. I took a long hot shower and hit the bed, lying there and thinking about what had just happened. Unskilled and untrained, Cash had nonetheless taken a chance and reached inside the dry mare and righted the foal, enabling it to come into the world, take a deep breath, and live.

Perhaps that's what Cash was trying to do for me...reach into the most barren, windblown parts of my soul, turn things completely around inside me, scaring me as she tried to save me, hurting me as she sought to help me.

And at this moment, my life, my beliefs, my fears seemed to be the very things that were in breech, and Cash Tate the person who could right them.

Chapter Twenty-three

After midnight, and I lay there. The night hot. The kind of heat that starts trouble—fights or infidelities. I tossed on top of the covers, then ripped off my nightshirt and thrashed half-naked on the cool sheets that became immediately overheated under my sweltering body.

Irritated and unable to rest, I jumped up and went into action, as if my flesh had decided to do something entirely on its own. Had it learned of my body's plan, my mind would have said it's late, where do you think you're going? As it was, my mind was uninformed.

Searching through my closet, I hunted for an outfit that was comfortable but sexy. In the back, I ran across something I hadn't worn in some time—years, in fact. Yet when I looked at it, the garment appeared brand-new. A pair of black knit pants I'd long rejected in favor of jeans. I held them up and was surprised at how small they appeared. Gingerly putting one leg through the pants, I marveled that the garment slid up and over my hips, fitting me like a glove. I turned to look at my butt in the mirror; the outfit actually made me look thin.

I pulled on the black top that billowed away from my skin and plunged in a V neckline, and I marveled that I looked great, surprisingly. Why hadn't I ever worn this? When did I buy this? Then I remembered purchasing it to have something to wear on a date that hadn't worked out, so I'd shoved it in the back of the closet. Next, I scrounged for shoes and settled for black flats...not exactly ranch wear.

Hoping to find Cash, I entered the living room but didn't see or hear her. After I uncorked a bottle of wine I poured myself a glass and drank it, as if I was short on heat spreading throughout my body and needed yet another stimulus. What was I doing? I could only think that the mind is an amazing symphony. Once it has experienced a thrilling emotion, the conductor can signal silence, even angrily demand the movement never be played again, but the exhilarating reverberation of the music remains in our DNA. That unnerving sustain keeps the body humming long after the music has ended. And so the mind believes it has driven out the sounds of lust or longing, but the body never forgets how those notes feel blended together, how they ripple across the heart and through the soul and into our consciousness, creating an unending need to replay them just to feel the music again.

Perhaps that's why, despite every rational thought, my body led the way as I reached into the cabinet and pulled down two clean wineglasses, the stems cradled between my middle and ring fingers and the wine bottle balanced in the crook of my arm. I opened the back door and walked toward the barn in the south pasture as the full moon carved a path through the darkness.

The closer I got to the barn, the nearer I came to the creek beneath the tree grove, where it was cooler. The little barn was aglow, interior lights illuminating stall windows and streaming from the open doors. Cash might be inside, perhaps in the tack room, so I wandered down the dirt trail, headed in that direction when a horse blew air through its nostrils in a contented snort. I glanced to the paddock just west of the barn. The barn lights dimly lit the ground from fifty feet away, and there Cash Tate, with a long riding crop, was lunging Mariah in circles, the white mare seemingly relaxed despite the nighttime workout.

The rope Cash held loosely in her left hand was attached to the ring on Mariah's halter, and she urged the mare forward with a light snap of the crop in the wind. Cash had convinced the mare to come to her and I stood still, smiling.

Perhaps the mare saw me and lost her concentration, or perhaps she was merely testing Cash, but Mariah jerked away from her orderly circling, creating mad triangles, in and out and away, causing Cash to tighten up on the line, her deerskin gloves protecting her from rope burn. As Cash reeled her in, the mare turned to face her, then took two decisive steps backward, planting herself and using her full weight to create a no-win tug of war.

"Loosen up just a little and she'll circle back to you," I said softly from the darkness, and Cash's body sagged, as if hearing my voice from the void had collapsed her knees. She let the line go slack and the mare relaxed, then looked at Cash and slowly began to circle her again, this time without the aid of a crop. Cash glanced at me for a second, then moved in and unhooked the mare's lead line and slipped off her halter.

She walked over to the fence, where I rested my arms on the top rail, my head propped up on my hands. "Why aren't you asleep?" Even I knew my voice sounded different, as if it were caressing the air.

"Can't," she said.

I nodded to the wine bottle and glasses propped against the fence post. "Can I interest you in a drink?"

Cash hooked the halter on the fence post, then put one boot on the bottom rail and sprang up and over the fence, landing on the ground beside me. She dusted herself off and yanked off her gloves, tucking them in her back pocket. The wind suddenly picked up, blowing her cologne around and through me, and the leaves on the trees shuddered in one unexpected orchestral whoosh, branches whipping in unison like the tails of a million celestial horses. A thrilling sound of nature that sent chills across my soul.

I looked up at the heavens for a moment, the stars twinkling down and around me, the night black, and the wind soft with possibilities. I took a deep breath, and then I reached for her, slipping my fingers slowly around her waist, narrow and tight, and up the back of her shirt, feeling her suck in air and freeze. She trembled beneath my touch, making me want her even more.

Tilting my head up I could see her strong features in the moonlight, and without sunlight to highlight her youth, I caught a glimpse of her bone structure. What a magnificent-looking older woman she would most likely become. Her pale eyes sparkled down at me.

"You look wonderful in that outfit," she said.

"Been saving it for a special occasion." I pulled her into me, signaling she was the occasion I'd awaited, and put my lips to hers, our mouths softly sliding into a fit so perfect that it frightened me. My mind was completely jettisoned from the equation, as my mouth enveloped hers as deeply as I could possibly go without crawling inside her. Our longing became urgent now, the desire so intense that it created a kind of passionate pain. Those pale eyes held a fever, her body temperature hot to the touch, perhaps a sickness of wanting.

A sound came from the south side of the horse barn, perhaps Perry moving around in the dark. I grasped Cash's arm and towed her back up the dirt path. Once concealed in the dim light I propelled her back against a tree trunk and held her face in my hands, pressing my body up against hers. Her hands searched beneath my shirt and I could easily have dissolved under their warmth or the intense probing of her tongue as it sought more and more of me, but I was determined to remain the aggressor. She would not go home saying she had seduced me; if anything she would have to tell the tale of innocence devoured. She had craved me, nearly to the point of stalking me, and now she would get her wish. And yes, beyond all the lessons my mind proposed to teach her, my body simply wanted her more than anyone I had ever wanted in my life.

I unbuckled her belt and slid my hand down the front of her pants, slipping my fingers into the wet hollow between her legs. She moaned and fell back limp and shaking.

A part of me wanted her and another part of me simply wanted to show her what wanting really was: more than a one-night stand, more than some bimbo she'd screwed after a wild night at a bar. She should know how incendiary true passion could be. Not mere flickers of emotion, infantile flames fanned by youth, but seasoned fire. "I've never been loved by a woman," I whispered to her, "but then neither have you."

When it appeared she had weakened to the point of collapse, I took her hand and pulled her with me toward the house. Then I broke free and ran ahead and up the back steps and turned out the lights, leaving her to enter in darkness, except for the sliver of moonlight that shone through the shutters. Leading her to my bedroom, I closed the door, placed my back to it, and let my eyes caress her tall frame as she stood expectant.

"I've hated that door that kept you from me. Every night I dreamed myself here in your bedroom," she whispered, as I unbuttoned her shirt and slid it off her shoulders, then slowly pushed her back onto the bed, this time slipping her pants off with ease. *Hadn't I done it a hundred times in my fantasies?*

Naked and stretched out across the bed, she was a painting from an Italian master of a young boy with smooth skin and radiant hair. I paused to take her in before tossing off my own clothes and sliding on top of her. She moaned in appreciation of my flesh meeting hers unhampered by clothing. And now, no longer able to hold back the emotion, I began to kiss her neck, her ears, her beautiful lips.

She whimpered as I kissed my way across her breasts, trailing down her belly to the bones at her hips, skipping the most sensitive areas in favor of her inner thighs, then spreading her legs and, as she begged me to touch her, simply placed my breast against her throbbing lips and looked up to register the ecstasy on her face.

Something about her giving in to me, completely in my charge, aroused by everything I chose to offer her, was in itself sensual and empowering, and it emboldened me. Her body was white-hot, and a light perspiration had broken out on the surface of her skin. I pulled away from her, then opened the delicate folds concealing the softest part of her and put my mouth there. She gasped and clutched my hair as she rocked and writhed and too quickly exploded. And even then I refused to release her until she had to give in again, complaining that I was killing her, and pushed against me rhythmically, her release total as she begged me to let her go. But I would not. And the river I created in her spread its tributaries down to me, and while she was sated, I was insatiable and would have taken her again had she not found the strength to suddenly pull me up to her and kiss me ferociously as she rolled me onto my back. And now the tables turned, and like a drug that had sent me out of my mind, she gained complete control, and I shook as her fingers sought solace in the refuge of my body.

I forgot where I was and who I was as next she held me, facing her with my legs around her, and kissed me, then suddenly fell backward and slid my hips onto her chest, where her face now rested between my legs and, before I could protest, made love to me again. She was everywhere all at once. Her breath hot inside my body like a summer wind, building to a fury that matched her incessant strokes, then slowing to allow me to linger in her soft breeze. The smell of her all around me, on me, and now in me was breathtaking. She knew from the twisting of my torso and the near-sobs that tore through me like a storm through the prairie that she had me, and she did not leave one piece of anatomical geography unexplored.

Unable to take the intensity any longer, I rolled off her and onto my back and tried to make light of my feelings. "Had I known you could make love like that I would have locked my front gates and never let you come for the summer."

"I want to do nothing more than lie here and come for the summer." She playfully tumbled me onto my stomach and slipped one hand under me, stroking me into an orgasmic eruption that nearly made me black out. I rolled over and fell into her arms and slept. When I awoke she was cradling me and looking down at me with those spectacular eyes.

"I love you," she whispered as I lay exhausted and yet on edge at her slightest renewed touch. "I want you forever." The surety of her voice was comforting but frightening. I kissed her to avoid responding.

Forever. This had never been about forever. A breeze blew through my heart as if reminding me that out here nothing survives the intense wind for long. It all blows away.

CHAPTER TWENTY-FOUR

Light came through the shutters signaling the dawn and, with it, reality. I lay in complete and utter ecstasy…beside a woman. And not just any woman, the daughter of a friend, a person put in my care, someone fifteen years younger and wilder and what in the world was I thinking. *Obviously only of myself.*

She rolled over and pulled me into the hollow of her larger body, and I closed my eyes to wipe away that thought as she slid her hand into the V between my legs, resting it there as if I were her own personal glove. I sighed and managed to assemble my thoughts as I reached for the phone by the bedside to warn Perry off. I didn't want to have anyone at the front door seeing me in my current condition.

"Are you dialing 911?" she said.

"No, I think I'll just put the fire out myself." I rolled over, kissing her mercilessly, then made love to her again, unable to count the number of times, the surges coming like the tide upon the beach. With the last spasms of ecstasy, she clutched me to her.

The phone rang and I struggled to free myself and answer. It was Perry, wanting to know if he could stop by and talk about some farm equipment he thought we should buy. I kept him at bay, saying I was a little under the weather and planned to stay inside today. I would contact him later. From his tone, I could tell he thought something was up, but I didn't care because Cash was already driving me mad with her lips buried between my thighs. And like an addict, all I wanted was to feel the euphoria only she could give me, again and again and again.

When I awoke at noon, storm clouds were gathering and graying the sky, the light through the windows dimming like our spent passion. A drunk awakening from a night of bingeing, I was in agony and a voice in my head reprimanded me. What have you done? What have you done! The longer we stay like this, the weaker I will become until I'm finally unable to do what I need to do. I sought to summon the courage necessary to end this insanity, like a sexual samurai, stabbing the blade into my own heart and putting an end to it.

As if she knew what I was thinking Cash held me closer. "I'm moving in with you," she whispered.

And there it was. The terrifying offer that could only make parting unbearable, for no one, certainly not me, could ever believe a young woman of Cash's age would move in and stay. *Imagine that her clothes are everywhere, her books, her photographs, her cologne, and you've spent years together, and then she leaves because you're too old or too boring or too something or, worse, she tires of you or finds someone else, someone younger.* She herself said, you think you want something until you get it and then it's not what you wanted at all. I could become that for her.

"No, you're going home, back to your life, and you can visit me sometime," I said calmly.

"You think I'm giving you up? Never." The resolve in her voice stiffened me, and all my fears came rushing back.

"You have given me the most thrilling day of my life," I said evenly, as she reached for me, but I pinned her hands to allow me time to talk. "You are a wonderful lover. You will make some woman a wonderful partner."

"What are you saying? Not *some* woman—you."

"It can't be, Cash."

"Why are you saying this?"

"For all the reasons you already know."

Tears gathered in her eyes and she burst into sobs, heartbroken. "Were you just messing with my mind?" she managed to say between muffled cries. "You told me to leave you alone and then you came and got me and now you don't want me."

For a moment, that thought seemed thematic for Cash, the very thing that had happened to her in every aspect of her life. People had come and gotten her but never really wanted her. I pushed those thoughts back and hardened myself to her crying. I couldn't let her stay out of pity. Life is difficult and I would only make hers more so.

"I wasn't strong enough to resist you," I admitted, ashamed that I had caused this mess and hating that it had happened so abruptly, but then she had gone from merely making love to making a nest—moving in rather than just moving on.

"Because you love me. Say it! You love me, Maggie, you know it. I've never made love to anyone like this, and don't tell me you have either."

I jumped out of bed as if I had some place I might run and, instead, paced. "It's the summer heat. It makes people do strange things they regret."

"Neither of us regrets this—"

"You haven't lived your life. This can never work out. I knew that when I came to you last night, but I chose to do it anyway because I couldn't help myself. It was selfish, Cash, and it's over."

"Maggie, stop it."

"You're fifteen years younger than I am, and aside from the fact that you have screwed me completely senseless, we have nothing in common that would ever keep us together."

"Except the fact that we love each other," she shouted angrily.

"Except the fact that when I'm sixty you'll be forty-five, which is a huge difference and something you never stop to contemplate when you're twenty-eight."

"Maggie, what happens in fifteen years or fifteen months or fifteen minutes is something we'll take as it comes."

"No, we won't. You're going home."

"I *am* home." Her tone was so soft that I was tempted to give in, so I clenched my jaw and spoke as I might have to some field worker.

"Start packing," I said as firmly and as harshly as I'd spoken to Jeremiah the day he lay face down and drunk in the bunkhouse. This crazy lust couldn't last forever, and when it subsided my life would be awash in the debris left on land.

"You're throwing me out of your life, just like that. Well, then you're as bad as I am, aren't you? You just fuck me and throw me away."

"Be grateful, Cash. If not now, later. You'll meet someone you truly love and I will be a very nice memory, and you will be mine." I choked on the last words.

She pleaded with me, eyes afloat in tears, but I left the room and headed for her bedroom. I yanked her clothes from the closet and stuffed them into her duffel bag, my heart pounding and my stomach churning. The change in my life had come on so suddenly that I was nearly sickened, and I lurched unsteadily from lust to leaving.

She followed me, her anger building. "Remember when we talked on the porch and you said you'd promised yourself you'd never hurt again, and I asked how you could make good on a promise like that, and you said, 'I choose to focus on things that don't hurt.' Well, you can focus anywhere you want, Maggie—on the ranch, on the weather, on throwing me out, it doesn't matter—but this is going to hurt. And never seeing me again won't stop the pain because I'm inside you now: in your head, in your heart, and I love you!"

"Stop it!" I shouted, and she grabbed me, holding me as if nothing could pry her loose. "I don't want to spend my life with you. I want to be with an adult, Cash." I threw the words like a javelin, knowing how they would wound and immediately sever the cord between us, all the while wanting to cry out that I was lying. Lying to save us both.

She let go of me and stood very quietly, as if stunned, then put her hands in the air as if trying to fend off the very phrase I'd flung at her. "Leave me alone a minute, please," she said, and I turned away, leaving the room, unable to look her in the eye.

Thirty minutes later she appeared in the living room in her jeans and boots and carrying her packed duffel. She was calm now and we were both quiet.

"Tell me you don't love me," she said.

"Cash, go on. I don't want to hurt your feelings any more." My hand gesture was meant to be dismissive, to let her know she was acting foolish.

"So you don't love me?"

"I want you to leave. Right now. It was all an interesting experiment, but it isn't my life. *You* are not my life." I stared her down but she never turned away, piercing my soul, searching for the truth, but I held strong. She picked Moses up and kissed her on the top of her head, then handed her to me. Turning suddenly, she raced out the front door, throwing the screen back with such velocity that the wind caught it and busted the hardware and its old wooden frame flapped in the gale forces, banging erratically against the side of the house and ripping the hinges from my heart.

She sat in her vehicle and stared back up at me on the porch, and I flashed on her having an accident on the highway the way Johnny did after we fought. I quickly wiped those negative images from my mind. She would be fine, I had to believe that. She was better off driving away from me than she would ever be staying. I gave her an encouraging wave as one might say good-bye to a friend. She cranked up the engine and spun the Jeep out of the driveway and drove away. The dust of her leaving settled in the wind, and I watched all the laughter and love in my life simply blow away.

Once she was out of sight, I let myself go, sagging into my own despair. *Why did she have to appear in this form, a woman, and why this age, too young, and why at this moment in my life when I am obviously vulnerable. And why despite any of that, did I have to drive her away.* Tears streamed down my face as I walked back inside the house, clutching Moses to me.

CHAPTER TWENTY-FIVE

Moments later, a timid knock at the door, and I tried to dry my eyes and look halfway presentable. Perry stood on the steps and, after a quick glance at me, kindly averted his eyes.

"You don't look so good."

"Thanks." I half smiled.

"Need anything from the pharmacy or...something?"

"No, I'm fine."

Only then did I spot the wineglasses and bottle in his hand. "Found these and didn't want the horses to step on them."

"Oh, I was just down there doing a little..." I didn't want to demean what had happened with another lie about my life.

He handed me the glasses and headed back down the porch steps. Then he paused as if contemplating what he was about to say. "You done it now, Maggie Tanner. You ran off the one person who counted." He left without making eye contact and I knew that he knew.

I closed the front door and sank down at the kitchen table, cradling my head in my hands, and tried to get control of myself. Across the battered wooden surface, I spotted Cash's diary sitting on the edge of the table as it had that night I first found it. I picked it up and stroked the soft leather cover before opening it and skipping to the last page. It read:

August 4th, Why would you let the number of
times you saw a sunrise before I was born keep us
from seeing the rest of the sunsets together?
   Signed Cash Tate

The racking sobs came in waves and would not be silenced.

❖

Everywhere I looked she was there—in the undulating summer grass, in the sunlight on the fields, in every moment worth capturing in a camera, and then, in the wind—certainly in the wind.

I did most of my talking to Mariah, riding her over the prairie, letting her have far too much control as I simply used the ride to think, wondering what to do to piece my life back together.

Two days went by before Perry screwed up his courage enough to ask me if I'd heard that she made it home all right, and I told him I was sure she had.

"She was a good hand," he said.

"There are other hands." I thought about hers and how they'd driven me over the edge of sanity.

"Might be time for you to think about happiness, Maggie."

His voice was not unkind but I snapped back at him. "What are you, the town shrink?"

"I wish I was. I'd give you a ten-visit discount." He stomped off, leaving me to my own madness.

I grabbed my truck keys and headed to town to do errands, deciding that the best thing that could happen to me was to get back into a routine. I picked up my khaki shirts and stopped by the post office for stamps, almost looking for something to do or buy or keep me busy, then finally parked and went into the 2-K, where Donnetta greeted me like a soldier returning from war: big hugs, an assessment of my person, and the offer of a huge chunk of chocolate pie.

"Eat!" she said, shoving the fork into my hand, but I set it down, my stomach inexplicably queasy. "You look thin, and not so good. What happened?"

"Nothing."

"You don't look like nothing happened. You look like everything under the sun happened. You sleep with her?" She lowered her voice.

"Yes." Weeks ago my response might have been pinched or nervous or giddy. Now it was merely a statement of fact.

Donnetta glanced around to see who was in earshot, which was ironic, since she often shared my secrets before anyone had a chance to overhear them.

"We made love for fifteen hours, nonstop, the most magical hours of my life."

"Fifteen hours?" she said under her breath to no one. "Where is she now?"

"I sent her back home to Colorado."

"That kind of lay and you sent her away?" When I didn't answer she confessed, "Perry said you're hung up on her age."

"What are you doing talking to Perry about my relationship with Cash?" My voice rose.

"Well, honey, he's the one closest to the situation and has the best information. He thinks you're in love with her and just won't let yourself be happy."

"Oh, for God's sake, this town!"

"Is he right?" *Her* question really, wrapped up in Perry's. I jumped up from the booth, no longer able to be civil, wanting to flee from my own body. "What are you going to do now?" she asked, and I pretended I didn't hear her as I waved good-bye because I didn't want her to see me crying and I didn't know what I was going to do now.

As I drove back to the ranch the radio sang Garth Brooks's plaintive song about exchanging the pain for the dance, and the only thing I knew for certain was that I wouldn't have missed making love to Cash Tate for any amount of pain. So that, I supposed, is what I would do—cherish our brief moment and embrace the pain it left behind.

When I got home, I went to the computer to check the weather almost idly, not really concerned with the results, just out of habit, assessing the elements. An e-mail dinged in at that moment, as if it knew of my arrival. My heart caught so suddenly that it nearly stopped my breath completely as I read her message:

> Maggie, life without you has been pretty unbearable, but you taught me a lot about staying focused, and that's what I'm trying to do. Some things I know now for sure: I have more confidence, I'm determined to do what makes me happy, and I've experienced a love that, for me anyway, was more than mere sex (although I want to give that an A+ rating, for the record). Hug Moses and Knight and Mariah for me. Hi to Perry. And of course, you already know, I love you.
> Signed Cash Tate.

My chest so tight I could barely draw air, I tried to formulate a reply and vacillated between "come back" and "have a nice life." In the end, there was nothing to say. I saved the e-mail and didn't reply. I would read it again when my wounds were less raw.

I opened the oldies Web site I'd stored in my Favorites after that night we'd danced and clicked on a selection. "Wayward Wind" filled the living room and tears, not unlike an accompanying storm, streamed down my face.

When the music ended, I went into the spare room she'd vacated so quickly at my demand. It was the first day I'd been able to enter her room, and I was doing it with the purpose of taking down the photos tucked into the edge of the dresser mirror and putting them, along with her diary and a few odds and ends, into a dresser drawer. I carefully slid the picture out of the crevice that held it up against the mirror. The shot was of me in the field that day, hot and sweaty, showing off for her. I looked absolutely on fire, alive. And next to that picture, another of me lounging on the chair just as she'd placed me, the night I gave her the camera and she tousled my hair and told me I looked sexy. I did look sexy, and relaxed, and dreamy…and in love. The truth about what I felt for Cash Tate was staring at me. I'd never seen that expression in my eyes, didn't know I was capable of giving anyone that look. On top of the dresser I noticed a slip of paper with Cash's handwriting, and I picked it up.

Things I learned this summer.

1. Mama's closing rule: mouth, fridge, gates... close them all!
2. Wear the deerskin gloves!
3. You can't fool a mare with cookies
4. Line-dance boots are out
5. Give Buck more credit for bull riding
6. To attract a horse, act like a horse
7. Country boys are terrified of Mama & Jesus
8. To rock on you need a porch
9. Ranch women are proud and stubborn and can break your heart
10. One-sided love sucks

I took a deep breath and lay back on the bed and gazed up at the ceiling and thought about her and the risk of loving and how taking risks changes everything. I could still faintly smell her cologne from the pillowcases, and it was intoxicating and heartbreaking.

I should never have touched her, I thought, and the voice in my head entered the conversation. And would never touching her have stopped you from wanting her? And are you decimated now because you not only wanted her, but you love her and you miss her?

Moses whimpered, stretching her little frame and begging to be lifted up on the bed as Cash used to do for her. I reached down and scooped her chubby body up, and she scurried around on the bed covers looking for Cash until I cuddled her in my arms. Tears streamed down my cheeks as we hugged her pillow, both of us searching for any scent of her.

CHAPTER TWENTY-SIX

Two-thirds of August spent, and two weeks since Cash had disappeared from my life, when Donnetta's old Mercury Cougar, its paint color long indistinguishable, chugged up the driveway. She climbed out lugging a cardboard box, and I managed a wave from the porch, where I'd been gaping off into space.

"Brought you something to eat," she said with wrinkled brow, and set the box down on the table and rummaged through it, setting up the porch as if we were two ladies at a tea party. Napkins, drinks, sandwiches, chips, all anchored with small rocks she picked up off the ground to keep things from blowing away. "There." She finally plopped down in a chair alongside me. "Now let's have a bite."

"So you've started a catering service?" I tried to smile.

"Yup, but very limited. You're my only client because I gravitate to women who are miserable, pining, and moving rapidly toward anorexia. Eat that," she demanded, pointing at a sandwich, and I took a bite. "What have you been doing?"

"Just running the ranch. This is good, Donnetta, thanks."

"Running the ranch from this rocker, I'm told. Don't see you in town any more." I tried to respond and I choked up and tears gathered in my eyes. Donnetta ate silently, pretending to ignore my emotional state. "My Cherokee grandmother used to say, 'Don't let yesterday eat up too much of today.' You chose a path for good reasons. Be strong enough to live with your choices."

I dried up and bristled at the advice. "Does this Indian lecture come with the burning of sage to ward off evil spirits?"

"Burning sage drives out ghosts…and seems to me you got one lodged in your heart. Have you talked to her?"

"She sent me an e-mail. I didn't respond."

"Boy, when you're done, you're done."

Perry came around the corner of the house as if he just happened to spot her car, but I was certain he was the one who'd told her I was a mess. "Well, look who's here!" He gave what I was pretty sure was a mock-surprise greeting. "I was just about to take a look at the hinges on this screen door," he said, and pulled a screwdriver out of his back pocket as if we required proof.

"Have a sandwich." She handed him a wrapped lunch and he took it. "You're looking thin too. This whole place is on the verge of shriveling up and blowing away."

I said nothing and continued to eat. I thought I saw the two of them giving each other the eye, but I was too worn out to care.

Finally Donnetta stood up, dusting off the crumbs on her pants, and cleaned up our dishes. "See that she gets into town for half a day on Tuesdays and Thursdays. I'll be waiting for her at the coffee shop. If I don't see her, I'm coming out to kick everyone's ass."

"Yes, ma'am," Perry said, and left when Donnetta did, to avoid any reprimand from me. I knew Donnetta was right. I needed to get on with today before I screwed up the rest of my life.

❖

Tuesday I drove into town to the 2-K, only because I didn't want to see Donnetta's Mercury flying up my driveway again. When I opened the glass door to the café, Donnetta flung her arms around me. She poured me coffee and tried to fend off anyone who came over to the booth to say hello, mostly because she knew almost anyone who showed up was just curious about my condition.

When Sven Olan couldn't get within a few feet of me, he hailed me from clear across the room. "Heard your ranch hand left. Must mean your hay's all in, then?"

Anyone could drive by my fields and see I was up to my eyeballs in uncut hay, so that was Sven's way of asking why she'd left.

"I've still got hay to harvest but Cash has gone home," I said, refusing to call her a ranch hand any longer.

"Verta could come out and give you a hand," he said, and I declined, wondering exactly what kind of hand was being offered and where it had been.

"Men are stupid," Donnetta said under her breath. "And speaking of stupid, here comes Verta herself."

Verta Olan wandered into the 2-K and almost went to the counter to greet her brother but, seeing me, glided over.

"So she's gone." Verta shrugged, obviously referencing Cash.

"Like a '57 Cadillac," I said wryly.

"She was frigid," Verta whispered loudly, wrinkling up her nose, and a tiny diamond stud in the edge of it caught the light. "I heard that, anyway."

"Really?" I couldn't contain a wistful smile.

"Yeah, really. I think she will be happier there in Denver. She had lots of hang-ups and there are many good therapists there." Having shared that piece of news, Verta sauntered off.

"Sounds like she didn't get laid. Now aren't you glad you came to town?" Donnetta grinned.

Despite the insanity of the commentary, the fact that everyone knew Cash personally made it seem as if she was still here. Maybe that's what little towns did—created a collective consciousness of love and joy and hate and sorrow, intensifying everything by their communal nature. Today everyone seemed connected to Cash's leaving or at least acknowledged that she'd been here, and somehow that helped.

❖

Long, hot weeks went by before the mid-September winds kicked up suddenly, coming in cool from the north and threatening torrential storms and damage to the hay that needed to get off the fields immediately. We'd cut two days earlier and raked, and now we had to get the balers moving and hay off the ground before the high winds carried it down to Oklahoma. The last cutting of the season and Perry had another worker from town helping him, a fellow I hardly knew and at this point didn't want to know, so long as he could drive a tractor.

"We'll barely beat the first frost." I smiled at Perry as he trudged toward me from the field. Something in the wind sent anticipatory tingles through my body, foreshadowing the cool shade of golden leaves and relief from the summer heat.

"Maggie Tanner, our hay never gets frostbit. We're old-timey ranchers and we have our wits about us."

"Glad to know you're so high on yourself," I said. "As for me, I think we're just plain lucky, and God gives fools luck when He runs short on brains."

"Well, I was at the head of the line. If they ran out before they got to *you*, well, that's none of my doing." He grinned and strutted off, full of himself again.

For the first time in weeks, I was happy for no apparent reason other than Perry's good mood and the fact that the seasons were changing again and I could feel excitement in the wind—the restlessness that comes as the heat's driven off and the cool fall air signals farm equipment can be cleaned up and put away for another year, the green grass turning brown ahead of the winter snows. The horses could feel it too, and they reared up and pawed at each other, battling playfully in the fields, then ran and whinnied as if the wind was a bellows for their soul, telling them secrets no human could translate.

The machinery made its last run of the season up and down the long rows all day long until late afternoon. Individual buyers came and went, loading up single rounds as they tumbled off the baler. Late afternoon, it was over, and the pastures looked picturesque. Perry and his crew headed into town for what would undoubtedly be a night of drinking, the harvest serving only as an excuse.

I went inside and showered and picked up a book, preparing to read, which I did a lot of lately to allow myself to leave my life and disappear into someone else's. Usually I read myself to sleep, going to bed early.

Tonight, I heard the sound of tires ripping down the driveway, and I hopped up and flew out onto the porch to see who was tearing up my road, leaving Moses watching through the screen door. The vehicle was surrounded by a cloud of dust. I wondered if one of Perry's workers had forgotten something.

Shielding my eyes to squint through the grit, I watched as the vehicle slammed on its brakes and a tall figure climbed out and sauntered toward me. As if my heart recognized her walk, it sped up to greet her as my body braced against the newel post and I watched the beautiful form approach, solemn and determined.

The handsome, somber figure, carrying a large duffel bag, crossed the front lawn and planted herself at the foot of my porch and I smiled, unable to speak.

"Cash Tate, Ms. Tanner. I was hoping you might be expecting me. Heard you need an experienced hand, and I damn sure am one."

"You have no idea how much I've missed you." My words were breathless and barely audible.

Her tone was serious but her eyes caressed me. "I hope you have your shotgun handy, Maggie Tanner, because that's what it's going to take to get me to leave you again. I swear, you'll have to shoot me."

"And what if you get bored with this…me?"

"I won't."

"When I'm sixty—"

"We'll dance in the moonlight."

"What will you do out here, for God's sake?"

"Love you."

I sagged in surrender as she picked up her duffel and slung it onto the porch, bounded up the steps, and gathered me up in her arms, pressing every inch of me to her. Then, like the hero in a bad Western movie, she picked me up and carried me over the threshold.

"Put me down, you'll break your back."

"I only intend to do this on special occasions. She tilted me so I could reach the screen-door handle. "Hold the door open, Ms. Tanner." As I did, she caught it with her foot and swung it back, twirling us both through the opening. Moses leapt up and down at her every step, overjoyed that she was back as Cash made a left turn away from the guest room and into my bedroom, where she lowered me onto the bed.

For a second, I realized Cash would never really fit in anywhere, except maybe out here, if given a chance, and I didn't fit anywhere either, despite the years I'd stayed. And none of that mattered any more for either of us.

"I said every terrible thing in the world to you—"

"And didn't have the courtesy to answer my e-mail," she said.

"—when the truth is, I love you. I've been desolate without you."

"I spent weeks trying to get over you, but I couldn't get you out of my head. And then I realized I could spend years trying to find the thing that makes me happy, when it's you. Just you." She buried her face in my neck and ran her hands down my back and cradled my body, nearly driving me insane.

"I was so lovesick when you left, I think everyone in town has taken pity on me," I whispered.

"That's what Donnetta said." When I pulled back from her, shocked, she grinned. "She said she'd seen you and you were pining away for me."

I moaned at the thought of Perry and Donnetta knowing I was lusting after Cash and then discussing it with her. Suddenly the specter of family dinners with Buck Tate loomed before me, with him summoning mental images of me having sex with his daughter. "And oh, my God, Buck—"

"He knows everything. The person he was coming back to introduce you to was me. I told him when he was here that I was wild for you, and he said if I could land you I should get a gold star."

I groaned even louder over Buck's discussing my sexuality with Cash. "This is sooo strange and complicated." I tried to catch my breath as she covered me in kisses.

"No, it's not," she whispered, and began making love to me in earnest, her hot hands pushing aside my clothing and caressing my bare skin.

"You don't think it is, because you're twenty-eight," I moaned before I completely lost my senses to her fervent lovemaking.

"I don't think it is, because it's not." She put her lips to my breast and the sensation liquefied me. Half rising, I thought I heard Perry tromping up the porch steps but the sound softly receded, Cash's deserted duffel perhaps serving as a Do Not Disturb sign. Her body pressed me down onto the sheets, telling me with each tender caress to let go. And now I could no longer blame my feelings on the summer heat but only on the heat generated between us.

Cash Tate had broken through the barrier, ridden in on the wind and brought love with her. My life would change, like the shifting gale forces that rocked this ranchland. What form that change would take, or how long it would last, I could not know, but I was willing to risk it—throw open the screen door and feel the wind's full force.

About the Authors

After theater school in New York, ANDREWS began her career as a broadcaster in morning drive on the number-one radio station in New York. She spent nine years in the advertising world as a writer/producer.

She moved to California for a career with a well-known motion picture studio as VP Network Specials. She later joined an international television and publishing conglomerate, becoming president of one of their largest entertainment divisions.

Andrews now serves as president of a national auction and brokerage-services firm and is CEO of an interactive television network. She is an accomplished writer, producer, and public speaker.

AUSTIN, a talented writer/producer and on-air personality, partnered with Andrews, to form their own production company in Los Angeles.

She has served as a segment producer for broadcast network specials, developed and written animation segments for broadcast network promotions, and developed movies of the week and theatricals for studios, networks, and independents.

Prior to owning her own production company, Austin was co-producer and on-air host of a regional shopping channel.

Books Available From Bold Strokes Books

The Pleasure Planner by Larkin Rose. Pleasure purveyor Bree Hendricks treats love like a commodity until Logan Delaney makes Bree the client in her own game. (978-1-60282-121-7)

everafter by Nell Stark and Trinity Tam. Valentine Darrow is bitten by a vampire on her way to propose to her lover Alexa Newland, and their lives and love are placed in mortal jeopardy. (978-1-60282-119-4)

Summer Winds by Andrews & Austin. When Maggie Turner hires a ranch hand to help work her thousand acres, she never expects to be attracted to the very young, very female Cash Tate. (978-1-60282-120-0)

Beggar of Love by Lee Lynch. Jefferson is the lover every woman wants to be—or to have. A revealing saga of lesbian sexuality. (978-1-60282-122-4)

The Seduction of Moxie by Colette Moody. When 1930s Broadway actress Violet London meets speakeasy singer Moxie Valette, she is instantly attracted and her Hollywood trip takes an unexpected turn. (978-1-60282-114-9)

Goldenseal by Gill McKnight. When Amy Fortune returns to her childhood home, she discovers something sinister in the air—but is former lover Leone Garoul stalking her or protecting her? (978-1-60282-115-6)

Romantic Interludes 2: Secrets edited by Radclyffe and Stacia Seaman. An anthology of sensual lesbian love stories: passion, surprises, and secret desires. (978-1-60282-116-3)

Femme Noir by Clara Nipper. Nora Delaney meets her match in Max Abbott, a sex-crazed dame who may or may not have the information Nora needs to solve a murder—but can she contain her lust for Max long enough to find out? (978-1-60282-117-0)

The Reluctant Daughter by Lesléa Newman. Heartwarming, heartbreaking, and ultimately triumphant—the story every daughter recognizes of the lifelong struggle for our mothers to really see us. (978-1-60282-118-7)

Erosistible by Gill McKnight. When Win Martin arrives at a luxurious Greek hotel for a much-anticipated week of sun and sex with her new girlfriend, she is stunned to find her ex-girlfriend, Benny, is the proprietor. Aeros Ebook. (978-1-60282-134-7)

Looking Glass Lives by Felice Picano. Cousins Roger and Alistair become lifelong friends and discover their sexuality amidst the backdrop of twentieth-century gay culture. (978-1-60282-089-0)

Breaking the Ice by Kim Baldwin. Nothing is easy about life above the Arctic Circle—except, perhaps, falling in love. At least that's what pilot Bryson Faulkner hopes when she meets Karla Edwards. (978-1-60282-087-6)

It Should Be a Crime by Carsen Taite. Two women fulfill their mutual desire with a night of passion, neither expecting more until law professor Morgan Bradley and student Parker Casey meet again…in the classroom. (978-1-60282-086-9)

Rough Trade edited by Todd Gregory. Top male erotica writers pen their own hot, sexy versions of the term "rough trade," producing some of the hottest, nastiest, and most dangerous fiction ever published. (978-1-60282-092-0)

The High Priest and the Idol by Jane Fletcher. Jemeryl and Tevi's relationship is put to the test when the Guardian sends Jemeryl on a mission that puts her not only in harm's way, but back into the sights of a previous lover. (978-1-60282-085-2)

Point of Ignition by Erin Dutton. Amid a blaze that threatens to consume them both, firefighter Kate Chambers and property owner Alexi Clark redefine love and trust. (978-1-60282-084-5)

Secrets in the Stone by Radclyffe. Reclusive sculptor Rooke Tyler suddenly finds herself the object of two very different women's affections, and choosing between them will change her life forever. (978-1-60282-083-8)

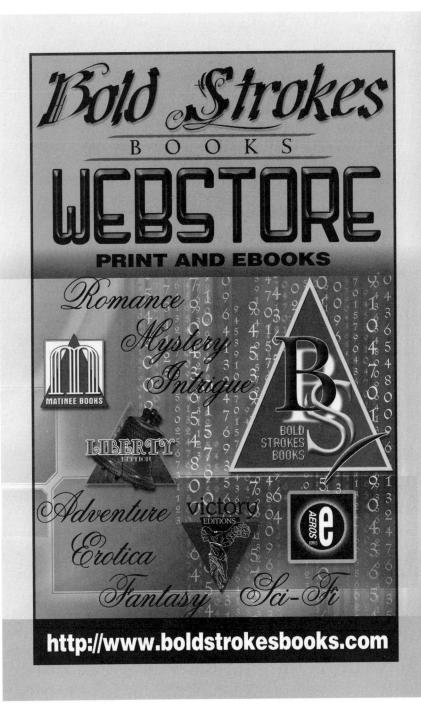